At the Mile End Gate

Also by Sally Worboyes

Keep on Dancing

The East End Sagas

Down Stepney Way
Over Bethnal Green
At the Mile End Gate

Sally
WORBOYES

At the Mile
End Gate

⚙CANELO

First published in Great Britain in 2001 by Hodder & Stoughton

This edition published in the United Kingdom in 2023 by

Canelo
Unit 9, 5th Floor
Cargo Works, 1–2 Hatfields
London SE1 9PG
United Kingdom

A CIP catalogue record for this book is available from the British Library.

Print ISBN 978 1 80436 349 2
Ebook ISBN 978 1 80436 142 9

Look for more great books at www.canelo.co

Printed and bound in Great Britain by Clays Ltd, Elcograf S.p.A.

I

For my uncle Johnnie Lisbon killed on the beaches of Dunkirk. And for all those fighting beside him who kept Britain free from tyranny. Also for the families who suffered and those who lost loved ones. Their courage – our pride.

Chapter One

Leaving the Forces for Civvy Street after the war, especially once the exhilaration of victory had dampened, was something of a let-down for the British troops. The euphoria of returning home to loved ones faded with the reality of a bombed-out country and with the sight of familiar streets where they once played, filled with rubble and debris. Having fought in a bloody battle against a fierce enemy and struggled to stay alive, the soldiers found their joy and longing to be in their own country tempered by the reality of the devastation back home. Tom Smith was no exception. For him, like millions of others, demobilisation had brought with it the hard truth. Britain may have won the war but she had suffered massive losses and destruction. *Why!* was the question that ran through Tom Smith's confused mind as he made his journey home to London's East End from the demob centre at Northampton. Over and over the same thought, the same question: Why had millions of innocent people been killed because of a handful of evil-minded, if not insane, heartless bastards? Had it been *so* impossible to have one bullet fired into Hitler's head at the onset of war? Especially since half the world knew that some of the men in power at the time were evil-minded if not mentally deranged.

'What's the point?' murmured the stranger sitting opposite Tom in the train carriage and gazing out of the window in a world of his own. 'Nah, no point. Forget it. Not worth it.'

Tom recognised his companion as every bit the soldier demobbed. He felt sure that this man would also be asking himself the same pointless questions.

'Not that easy though, is it, mate?' said Tom. 'Will we ever forget it? I don't think so.'

'Easy? Huh. Easy Street, blown to pieces.' A sardonic chuckle escaped the man opposite. 'It'll never be the same. No point.'

Tom pulled out a packet of ten Woodbines and offered him one. 'Give it a decade,' he advised.

Taking the cigarette, his eyes still fixed on the passing scenery, the man thanked Tom and put it behind his ear. 'May to December, bastards. Kept us out of the way 'cos of the food shortage. You get sent to the other side of the soddin' world to fight their battles and then they make you wait months before they send you 'ome.'

'Where was that then?' said Tom with a yawn, not really understanding what he was talking about. He guessed that the stranger's demob had been delayed.

'In hell. What difference does it make anyway? What's the point of it all?' The stranger held his gaze out of the window and so far hadn't even glanced at his travelling companion.

'You're right there, mate,' said Tom. Yawning again, he shifted in his seat, stretched a leg out into the aisle, folded his arms, rested his head back. Glancing along the aisle he saw two women pouring tea from their flasks and wondered if his wife Jessie had changed her pretty blonde looks. The women he'd seen so far on his journey home

2

all seemed to have put glamour to one side. They were wearing turbans, dungarees or slacks, and stout crepe-soled shoes on their feet. They seemed to walk differently too. Gone was the easy stroll and the teasing arse. It was all no-nonsense and hard work now. The mumbling of the man opposite broke into his thoughts.

'May to December...' he said again, shaking his head, despairingly. 'I'd 'ave bin all right if they'd let me go sooner.'

Why the man had had to wait this long to be demobbed was of no interest. Tom knew why they had kept *him* back – in the punishment block. He'd got away with desertion by the skin of his teeth. But as far as Tom was concerned it was much better than having to come home and face a long prison sentence. The word desertion made him smile. To his mind a few months AWOL didn't compare to the years of fighting for his country. The man's voice drifted across his head.

'Your demob suit fit yer, does it? 'cos mine don't. Only seven to choose from by the time I got to the stores. Tight round the arse and short on the ankles. All the caps 'ad gone. I 'ad to settle for this thing. A porkpie that sits on me ears. There you go. Don't matter now anyway?'

Opening an eye and giving him the once-over, Tom had to stifle his laughter. All that he'd said about his new civvy rig-out was true and, to top it all, the woollen courtesy gloves were too big and his raincoat, with its brand new creases, was big enough for two men his size.

'I know what you mean... the socks are itchy as well,' said Tom.

'Don't make no difference. I've got athlete's foot anyway. They let me keep some of me gear as a reminder:

hairbrush, shaving-brush, shoebrush, toothbrush, and me razor.'

Closing his eyes again, feigning another yawn, Tom murmured, 'Soon be 'ome.'

'Wherever that is. I'll go to my sister's in Canning Town. Marjorie's place never got hit.'

'Yours did, I take it,' said Tom, keeping his eyes shut.

'No idea. I could go to the Borough though, see what they've got.'

'You must 'ave lived somewhere before they called you up.'

'Oh yeah. Course. Big mansion in the country. Well, not a mansion exactly. Still… there you go.'

His curiosity piqued, Tom had to know more. At the risk of having his ears bent, he opened his eyes, lit a cigarette and studied the man's side profile. He was still looking out of the window. 'So why can't you go back there, then?'

'Wouldn't want to.'

'Oh right. Someone else got 'is feet under the table?'

The stranger didn't seem to have understood. 'It's bound to be different now. Well it would, wouldn't it. Different staff and so on.'

'Staff, eh? You must've 'ad a few bob.' Tom started to suspect this man had a screw loose somewhere. Staff? Come off it.

'Oh yes. Bank balance was always healthy. I used to drive a Bentley, on my chauffeur's day off.' The man's voice had gone from cockney to upper class within minutes and both accents were convincing. Tom was intrigued, not to say amused.

'I thought it great fun to drive one of Mother's cars,' the stranger continued. 'You can imagine the ladies, at least, those not used to that kind of lifestyle. You know a day never passed without a roll in the hay. I shall miss some of it, obviously.'

'What about your sister? Did she used to visit you there? For lunch and that?'

'Sister?'

'Marjorie.'

'She's wasn't my sister. She was a servant. Took care of the laundry room, that sort of thing.'

'Oh right,' said Tom, wondering which of the two of them was most confused. 'So Marjorie, the servant, she now lives in a flat in Canning Town and you'll stay with her.'

'I might. Dunno. We'll 'ave to see. No point making plans. She's a filthy cow, that's the trouble. No idea about personal hygiene.'

Convinced that his travelling companion had lost the thread, Tom was reminded of his older brother, Johnnie. Johnnie the entrepreneur, who had received a bullet through his head at Dunkirk. Had the wound not been fatal he would, without doubt, have been in a far worse condition than this man. Sadness swept over him as he remembered earlier days playing football in the street with both his brothers. Allowing his memories to flood freely, something he had resisted throughout his time away from home, he found himself smiling at happier memories and good, times. He closed his eyes and drifted off into a light comfortable doze while his travelling companion continued to gaze out of the window.

It was the sound of the train pulling to a halt that brought Tom from his sleep. He'd dreamt that he was on the beaches of Dunkirk, wounded and dragging himself along the sand to where he thought his brother Johnnie lay dying, only to find his lovely wife Jessie covered in blood. The sweat on his brow felt icy cold.

'You're in for a shock, son.' The stranger was talking again and calling him son when he was no more than a few years his senior. 'I didn't wanna wake you. It's not a pretty sight, half the streets 'ave bin flattened.' Now the man was talking as if he were three times his age.

Letting that drift above his head, Tom closed his eyes and tried to bring Johnnie's face back to mind, his smiling face – before the war – when the two of them went almost everywhere together.

'Don't you worry about me, you've got enough on your plate. I might go with the Sally Army. They wait for us you know, at the station.' The man splayed his hands and stared at his oversized gloves. 'I swear these are not my hands.'

Collecting himself, Tom nodded, saying that there would be bound to be kiosks set up ready to give them both some soup and bread. All he wanted right then was to get home as quickly as possible to see his Jessie and their two children, Billy and Emma-Rose. His daughter who hadn't even seen her dad. Tom had seen photographs of her which Jessie had sent out to him and, as far as he was concerned, she was the spitting image of her mother whereas Billy, who was almost six years old, looked like himself. Which, to his mind, was how it should be.

The piercing shrill of the whistle from the guard and the opening and slamming of the heavy carriage doors sent an icy chill through Tom for no particular reason. 'Right, good luck then, mate,' he said to his companion, lifting his gear from the luggage rack. 'I think we're both gonna need a bit of that some'ow.'

The stranger didn't move, but just sat in the same position, staring out of the window. Annoyed with himself that he couldn't simply walk away and leave him to it, Tom sighed, irritated. 'Come on then, move yourself. I ain't got all day. I've got a family to get back to.'

'Don't you bother about me. You'd best go.'

'I am going, and so are you.' Irritated by the crowd of jostling civvies, pushing and shoving as they made their way down the aisle, Tom pushed his face closer to the man's. 'Move your bloody self, get up.'

'Ah, don't be like that, son. Your dad's getting on, you know...'

Clenching his teeth, Tom tried to be patient. 'Come on... we're 'ome now, you silly sod. The war's over and we've come back 'ome.' Since the man was obviously suffering from severe trauma, he felt it best to go along with his fantasies. He'd seen worse than this, much worse. The Government was sending home thousands of poor bastards with wrecked brains. He thanked his lucky stars he wasn't one of them. Taking the man's small kitbag from the rack, he hooked it over his free shoulder. 'Come on. We'll get ourselves a cup of tea.'

The stranger looked up at Tom as if he was seeing him for the first time. 'Is this it, old chap? Is this the prison camp? I've been asleep, haven't I?'

'What's your name?' Tom's voice was now filled with compassion. 'Mine's Tom. What's yours?'

'Love a duck if I know.' The approaching sound of a steam-train and its loud whistle caused the stranger to freeze. His eyes wide and glaring he grabbed at Tom's arm.

'Its all right. It's only a train coming into the station,' Tom said with a smile 'Were in London, at the station.' Giving him a wink, he did his best to reassure him.

'So we are,' said the stranger, a smile spreading across his face. Cocking one ear, he listened intently. 'On the next track I should think.'

'Sounds like it. I'm getting off now, you can stop there if you want, it's up to you.'

'My kitbag. Where's my kitbag?' said the stranger.

'I've got it here. Come on, let's get off.'

Hoping the sight of himself walking along the aisle might spur him on, Tom didn't look back. And then an awesome, spine-chilling scream filled the carriage. Spinning round, he saw the open doorway and the look of horror on the faces of the other passengers. The poor bastard – whose kitbag was still on Tom's shoulder – had jumped in front of the arriving train.

Sickened by the horror of it, he turned and wove his way rapidly through the packed aisle of shocked travellers. Stepping down off the train, he felt very peculiar, as if his body wasn't capable of holding up. Had he not dropped down on to one of the benches on the platform, his legs might well have buckled under him. It seemed laughable that one man's death should almost bring him down, after all that he had seen during the past few years. The word horror did not cover what he had witnessed – seeing men being blown to bits. Luck had been on his side so many times that he wondered if, now that he was back in the land of sanity, it might run out. Afraid that he was about to suffer some kind of breakdown, he did his best to get a grip and waited for the sickly, ice-cold sensation sweeping through him to pass.

Tom gazed at the floor with beads of sweat breaking on his brow. Blocking out the noise of people greeting their loved ones he tried to visualise his Jessie whom he was longing to have by his side again. Rubbing his eyes hard, he felt a hand on his shoulder. It was a Salvation Army officer and the gentle smile and voice were exactly what Tom needed right then. The man's thin face was lined and at some time he'd suffered a broken nose but still he looked as if life was worth living. He was asking Tom if he'd like a blanket. Tom narrowed his eyes. 'What for? I'm not the one who wanted to end it all. It was my travelling companion who jumped.'

Eyeing him cautiously, the man placed a thick grey cover around Tom's shoulders and then sat next to him and waited.

'I don't know why I didn't think it would be this busy. People everywhere,' Tom finally murmured.

'Have you a home to go to, soldier?'

'The name's Tom. And yeah. I do 'ave somewhere to go. Why?'

Smiling at him, the man shook his head. 'You'd be surprised how many don't have homes any more.'

'Surprised? Don't bet on it,' said Tom, remembering the look of misery on the faces of some returning soldiers. 'Tell me… what makes someone jump in front of a train? He was gonna die anyway, one day. Why bring it forward?' He shook his head. 'The poor bastard 'ad everything to live for. The nightmare's behind us now. We've won ourselves a future.'

The man laid a firm hand on Tom's shoulder. 'Come on, let's get you away from this. It's quieter outside and the sun's come out.'

'Sun? It's cold enough to freeze a brass monkey's—'

'So,' said the Salvation Army officer, 'you'd appreciate some hot soup or a mug of steaming tea?'

'That's all right, mate, give it to the other poor sods over there, cheers for the thought. I'm all right, I'll just stop 'ere for a minute then I'll be on my way. They're expecting me.' He gazed out, remembering. 'My wife Jessie, my little boy Billy, my baby girl Emma-Rose, my Mum and Dad, and with a bit of luck, my brother, Stanley – last heard of missing in France.'

'That's good. They'll have the flag out for you then.' The man sucked on his lip and looked Tom in the eye. 'Mind if I give you a little advice?'

'Give me what you like, mate, I'm easy. Anyway, I reckon you know more than I do right now, the way I'm feeling.'

'And what *are* you feeling?'

'Like a stranger, in my own neck of the woods. Am I going soft or what?'

'Look. Don't expect too much of yourself. Give it time.' There was a pause while Tom tried to take in what he was saying. 'It's not been a bowl of cherries for wives and mothers.'

'What exactly you getting at?'

Treading carefully, the Salvation Army officer explained that the women had undergone dreadful and endless routines of war: long working hours, broken nights in damp air-raid shelters, food rationing, endless restrictions and interminable queuing. 'The problem is that thousands of soldiers thought it best to paint a false picture of what they were *really* going through so sent letters home which painted a picture of adventure and excitement.'

'So the women thought, sod it… if that's the case I'll have a good time. Is that what you're saying? That some of us might not find our women at home waiting?'

'No. I'm just trying to prepare you for the mood your wife might be in, that's all. Just try and see it from her side if she does start to accuse you of having enjoyed yourself abroad. You've got a tan… that'll rankle for a start,' he said, light-heartedly.

'Good. Keep 'em a little bit jealous, that's what I say. Right, I'm off,' Hitching his and the dead man's kitbags on to his shoulders, Tom stood up and strode out of the busy station, leaving the man of religion to stare after him. Tom raised a hand but didn't look back. Once outside, he pulled his collar up to keep the chilly air from his neck and walked past the Salvation Army band as they played 'Abide With Me'. He walked quickly, preferring that to catching a bus. Red buses, gliding by, symbolised London to him, a heart-warming sight, and he preferred to be outside looking on than inside looking out. He pushed the suicide episode from his mind but kept a firm grip on the man's kitbag. Once at home he would hide it away until he was ready and strong enough to look through for evidence of a living relative. Depending on what he found, he would either dispose of it or deliver it to the dead man's family. For some reason, he had a feeling that there was no one and hoped he was wrong. He couldn't imagine what it must be like not having someone crying over you once you'd popped your clogs. No, thought Tom, I wouldn't like that myself. I want all of them – family, friends, neighbours – crying their eyes out at my funeral. After they'd sung a couple of heart-rending hymns. Sod death, I want to live, he thought to himself.

Striding out towards home, he brought his Jessie's face to mind and the memory of her sweet smell. He had missed out on so much but there were better times to look forward to. He would treasure every single day from now on. He thought about his mum and his dad who had taken his small family in for safe keeping. No doubt there would be a fire burning in the grate when he got home and maybe a cake in the oven. He thought about his two-up two-down and wondered how long it would take him to fix it up, make it as good as it was when he left. He was a good painter and decorator and once he'd chased the Borough to do the building work on his bomb-damaged house, he would get stuck in. After that he would find himself steady work. From what he'd seen of the devastation all around him, finding regular employment would be easy. His plan long-term was to work for himself and maybe start up his own little business. Glancing at the sign above a shop which read 'Smith & Son' Tom smiled and murmured, 'Smith Brothers and Company'. He was thinking of himself and Stanley, his younger brother, the clever one who had nestled himself away under a French feather eiderdown while others were firing bullets at innocent conscripts or being butchered themselves.

If Tom hadn't been so preoccupied he might have picked up on the unrest that was in the air. Food shortages and flattened houses were the major problems. There would be thousands of demobbed soldiers who couldn't find the work they had before the war. Able-bodied men wouldn't be able to get used to the idea that there were *no* jobs. Hundreds of factories, office blocks, buildings of all sorts had been flattened during the Blitz. Worse still, some men discovered on their homecoming that their children called the coalman, milkman or baker, 'Uncle'. Extra coal or milk or bread had meant a great deal to thousands of mothers. Consequences at the time were not uppermost in their minds. Fortunately for Tom, Jessie Smith had been strong throughout the nightmare ordeal and had managed to see her way through without help other than from family and a handful of friends.

Chapter Two

While Tom was nearing Grant Street, Jessie was in the kitchen decorating the iced, cake she had made in honour of his return. Of course she was looking forward very much to seeing him and having his strong arms around her but there was little that could take away the worry in the pit of her stomach. In the few letters which had managed to get through to Tom during his time posted abroad, she had lied. She had lied over one of the most important things in the world – a baby daughter Tom had not yet set eyes on. Jessie had suffered so much during the war and trying to save him from the same heartache might now have traumatic consequences. Jessie was so deep in thought as to how she would find the right words to explain *why* Emma-Rose had been placed in a home, that she didn't hear Billy creep into the kitchen.

'Gran said put the kettle on Polly.' Giggling at his and Emmie's shared joke, Billy's gappy grin brought Jessie out of her sombre mood. After all, Tom's mum and dad were making an all out effort to decorate their front room as well as the outside of the house with streamers and Union Jack for the homecoming celebration. Even the neighbours had put out the flags to welcome Tom back.

'Have you put that tooth under your pillow yet, Billy-boy?' Jessie asked, giving her boy a hug.

'Nope. Granddad said I should leave it on the mantel-piece under his magic hanky and one tooth might turn into two and I'll get two threepenny bits instead of one.'

'You'll be a lucky soldier,' said Jessie, smiling.

'I am lucky. Granddad said I'm a lucky little bleeder!'

'Billy! How many times 'ave I told you! Don't parrot Granddad!' Jessie stormed into the front room where Charlie was taking a five-minute kip in his old armchair. She was stopped in her tracks by Emmie.

'Don't wake 'im up, for Christ's sake. He's been driving me mad – up and down, up and down, back and forth, back and forth. The mat'll be worn out time he's finished. And he's smudged the bloody window keeping on rubbing it when he thinks he can see Tom coming.'

Looking from Charlie to Emmie, who was standing on a chair, pressing a drawing pin through a paper chain and into the picture rail, Jessie said, 'You're gonna have to have a word with him, Em. Teaching Billy to swear. You should 'ave heard what he just said.'

'I did hear. The kitchen's not that far away.' Emmie hid her smile. 'Have you decided yet? What you're gonna tell Tom as to why Emma's been—'

'Emma-Rose,' corrected Jessie.

'If you say so. Look Jess, I know how difficult this is gonna be, love. But you know that me and Charlie are behind you all the way. Tom'll soon come round, especially when we tell 'im that we can go and get her back.'

Looking away, Jessie took a deep breath. 'It's not as if it's a horrible place there and she does like it. As soon as our house is ready to move into we can fetch her home. The Welfare woman said that, you know she did.'

'Don't mention that woman to me. Overcrowded? Cheeky cow,' Emmie said, heaving her frame down from the small ladder. 'Me and Charlie'll go up the pub while you explain everything. Best to tell the truth.'

'Is it though? He's gonna feel really bad once he learns that he was mostly to blame. After all, if he hadn't gone AWOL during the war I wouldn't 'ave had my army pension stopped and the landlord wouldn't have thrown me out of that little house in Whitehead Street.'

Emmie didn't like the sound of it. She tried to persuade Jessie to leave that bit out and simply tell Tom there was such a shortage of housing that she had to move in with her and Charlie... even though they'd already taken in young Molly McGregor and her two small children. But in her heart Emmie knew that it wouldn't be that simple. No matter which way it was explained to Tom, he would be very upset that his own mother had put strangers before his little girl. 'Not quite the homecoming he's expecting, but there we are. He's not the only one, many a poor devil's come back to worse.'

Glancing at the framed photograph of Billy and Emma-Rose, Jessie felt herself go cold. Of course they should all be together but there had been a world war and families had been parted – thousands for eternity. The worst of all things, in so far as Jessie could tell, were those men who had gone to war strong and healthy and returned mutilated. Some with artificial limbs, others with painful body wounds and scars and many who had had their spirits broken as well as their sanity.

Going back into the kitchen, Jessie felt the tears welling at the back of her eyes. But with her five-year-old son looking forlornly up at her she summoned all her will-power to be strong until bedtime, when she would let the tears flow on Tom's broad shoulders. Yes, Jessie could put a brave face on it, she was well practised. After all, it was *her* adorable three-and-half-year-old daughter who had been taken into care six months before the war ended.

The home in Essex, where Emma-Rose was at present, had once been a residential school for hundreds of poor children from the East End of London at the turn of the century. In those early days, the boys learned a trade before they left so that they would not have to follow their parents into the workhouse and the girls were given training in all domestic skills. Hundreds of children were saved from having to beg for a living, prostitution, or a life of crime. By the time war was declared in 1939, the residential school was no longer home to paupers and foundlings due to the end of the Poor Law system in 1929. During the Second World War this haven was sometimes used as a retreat for wounded servicemen and those children, like Emma-Rose, whose homes had been bombed. A Welfare Officer had persuaded Jessie that to place Emma-Rose in care at Ongar was the best she could do for her little girl. And so it was. Convincing Tom of this, however, was not going to be easy.

Giving Charlie a gentle nudge, Emmie spoke quietly to him. 'Come on lazybones, wake up. Charlie, rise and shine!'

Opening his eyes wide, Charlie stared at her, puzzled. 'Whassat? What's 'appening? Eh?'

'Go and have a quick sluice to wake you up, Tom could arrive any minute.' She couldn't help smiling at his faraway expression. 'We've won the pools,' she joked, knowing full well that that would liven him up.

'Have we? Blimey. How much?'

'Five bob. Now move yerself.' It was worth a dollar of anyone's money to see his expression change. This was the smile she wanted Tom to see when he walked in the door. For all Charlie's faults – secret drinking being one of them – he did have a big contagious smile that could lighten any heart. 'Put on a clean shirt as well, we don't want our son to think we've let ourselves go to the dogs, do we?'

Rubbing his chin, Charlie agreed with her. 'I'll 'ave another quick shave an' all. Where's Billy?'

'In the kitchen with Jessie. Helping 'er decorate Tom's cake.'

'Yeah, I'm sure. Pinching the icing while she's not looking more like. Poor little bugger.'

Emmie shot him a look. 'What's that s'posed to mean?'

'This morning he asked if little Emma didn't live with us no more. While he was sitting on the lavatory. He knew I was 'aving a shave and called out through die door. Can't look us in the face when he asks. You never know what's goin' through a kid's mind. I said she'd be back soon. That's right, innit?'

'Course it is, Charlie. How soon though, depends on how quick our Tom can get their place back to what it was. A bit more of the roof caved in yesterday.'

'You never said.'

'No, I didn't wanna worry Jessie over it.' She gripped his arm and helped him up out of the armchair. 'And don't forget, once we've welcomed him home, we're to slip next door to Sarah Damps for a cup of tea, while Jessie explains to Tom.'

'Too right. I don't wanna be in the same room, it's gonna break 'is 'eart.'

'Don't be so bloody soft, course it's not. Many a child was evacuated.'

'Yeah, and most are back 'ome by now. I'm telling you, Em—'

The sudden rat-a-tat-tat on the door knocker stopped him short. 'Oh gawd. I've not 'ad time to change or that!' Emmie wasn't listening. She was out of the living room in a flash and at the street door. Her son was home. In the flesh: her son Tom.

'Hello, Mum,' Tom said, giving her a wink. 'How's tricks?'

With all her expectations of a mother hugging her son fast disappearing, she held her hand to her mouth, speechless, hardly recognising him. Tom's face, although tanned, was drawn and his eyes were dead. The. twinkle had gone and so had his cheeky grin. He was smiling but it was forced or her name wasn't Emmie Smith. Her eyes filling with tears, she was too emotional to speak. Shaking her head in despair was not the way she had planned it but Tom had aged in the few years since she last saw him and his once thick hair was much thinner. 'You gonna let me in then, Mum, or what?'

Before Emmie could bring herself round, Jessie was there, pushing past, anxious to get to her husband and when she did they simply looked into each other's eyes; there was no need for words. The love they had for each other flooded from one to the other. Holding out his arms, the tears rolling down his face, Tom tried to speak but nothing came out other than a heart-rending sob. Slipping into his arms, Jessie seized him, suddenly aware of how much she had missed him. The next one to appear in the passage was Billy, looking from his parents to his gran; he narrowed his eyes, his face full of question as he whispered, 'Gran… who's that man?'

Forcing herself to speak, Emmie murmured, 'It's your daddy come home.'

It hadn't been a secret kept from Billy and he had been well aware as to why he was decorating the cake and his grandparents were dressing the front room with paper-chain and flags but this man holding his mother wasn't what he expected. He didn't look right and he didn't smell right.

'It's not him.' He spoke with urgency as if a terrible mistake was being made. With his back to Tom he splayed his arms and hunched his shoulders, a habit he'd picked up from Charlie. 'He's not a soldier. *He ain't got a gun!*'

Emmie put a finger to her lips and gave him a scolding look. Determined not to cry, even though he was disappointed and confused, he began to back away along the passage to fetch his granddad, but Emmie grabbed him by the shirt collar and hauled him back. Struggling, he pushed Emmie aside which did not go unnoticed by Tom who smiled at him, saying, 'Well, Billy? Ain't you gonna give your dad a hug then?'

Freezing on the spot, his eyes wide, Billy pursed his lips and pushed himself hard against the passage wall. 'Next door. Their dad's not back yet. Knock next door.'

Tom's roar of laughter startled him more so. 'I'm *your* dad, Billy.'

'No… my dad's been to war! You've knocked on the wrong house!' Now he was crying, 'Tell him, Gran – tell him!'

'Don't be so daft, Billy,' said Jessie, half-smiling, 'this *is* your Daddy.'

Stepping closer to Billy, Tom said, 'Has granddad taken you fishing yet, eh? I bet he has. And dog racing if I know 'im.'

'We never go fishing!' Billy shook his head rapidly. 'And we 'aven't got no dog!'

Kneeling in front of him, Tom gently ruffled his hair. 'Well, we can soon change that, can't we? Fishing I mean. You, me and granddad'll go down the cut and catch a few roach.'

'Bloody hell!' Charlie stood at the end of the passage scratching his head and grinning. 'What'd they feed you on – lettuce leaves?' Pushing his way through, he wrapped his arms round Tom and hugged him tight. 'Welcome home Tom,' he said. 'Welcome home son.'

'Its good to see you, Dad. Really great.'

'Go on then,' murmured Emmie at last, finding her voice. 'Inside the lot of you, before one of the neighbours knocks. Someone 'll 'ave seen 'im coming along the road, you can bet your life on it.' With that Emmie shut the street door and ushered them all into the front room.

Still convinced that this man was in the wrong house, Billy stayed back as Tom opened his kitbag and pulled out a present for his son. A brightly coloured hand-painted flute from Africa.

'Cor, ain't you a lucky boy, ehf!' But Charlie took the flute from Tom and put it to his lips. As a boy, he had entertained many with his tunes from his own penny whistle.

Emmie, who had rummaged in a drawer and found a photograph of Tom which would convince Billy of who he was, imagined that she would have to coax him to look at it. But she was wrong. Billy grabbed it from her and peered at it. Three or four times he looked from the picture to Tom before he slumped down on to an armchair and went quiet. Deciding that he was best left to himself, Tom winked at Jessie. 'Where is she then? Where's my little girl?'

Emmie, awkward and afraid of how Tom would react began to mumble about her and Charlie having to pop next door. But Jessie was having none of it. From somewhere deep inside she had found not only courage but a feeling of justness. She had done what was right for her daughter and any nagging doubts which had kept her awake the previous night had gone. 'No, you're not going next door, Emmie, you're stopping right here, and you, Charlie. No slipping out the back door.' Stretching herself to her full height, shoulders back, she pushed her dark blonde hair off her forehead and looked Tom in the eye. 'She's not here, Tom. But she will be back home soon. Once you've settled in we'll visit 'er.'

'What d'yer mean, visit?' The smile had gone and that pinched expression was back. 'Where is she... what's happened to her...?'

'She's all right and she's as healthy as you like.' Jessie continued to look him in the eye, defying him to start ruling the roost over something he knew nothing about. 'She's been staying in a country mansion in Essex with other children and being looked after as well as she would be if she was here with us.' She reeled the words off as if she had rehearsed them, which was not the case. She was simply not going to let what should be a great day for all of them to go wrong. Calling Ongar Residential School a mansion might have been an exaggeration but as far as she was concerned, the lovely environment with its cottages and village feel was a palace by comparison to being cramped up in an overcrowded terraced house with bombed houses for a view and with rats in the backyard.

Tom looked to Emmie for an explanation. 'It was for the best, Tom. Jessie was homeless but when it 'appened Molly McGregor and her little ones had moved in with us. You remember the McGregors, they was always...'

'So there was no room for *my* family? Is that what you're saying?'

'Steady on, son,' said Charlie. 'Me and your mother did what was right. If you'd 'ave bin 'ere you'd 'ave gone along with it. Our Emma's all right where she is. She loves it there and they don't mind when we visit. Don't begrudge the poor kid just 'cos you feel bad about it, none of us 'ave bin selfish so don't you start now. I've bin sleeping on the couch son, which ain't done my back much good I can tell you.'

Tom stared down at the floor. 'Why was you 'omeless, Jessie? How comes the Borough didn't give you a place of your own when ours was hit?'

'They just didn't that's all.'

'That's not an answer.'

'Well it'll 'ave to do. I don't wanna dig all of that up now. The war's over, you're home and soon we'll all be together again, in our little house.' Jessie prompted Charlie to open the bottle of sherry they had saved for the occasion. 'As soon as you feel like it, we'll catch a train to Ongar to see Emma-Rose. We've told 'er you're coming home and she can't wait to see you.'

Gutted, Tom pushed his hands through his hair. Fatigue had finally caught up with him. 'Fair enough. If that's the way it is then that's the way it is.'

'Did you bring a present back for Emma as well?' said Billy, finding his voice.

'Emma?'

'Yeah. She don't need *two* names.'

Laughing at his son's bluntness, he ruffled his hair. 'Well as long as your other gran don't mind I s'pose it's all right.'

'Granny Rose never comes to see us now. Mum 'ad a row with 'er.'

'Is that right? Well, there're no flies on you son are there? I 'ope you're as bright with your school work, with sums and words.' Pulling a face, Billy left the room, using the lavatory as an excuse. The fact was that he didn't like school and, he certainly didn't like having to learn his tables and alphabet. Billy was much happier messing around with paints and plasticine, when he wasn't outside kicking a football about.

'He seems to 'ave accepted it then. That I'm not the big strapping soldier he was expecting,' said Tom, rubbing his eyes.

'You look all in, son.' Patting him on the hand, Emmie suggested he have a short nap while she laid the table for his welcome-home tea. Ideally, she would have loved to have him to herself, there were so many questions she wanted to ask and so much she had to tell him.

'Yeah, I will 'ave a doze, in a minute. You and Jessie go and sort things out in the kitchen so I can 'ave five minutes with Dad.' He wanted to ask about his brother Stanley, but not in front of his mother. He knew she must be breaking her heart over him.

'That's more like it,' said Charlie, his spirits raised. 'Go on the pair of you. Me and my son should 'ave a bit of time together.'

Satisfied that things hadn't gone too badly, Emmie gave Jessie the nod and they both left the room, closing the door behind them. 'One question Dad and then you can ask me what you like. I know you, you must be dying to know what it was like out there.'

'Yes and no, son. Yes and no. And before you ask, no, we've 'ad no word as yet.' He looked Tom in the eye and smiled. 'I'm telling you, Tom, as sure as I sit here, our Stanley's all right. I feel it in my bones. Trying to get it across to your mother though... won't talk about it other than to ask every bloody morning if there's anything in the post.'

'As it 'appens, Dad, I think you're right. When Johnnie was killed I felt it inside, *before* I was told. I've not had the same feeling about Stanley, the opposite in fact. I swear the lucky bastard's holed up in France with a gorgeous tart. They were all over 'im before he got into uniform so...'

'I know. Too good looking for 'is own good, which can be worse than being ugly. Anyway enough of that, how was it out there?'

'Oh, not now, Dad, please.'

'You said you'd tell me!'

'I know, but...' he flapped his hand, '...I'd rather you told me what's going on here. How long are the neighbours gonna be boarding?'

'A couple more weeks, if that. Their place's nearly ready for 'em to move back into. Give it a fortnight and we'll fetch Emma-Rose 'ome.'

Tom shook his head slowly. 'What's it all been about, eh? I've lost the best years of married life, my own son don't recognise me and they've taken my baby girl away. My little daughter who I've never set eyes on. And our house won't be ready for a while by the sound of it. Not to mention our Johnnie. I'm gonna miss 'im more than ever now I'm back in my own surroundings.'

'Freedom. That's what it's all been for, we're still a free country thanks to blokes like you, Tom. The worst is over and you'll be on your feet soon and back out there as if the war 'ad never 'appened.'

'You reckon? Settling down after a different way of living won't be easy. I'll miss the camaraderie. Where are they all now? Where are the blokes I fought alongside? Spread out across the country and no doubt as shell-shocked as I am at what we've come back to.'

'You'll be all right once you meet up with your old mates again.'

'Yeah, but how many survived? And don't start saying I'll make new friends. I don't wanna make any more friends. Some of the best blokes I've known are still out there somewhere, rotting away. Any of my old mates who did come through'll ave enough of their own problems to sort out.'

'Blimey, son,' said Charlie, scratching his head, 'you are in a black mood. I never expected this, never had you down for someone who'd feel sorry for 'imself. I'm a bit fazed over it to tell the truth, don't know what to say to you.'

'I can't help it. I wish I could be like I imagined. Happy as a sandboy to be back with my family but all I want to do is to walk along a quiet lane by myself. Think it all through and pick up from where I left off, before Dunkirk.'

'You'll be lucky. Billy ain't gonna let you out of 'is sight now, he's not stopped going on about when you come 'ome. Drove me mad at times.'

'Come on, Dad. He didn't even know me. You might 'ave shown him some pictures to remind him.' Unscrewing the cap of his whisky bottle, Charlie told Tom to get two glasses out of the sideboard. 'Course we showed him pictures, you silly bugger. But you've lost a lot of weight and you've aged.'

'Thanks, just what I needed to hear.'

'Don't mention it. Now then, get this whisky down you, and then go and have a lie down. In a couple of hours we'll be 'aving a few visitors. A few of the neighbours are popping in, they've all been waiting for you, Tom. Whether you like it or not you ain't gonna be able to mope around.' Charlie raised his glass to his son and winked. 'Upwards and onwards, son. Here's to the future.'

'Cheers, Dad.' Tom drained his glass in one gulp, and made his way to bed.

Charlie realised his optimism was shaky – he knew only too well that things were not turning out the way people had hoped they might. Tom's chances of getting back into regular employment at all were slim. For every thirty thousand vacancies throughout Britain, a million men were applying for the work. The Government knew this was going to be the case and compensated by giving gratuities to the men on demobilisation. But so-called voluntary societies were there, like vultures, waiting to pick the bones. Confidence tricksters who managed to persuade many of them to part with their cash in fast schemes that came to nothing and the con men disappeared with their pockets lined, never to be seen again.

Others not taken in by the crooks were buying lorries from the Government who were selling them at a reasonable price, enabling the ex-servicemen to start up on their own. Needless to say, the majority of the working classes, who had no idea how to run a business, had lost or were losing their money within months. Charlie knew about the lorries on offer and felt sure that given time, his son would be a prime candidate for setting up his own painting and decorating business. But he hadn't bargained on Tom looking so beaten and tired and more than anything he now needed encouragement. And Charlie was determined to play his part. But to do that he would need a clear head – the booze would have to go. Well some of it anyway. It was time for him to pack in the whisky.

It wasn't easy to pour the whisky down the drain in the kitchen sink. But he did it. Not only for his son, but for all his family. Raising his eyes to see his reflection in the small mirror above the sink, he felt ashamed. It was as if he was seeing himself for the first time. He didn't like what he saw and he didn't like what he reminded himself of: the down and outs of the East End with their glazed red-rimmed eyes and swollen drink-sodden faces – poor bastards who had had to face what Tom was now facing, when they had returned from the First World War. Well that was not going to happen to his son. No, not his son.

Charlie had had enough. He now acknowledged that he was more than a little dependent on the whisky, something he had always denied. *Now* he was determined to turn over a new leaf – well as far as the whisky was concerned!

That night, Charlie got into his makeshift bed on the settee, drunk it was true, but in his mind, drunk for the last time. And it was his choice and no one else's. *His* decision. 'Sod the lot of 'em,' he murmured as he pulled the covers over his head. 'I've got nothing to prove to no one… only myself.

Chapter Three

Riding on the bus to Fenchurch Street where Jessie, Tom, Emmie, Charlie and little Billy were to catch a train to Ongar to visit Emma-Rose, Jessie felt as if she were looking at the devastation of buildings and houses through different eyes. So used to conditions throughout the war, she had almost forgotten the way things were before. Sitting next to Tom, their hands held tightly, she was seeing it in the same light as he was. The queues of people outside the butcher's shop, the fishmonger's, the baker, the grocery shop and the greengrocer's added to the feeling of a war not quite over yet. Everyone in the sorry queues were clutching their ration books and most of them had been queuing for hours. Not all were as sharp as Tom's mum and dad who had made it their business to exploit the so-called black market trade. Emmie and Charlie had been busy during the war and not just for themselves and their neighbours but for other poor families in surrounding streets who had been able to ward off hunger pains and humiliation only due to the work they had secretly carried out. Given help, the two of them could have done so much more and for all of the East End families. As it was, Emmie Smith and her old man Charlie were held in very high regard throughout the neighbourhood and they weren't the only unsung heroes.

'Five years and it'll all look different,' said Jessie, giving Tom a kiss on the cheek. 'The capital's been in a worse state than this, or so the history books tell us.'

'We'll see,' he said, despondently. 'Come on. This is our stop.'

Once they were settled on the train, Billy came to life. He'd been quiet on the journey up until then and Jessie had left him alone telling Tom not to let it worry him. It had been the same each time they'd gone to visit Emma-Rose. When Jessie had asked him what the matter was, Billy had simply replied: 'I'm sad.' Now, sitting opposite his mum and dad with his grandparents on either side of him, he was smiling and his smile reminded Jessie so much of Tom. 'Look at him,' she said, 'he's a dead ringer for you.'

'Course he is,' said Tom, giving Billy a wink. 'He's a chip off the old block, ain't you, son?'

'That's what Granddad says. He says I'm a chip off the old block. What block?'

'It means,' said Emmie, warming to her day out, 'that when your dad was your age, he looked just like you. So if you think of a big bar of Cadbury's chocolate and imagine a small bat exactly the same next to it... that's what it means. You're smaller but you're just the same.'

'If I was a bar of chocolate I'd eat myself,' he said, his face serious. 'And if Dad was a big bar we'd 'ave shared 'im out by now.'

'I bet you would 'ave an' all,' said Tom, a wry smile on his face.

Staring out of the window, Billy went quiet again. Quiet and pensive. 'We fetching Emma back with us today, Mum?' he asked finally.

'No. I've told you before we have to wait until our house is finished.'

'Can I stop there this time? I've got some clean pants in my pocket and a pair of socks.'

'Don't start all that again, Billy,' said Jessie. 'Your Dad's back now and things are gonna change. That's right, eh Tom?' she said, giving him a nudge. Tom was disappointed that his son, from the sound of it, would rather be in a children's home now that his dad was back from war.

'Let 'im stop there if he wants to. They can lock 'im up and throw away the key. We won't—'

'Emma *ain't* locked up!' snapped Billy.

'Maybe not, but odds on they lock up the boys and make them go up the chimneys to clean 'em.'

'They don't 'ave to learn their tables and alphabet though.'

'Oh give it a rest, Billy,' said Emmie, tired of hearing the same old thing from her grandson. 'Shut your eyes for five minutes.'

'I'm not tired,' he said, folding his arms and fixing his eyes at the passing scenery. 'Anyone'd wanna live in the countryside instead of our smelly old street.' There was a pause while they waited for his next stream of words. 'I might go with Uncle Alfie, he's always on the run. If he goes to Australia I'll go with 'im, and dig for gold.'

'If you knew what "on the run" meant, Billy, you wouldn't want to go anywhere with that wayward brother of mine,' said Jessie.

'I do know what it means. Alfie told me but I'm not to put it about.'

'Alfie?' said Jessie.

'*Uncle* Alfie,' sighed Billy.

When the train finally pulled into the sidings at Ongar, Billy was sound asleep and had to be nudged by Charlie. 'Come on, soldier, wake up, we're there.'

'I *know*!' he said, hating to be caught napping. 'Can I 'ave a sandwich?'

'Not now, no,' said Jessie, 'wait till we're there. We'll have a picnic then.'

'If I don't die of starving hunger. We gonna get a bus?'

'No. It's only a ten minute walk up the road,' said Jessie hauling him out of his seat. 'Stop performing.'

Impressed with Ongar and surprised at the bustling railway station with London and North Eastern trains running out to this terminus, Tom's mind began to work overtime. He liked the compact town and the country village atmosphere. Looking around he could see a butcher's that would be right down his mother's street. Hanging in rows of six on large metal hooks just inside the open-fronted shop was a display of poultry and game: chicken, rabbit and pheasant. 'I take it that meat's still on ration?'

'Yeah,' said Emmie. 'I was thinking the same thing myself, Tom. Wouldn't it be lovely to 'ave a roast chicken, eh?'

'I might go in and talk to the guv'nor on the way back. See if he'll take cash.'

'Course he will, Tom, but you'll need every penny of your demob money. Make it last best you can.' Emmie guessed she was talking to a brick wall. Money had always burned a hole in Tom's pocket.

'One little chicken ain't gonna break the bank, Mother.'

'You'd be surprised. The butcher'll ask for a tenner you see if I'm wrong.'

'Don't be daft.' Tom suddenly realised just how much he'd missed home cooking and everything else about England, especially the pubs. 'Not a bad place to live, eh,

Jess?' he said. 'Chipping Ongar? Bit of 'istory everywhere you look.'

'Here we go,' said Charlie, 'he's off again. Gonna come and live 'ere with the carrot crunchers are you?'

Tom was right in his observations. Ongar *was* steeped in history. It had strong connections with William the Conqueror and once boasted a very impressive castle.

Arriving at the wrought iron gates Jessie felt her stomach turn the way it did every time she went to visit Emma-Rose. Her own acting ability only stretched so far, underneath the surface she was a grieving mother and after each visit to see her little girl she was left broken-hearted. This wasn't what she had planned when she married Tom. Her dreams of a happy family together had been blown apart, but still she'd had to keep on smiling through it all, for the sake of Billy and Emma-Rose.

Once inside the grounds, Jessie could see that Tom was impressed and breathed a sigh of relief. This place *was* heaven compared to the back streets of London. From every chimney, smoke curled upwards and from every house a light shone out of a window and the gas lamps circling the oval had been lit early. It being early December, rehearsals for the Nativity plays and carol services were already taking place and from the assembly hall came a din which could be recognised roughly as the practising band and chorus turning out 'Once In Royal David's City'.

As the other children were playing on the green Emma-Rose was standing by a tall fir tree, wrapped up warm and clutching her much loved toy bear. Her eyes were fixed on the entrance gate and once she had spotted Jessie she came running across the oval.

'Here she comes,' said Billy. 'I bet she falls over, she can't run properly yet.'

'Course she can. Same as you could when you was 'er age.' Taking Tom's hand and squeezing it, Jessie tried to be brave. The sight of her little girl in a pair of Billy's long grey socks and her old blue coat, with her long curly blonde hair blowing in the breeze as she ran towards them with her arms outstretched, was almost too much to bear.

Falling to her knees, Jessie opened her arms and waited for Emma-Rose to rush into them, and as she did so, she wet herself. 'Never mind, sweetheart. Mummy's got a dry pair of knickers in her bag.' This was a normal occurrence.

'I w-w-went wee-wees b-b-before. It's not *my* fault!'

With Emma-Rose snuggling into her breast as if she was trying to get back inside her mother where she would be safe, Jessie couldn't be blamed for ignoring everyone else and smothering her with kisses. 'Guess who's come to see you, baby?'

'B-blinking Granddad. Mustn't t-t-torment me, eh?'

Looking into her daughter's lovely round pale face, Jessie brushed her fingers across her long fringe so she could see those big wide pale blue eyes. 'It's your Daddy, Emma. Daddy's come back from the army.'

Squinting up at Tom, Emma-Rose moved closer to him and sniffed the sleeve of his overcoat. 'B-b-blinking mothballs. Just like m-matron,' she said, looking up into his pinched face.

Tom was speechless. His emotions getting the better of him he could only look at her. Look at his beautiful little girl with snow-white hair. He opened his mouth to say something but his throat was dry as he struggled with his emotions. Falling to his knees he cleared his throat and tried again. 'I brought you some sweets and a present.'

'Shall we go inside,' the soft voice of Emma-Rose's foster mother took Tom by surprise. He hadn't seen her coming. 'We'll go into my flat and have some tea and biscuits.'

'B-B-Billy live 'ere now, eh?' said Emma, wiping her runny nose on her coat sleeve.

'Let's go inside, Emma, Mummy's freezing. See how cold my hands are.' She laid the back of her hand on Emma's cheek.

'Wh-wh-what about my present?'

'Daddy'll give it to you once we're inside.' Peering up at Tom with one eye closed, Emma examined his face. 'You got an art and-and-and-ficial leg?'

Bursting out with laughter, Tom shook his head. 'I don't think so. They've both got hair growing on 'em so...' He started to laugh again which started Emma crying. The others couldn't help smiling.

'But, but Richard's dad's got one from the war.' She wailed.

Lifting his daughter up and wiping her tears away, Tom beckoned for the foster mother, Julie, to lead the way. Striding along, he couldn't stop kissing Emma-Rose on the cheek. 'You look just like your mum – did you know that?'

'Is, is, is it in your bag?'

'What your present?'

'Is it, Daddy?'

'Yes, sweetheart, it's in my bag.'

–

When it was time for them to go home Tom slipped away and had a quiet word with Matron, the headmaster's wife.

He used every bit of his charm to try and persuade her to let them take Emma-Rose home with them that day, but she would have none of it. The authorities would come down on her like a ton of bricks had she have given in. As far as Matron was concerned a soldier returning from war *should* have all his family round him and a small child of three-and-a-half should certainly be with her parents, but officially Emma-Rose had been listed as a child in need of short-term fostering and she would have to approach the Board of Governors in Hackney before she could agree to anything.

Waving goodbye to the sad little figure as she stood at the gate holding her foster mother s hand and clutching her black and white panda tightly was too much for Tom. Once Emma-Rose's carer walked her slowly away across the grassy oval towards the main building, Tom started to cry.

'This ain't right, Jess,' he said wiping his face with his clean, white handkerchief. 'Look at her... she's still a baby...'

Placing an arm round his son's shoulder and gesturing for the others to go ahead, Charlie gave him a squeeze. 'You get used to the idea after a while, Tom, and it don't hurt so much. You've gotta think of *her*, son, she loves it at this place. She only gets upset when we come to visit.'

'I'm sorry, Dad, it's not right. It's just not right. All I want is my little girl, you can't blame me for that.'

'No, I don't blame yer, course I don't. I knew it'd tear your heart out but' – he shrugged arid gave him another squeeze – 'it had to be done. You 'ad to come and see for yourself what it's like and—'

'That's not why I came, I came to get her back. I don't give a toss what the place is like.'

'Now then, now then. Don't say things like that. If it was a lousy run-down home with strict rules you'd be feeling a lot worse and you know it. She's better off than most there, it's yourself you're feeling sorry for, not Emma. I should know, I'm always gutted for myself as well, so's your mother, never mind what poor Jessie's going through. And Billy… he might not say much but he misses 'er. It's making 'im grow up too soon.'

'Poor little lad, he must be confused by it all, Dad, You're right as usual, come on, we'd best catch 'em up.' He looked at his wrist-watch. 'We've got fifteen minutes before the train leaves. Fancy a drink?'

'Sounds good, lead the way, son, lead the way. Just a beer, mind you – no whisky.'

Tom nodded. If his dad was saying that he'd given up drinking spirits, that was fine by him. He was worried when he saw how much damage the drink had done to his dad. He needed his old man. Needed him more than he'd ever let on, 'I was thinking of a pint not a short. Let's 'ope that Mum and Jessie go for it.'

'Course they will, son, and Billy, don't forget Billy. Lemonade and a packet of crisps if you can run to it.' He winked at his son.

'Course I can. They did give me *something* to come 'ome with.'

Giving Charlie two half-crowns to buy beers all round, Tom went to see the butcher, hoping to get one of those chickens. Going inside he didn't beat about the bush when he asked the man how much he would take for one of his fowls.

'Sorry, sir, but they're not for sale. Orders, every one of them.'

'Is that right? They've all bin saving up their coupons right through the war 'ave they?'

'Not that long, sir, no, it's a collective, that's how we do things here. Each one will be shared between three families if not four, the same goes for rabbit. I'm truly sorry to disappoint you.'

'And that's cut and dried is it?'

'Afraid so. If I had a chicken to spare I'd take it for my own family. Just back are you?'

Tom, suddenly tired, rubbed his face and yawned. 'Yeah. You don't mind if I sit down for a minute do you?'

'Of course not.' The butcher eyed him with caution. 'Where were you posted?'

'North Africa.'

'Ah, that'll be why you're late coming home.'

'Yep.' Stretching his face and widening his eyes, Tom asked if he could have a glass of water.

'Of course, sir. All right are you?'

'Yeah. Tired that's all, only got back yesterday. I've been to see my little girl at the Cottage Homes. Our place in London was bombed out and she had to come here.'

Going into the back room the butcher made a chance remark about the handicapped boys who stayed.

Tom was puzzled, and when the man returned with the water he quizzed him, 'I thought it was a children's home,' Tom said.

'Well it is in a way. It started out that way at the turn of the century but things changed. Now it's a residential home for boys who need special attention. Different during the war of course. Ongar families took quite a few evacuees but as we all know, there is never enough accommodation. So the home seemed the most appropriate place for children, like your little girl, to be taken in and looked after. I shouldn't think there are many left now. Almost back to the way it was before the war began.'

'Let's hope *everything* will soon be back to normal, eh…? Anyway, I've got to go, mate. See you again, and thanks for the drink.' Tom gave him a nod and turned to leave, but the butcher stopped him.

'Just a minute. I've got a bit of something that you might like…' No sooner had he gone out the back, when Tom grabbed a small chicken off the rack and stuffed it inside his coat.

Returning with a chunk of fatty stewing beef, the butcher smiled kindly at Tom. 'You could get a few meals out of that if you thicken it up with dumplings.' He wrapped it then winked at Tom and wished him luck. When Tom shoved his hand in his pocket to pay, the man smiled. 'Consider it a small gift.'

'Good on you. Much appreciated. Here's my hand,' said Tom, taking the man's and squeezing it firmly. Once outside his expression changed. His pride had been hurt. No way would he come back to Ongar where he would be known as the man whom the butcher took pity on with a handout of the cheapest beef on the market.

Just as well I did grab that chicken, he told himself, pleased that he still had the knack. After all, this wasn't the first time Tom had stolen something. Far from it.

Chapter Four

By the time Jessie and her family arrived home from the visit, Billy was fast asleep in Tom's arms. They were all tired from the long day, especially Emmie and Charlie who were beginning to feel their age but wouldn't admit it. Pushing the key into the front door, Jessie had the sensation of something not quite right. The house was in darkness and there was nothing unusual about that, but her sixth sense was working overtime. Shrugging it off she put it down to her sensitive state of mind. She had just returned from one of those visits which always left her with a deep feeling of loss which she usually kept to herself.

Jessie's imagination had not been playing tricks, when they had turned the comer into Grant Street, there had been a dim glow from the window but she hadn't consciously registered it and now the house was in total darkness. Unlocking the street door, her hand felt for the light switch in the passage but before she had reached it another light came on – from the living room. Puzzled, she glanced at Emmie who was looking a touch worried.

Walking cautiously along the narrow passage towards the open door of Emmie's front room, Jessie and Tom were confronted by several smiling faces and a chorus of 'Surprise!' which Could probably be heard all along the street.

There were tears all round, as one by one, family and friends embraced Tom, expressing their joy at having him back safe and sound. The noise woke Billy who lost no time in attacking the buffet table which had been laid by the neighbours. There was a large vegetable pie, fruit pies and plenty of sandwiches not to mention a crate of beer. This was Tom's secret welcome-home party which had been organised by Jessie's sisters, Dolly and Hannah. Hannah was keeping out of sight, upstairs. She had another surprise in store, one which had been the best kept secret of all.

Knowing it was going to be a shock as well as a surprise, Jessie's twin sister had to handle her treat in a certain way. After all, Stanley, Tom's younger brother, had been missing presumed dead for a long time. With the war over earlier that year and still no news of their son, both Emmie and Charlie were beginning to think the worst really had happened, but they were wrong and they were in for a big surprise.

Squeezing Stanley's trembling hand, Hannah asked him if he was ready to face everyone. 'Course I am. Can't wait to see Mum and Dad or our Tom. Do I look all right?'

'A feast for their hungry eyes. To see you here is all they could ever wish for, Stanley.' Hannah swallowed against the lump in her throat. 'You are sure that you wouldn't rather I brought Emmie and Charlie up here to see you before the rest of them get—'

'Nah, don't be silly,' said Stanley. 'I've planned this for weeks. I just wanna walk in on 'em and see the look of surprise on their faces.' His expression suddenly changed from mischievous and fun loving to serious. 'Don't start confusing me, Hannah,' he said, rubbing his forehead.

'Should I do it this way or that way? I'm doing it, ain't I? I've got this far.' He was just a little bit apprehensive.

Hannah gave him a hug and kissed him on the cheek. 'Come on then, before I lose my nerve.' Underneath her bravado Hannah was also nervous and hadn't stopped questioning herself. Had she been silly, in going along with Stanley's wishes to keep him hidden away, until Tom's homecoming party?

Still working as a civil servant in London, Hannah had been shocked to catch sight of Stanley at Liverpool Street railway station, where she had been waiting on the platform for her train home to Walthamstow.

'I wanna walk into the front room, as bold as brass,' said Stanley, checking himself in the mirror. 'Show them that their son, one arm missing or not, is a very 'appy bloke. I look all right, don't I? Not as skinny as I was?'

'You look great, Stanley,' she said, kissing him on the cheek. 'Handsome as ever.' How could she tell him he looked only half the chirpy, happy-go-lucky lad he was before he left for the war? The Japanese POW camp had left its mark.

'Main thing is that I feel really 'appy. I've given myself face-ache from smiling, I've bin smiling for two weeks solid.'

'Good,' said Hannah. It was true, pale and thin or not there was a warm glow about him which came and went, but at least it was there. Stanley was always the warm, friendly, youngest son of Emmie and Charlie and nothing ever seemed to get him down.

'I'm alive, that's all I care about, I'm alive and I'm back 'ome. And I'm about to see my Mum and Dad again.' His face lit up. 'Can't wait to see Tom's expression. What's the betting he cries?'

Downstairs, standing on a low chair, Charlie clapped his hands for attention and raised his voice above the racket of laughter and conversation. 'All right you lot! Shut up for a minute! I wanna make a speech!'

Astounding him, they did shut up. Whatever anyone might say about Charlie Smith he was a respected man in the street, a wise old chief of the tribe. 'Now then, I don't 'ave to tell you how me and Emmie feel about 'aving our Tom back. Things are not tickety-boo yet, what with our granddaughter not back from evacuation and that but we're on the way. Once Tom and Jessie's place is looking like a little palace again it'll be like old times!' His voice dropped as he said, 'Well not exactly like old times but…' The sudden silence and change in mood stopped him in his tracks. Slowly he turned to see who they were staring at. It couldn't be…

'But what, Dad? Cat got your tongue, 'as it.' Stanley, grinning, stood in the doorway. 'All right, Mum?' All eyes were on Stanley but all he had eyes for at that moment was Charlie. His Dad, his skinny old Dad. 'I told you I'd be back, Dad, didn't I?'

It was little Billy who broke the awesome silence. 'It's a blooming-well soldier, Granddad! They've shot 'is arm off!' There was no laughter, no scolding Billy for cursing, nothing. Charlie stepped down carefully from the chair and walked towards his youngest son arid looked into his face, hardly believing it was true. Finally he managed to speak, 'Stanley?' he said, croakily.

'Yeah, course it's me, ain't a ghost am I? It's me, Dad, I'm back.' He patted the empty sleeve of his jacket and grinned. 'I've lost a bit of weight though.'

Charlie turned to Emmie as if he needed confirmation that this was real. That his youngest son had returned as well as Tom. But Emmie couldn't help him out, she couldn't speak either. The held-back tears from stress and worry were now cascading down her cheeks. The fact that he'd lost an arm, the fact that he'd lost weight and was as pale as a ghost didn't matter. Her Stanley, her youngest, her baby, was here in the room. The waiting, the uncertainty, the worry – it was over. Slowly and not too steady on her legs, she went to him and gently, wrapped her arms round her son, murmuring, 'I love you, Stanley. Well done, son, well done.'

Stroking Emmie's grey hair, Stanley murmured, 'I love you as well, Mum. I love you so much.'

That night, not one neighbour complained of the rumpus coming out of the Smiths' house. Charlie played his banjo-mandolin until his fingers were sore and sung as he'd never sung before. He also enjoyed a good drink, promising himself that *that* would be the last time.

The dancing, the singing, the laughter were good reason for anyone to complain but most of the neighbours were there – a part of it. News spread fast in the back streets of the East End, especially good news and this was the best. Not just one of their own had returned but *two*.

With Tom holding Jessie close in their bed into the wee small hours of the following morning and with the party still going on below, she thanked God for sparing young Stanley as well as her own precious husband. 'You can stop feeling guilty now, Tom.'

'Guilty?'

'Well you know… you were back home safe and sound, the only *one* out of three sons. I thought you were feeling down because of that.'

'Not really, Jess. You can't expect me to be full of smiles. Anyway, Stanley's back safe and sound so Mum and Dad can stop worrying over 'im.' He stroked Jessie's hair and looked into her lovely face. 'Did you ever wonder if I'd get back alive?'

'Not really, Tom, no; I was more worried over you when you went AWOL. I don't think you realised then how dangerous that was.'

'Wasn't dangerous, Jess. I only went back 'cos of you. You never 'ad enough to live on. Tight bastards shouldn't 'ave stopped your army pension. Anyway, that's over and done with,' he said, stroking her leg. 'In a week's time I'm gonna 'ave our place ready for us to move into and we'll fetch our Emma-Rose back. And do you know who's gonna help me with all the work? Our Stanley, our Stanley *and* Dad. We'll work together as a threesome and while we work we'll talk about Johnnie, you know, bring it out in the open, face up to what's happened. I'll rope in some of our old mates as well. I'll make up for my past mistakes, I promise.'

'We'll see,' she said, unconvinced by his words. He had let her down so many times in the past she daren't start to rely on him one hundred per cent now. She wanted to – and she needed to – after all she'd been through, but she couldn't. Not yet.

His eyes closed, Tom was sinking into a deep sleep and soon he would be snoring. She smiled at the thought of actually missing that sound during his time away. Alone with her thoughts in the dark room she wondered whether her bit of good news was best kept to herself in case it came to nothing.

Shopping down the Bethnal Green Road earlier that week she had bumped into Max, her old flame and first boyfriend whom she very nearly married. Max had been turned down for the army so never went to war. He had been born with two left feet according, to *his* version of the medical diagnosis. As a good, qualified bookkeeper he could easily afford to move out of the East End and move on to better things, but the East End was Max's life and the people here were his people and furthermore, he had never quite given up on Jessie. His face had lit up when they bumped into each other in the market for the first time after almost a year.

On this occasion, they had taken time out to enjoy a coffee together and like old times, had chatted ten to the dozen, catching up on all the news. Max's mother, whom Jessie had been fond of, had had a massive heart attack and died in her sleep. Jessie felt ashamed for not visiting them when she was able, after her own long run of disastrous events had eased. Max's father had continued to run the delicatessen without his wife and according to Max suffered his grief openly, talking about his loss to any customer who was prepared to listen and some who weren't.

When Jessie had filled Max in on all that she had been going through, he made an offer impossible to believe. He said that she could live in the two-bedroomed flat above the delicatessen, which he'd bought as an investment. He even offered to take her in his car to collect Emma-Rose. Max had assured her that there would be enough room for Tom too, once he returned. Now that Tom *was* back, she wasn't too sure how he would take it. Tom had always been a jealous man but when he had asked her whether she had gone out in the evening while he had been posted abroad it seemed more like interrogation than anything else. She now wondered if she dare mention Max and his offer. Tom had always been especially jealous of Max.

Wrapped in her thoughts Jessie made up her mind that she would go through with the meeting which had been arranged and tell Max that it was best they stayed with Emmie until their house was ready. She was to meet Max at the Mile End Gate.

'What you thinking about Jess?' said Tom sleepily, wrapping his arm round her.

'Our house and us all together again. I thought you were asleep.'

'I was,' he said, yawning and drifting back off again.

Try as she might, Jessie couldn't sleep. All that Max had told her ran through her mind for a second time. His mother's heart attack had been brought on by the worst kind of headline news. His mother had recognised a cousin in a photograph in one of the newspapers. It was a picture taken by one of the American troops who overran the East German Buchenwald concentration camp where 21,000 starving survivors had been existing amidst thousands of corpses. Bodies which had been dumped into a huge open mass grave. Max's aunt was one of them.

Jessie understood that the atrocities had to be told to the world but wished that such photographs weren't published. It had destroyed Max's faith in God and his faith had been strong, once upon a time. To lose a faith was worse than never having one and now Jessie was also beginning to have doubts, having been brought up a Christian. The world had gone mad.

Despite these horrors filling her mind, Jessie – exhausted enough by the day's activities – at last succumbed and fell into a deep but restless sleep.

–

As Jessie made her way past Wickhams department store, on her way to the Mile End Gate to meet Max, she was conscious of Christmas drawing close. Several stalls along the Waste were out and the street vendors were in fine voice as they promoted their wares to the shoppers who were on the lookout for things which were no longer on ration. Although, here, as in most London street markets, almost anything could be bought for the right price, on ration or not.

Thinking about Emma-Rose being home for Christmas made Jessie very happy and it was all she could think about. She imagined her sitting by the Christmas tree, opening a present or pulling a Christmas cracker with paperchains hanging across the ceiling and the candles lit around the Christmas tree.

So deep in thought was Jessie, that until her brother, Alfie, stepped right in front of her, she had neither seen nor heard him call her name. Stopping short, she looked up at him, surprised as ever at the way he had grown tall and was still growing. Smiling he gave her a chiding look. 'Still living in a dream world, Jess?'

'Alfie! I wish you wouldn't do that. I was miles away.'

'Give us a hug then.'

'No. You give me one.'

'I asked first.'

Laughing, the pair of them linked arms and strolled along together. 'So what are you doing down the Waste, Alfie, swaggering round as if you own the place?'

'Eyeing up the crumpet. Bit different now that their old men are back from the war, can't get a look in.'

'You sound just like a yobbo. When are you gonna grow up?' Jessie was determined to keep her place in the family pecking order. As far as she was concerned, Alfie was still her little brother. At any rate he was younger than her and that counted for a lot in her eyes.

'So…' he said, forgiving her patronising tone, '…you gonna take up the offer then, Jess?'

'What offer's that?'

'Shacking up with Max.'

Stopping in her tracks she pulled her arm away from his. 'That's not funny! If you ever say anything like that in front of Tom—'

'Don't be silly, course I wouldn't. Mind you, as nice as he is, I think you'd do better with Max. He's going places that one and all in the name of a "straight chap",' Alfie chortled. 'If only his clients knew, eh?' At least he was enjoying the irony. 'He'll 'ave a million in the bank by the time he's forty-odd. See if I'm wrong.'

Jessie was surprised. She had no idea that Alfie and Max saw each other, apart from meeting at the local boxing club, to which her old boyfriend made donations and where he was a member of the board. 'You're not suggesting he's bent, Alfie?'

'He's a bookkeeper, Jess, wise up. You should see who he drinks with at lunch-time only his clients who've got a few bob and run nice little shops and that. Betting shops mostly. Still, can't blame 'em for sticking together.'

'What are you talking about – who stick together?'

'The Jews, they're worse than the funny handshake lot.' He looked sideways at her and spoke as if she was ignorant to the ways of the real world; 'Freemasons, Jess, Freemasons.'

'Max's not a Freemason!'

'No, he's a Jew. Can't be in both camps, they look after their own is what I'm trying to tell you, that's all. No need to fly off the handle. How is Tom anyway?'

49

'All right, all things considered. Stanley's back, by the way.'

Alfie looked genuinely pleased. 'No one told me. Well, well, well, that's the best bit of news today. Good for 'im. *Was* he shacked up in France then?'

'No, a Japanese prisoner-of-war camp. He lost an arm and a lot of weight but not his spirit. He'll be all right, but if you *do* see 'im don't ask about it, he still has nightmares.'

'I won't say nothing, Jess, course I won't. Poor bastard, prisoner of war, eh.' Alfie let out a low whistle. 'Which arm did he lose?'

'Left.'

'Thank Christ for that, unless he was left-handed?' Always the wisecracker. 'Was he?'

'Shut up, Alfie. I'm not in the mood. Anyway, how comes you know about Max's flat? The one that he said we could *all* live in; including Tom.'

Alfie tapped the side of his nose and winked at her. According to his story, he and Max had been associates right through the war. Associates and good mates and it had all started with Alfie joining the anti-fascists before the war. Max might have been taken in by his so-called passion to drive Mosley out but Jessie knew different. Her brother, with no trade or profession to speak of, was and always had been, clever – streetwise to say the least. He knew where his bread was buttered and for his own reasons he would have got in with Max's lot.

'I s'pose they gave you cover when you deserted?'

'I never deserted, Jess, I was a conscientious objector. I don't expect you to believe me though. It wasn't always a bowl of cherries; but as it just so 'appens they were all right to me. I stayed in some nice family 'omes. They know 'ow to cook them Jewish women. I 'ad a few good breakfasts in bed.' His grin was back.

'While their husbands were out at work no doubt?'

'Least I could do, wasn't it? Kept the women happy while the men went out and earned the bread.' He then went on to give his version of his own politics. If certain businessmen and tradesmen didn't have to go to war, he couldn't see anything wrong by staying low and keeping the engines running himself. 'I was small fry, Jess. But a strong tree needs as many leaves as it can grow. Anyone'll tell you that.' He looked at his wristwatch. 'Blimey, look at the time, tell Max I'll see 'im later on down the snooker club. Let me know if you and Tom need anything, eh?' He patted his top pocket to indicate that his wallet wasn't empty. He then ruffled her hair and swaggered off home to his flat above the Italian cafe.

Continuing on her way Jessie was disturbed, not just because her brother walked on the wrong side of the law, but he had mentioned Max once too often. She couldn't believe her old boyfriend would be working for any of Alfie's associates. Were they that chummy? Had Max forgotten Alfie's early involvement in crime? He was stealing chocolate and sweets before he was six years old and now mixed with criminals and wore tailored suits and cuff-links.

Alfie was more ensconced in the East End under-world than Jessie imagined. The protection racket had grown into a profitable business in most large cities. Gangs offering to protect dubs, pubs and shops from other gangs in return for a fee, was a guise. More often than not, the business concerned was not in any danger from such threats, but as many owners who refused to pay a protec-tion fee had discovered, their business would soon be burgled, set alight or trashed. The sorry victim was then ready to become a client of the gang they had rejected. A detestable form of crime but ironically one that did in some cases help to keep law and order.

Max was not involved in this low side of life but if asked he would have to admit that some of his clients probably did brush with such villains and not all of his patrons walked the straight and narrow, but that was life as far as he was concerned and much worse things happened at sea. All that Max was concerned with was to build up his own small and legitimate accountancy business. What his clients did for a living was their affair and not his. Socially, he was bound to come into contact with some of the rogues in the East End – his recreational passion was snooker and some of the billiard halls were like magnets for all and sundry, providing that membership was given and it was only given to the chosen ones.

Max, unlike the people he sometimes mixed with, was not a big drinker nor did he go to the dance halls or pubs. A quiet drink in his preferred club in a select area of the West End before or after a meal in one of the small restaurants was where he would take Jessie if the opportunity arose.

Arriving ten minutes early, outside the Blind Beggar pub, at the Mile End Gate, she was hardly surprised to see Max already there. Without trying, he stood out in a crowd, as smart as ever in his dark blue suit and black overcoat and trilby hat, he looked the respectable gentleman. As soon as he caught sight of her, his face lit up.

Brushing a kiss across her cheek, he looked a touch embarrassed and was possibly blushing. 'Trust you to be early,' said Jessie.

'You've just missed Alfie,' he said, as casual as you like, containing his joy at seeing her again.

'No I didn't. We bumped into each other. He said to tell you he'd see you down the snooker hall later.'

'Good. You must be pleased with the way he's turned out, Jessie. He's so well-mannered and friendly, I'm impressed. He could so easily have turned to crime.'

'Let's hope he hasn't,' she said, smiling, tongue in cheek.

'Of course he hasn't, he's got a regular job, a flat of his own...'

'Rented, Max, he hasn't bought it, if that's what he tells you.'

'You know what I mean. Now, do you want a drink and a sandwich or would you prefer to have lunch in the West End?'

'A quick drink. I mustn't stay long, what with Tom only having been back a week I—'

'Tom's home?' The smile disappeared but once again he covered his disappointment well. 'Alfie didn't say. How is he?'

'Fine. Almost back to his old self and right now he's taking the tarpaulin off our roof to see just how much damage there is. He's already been to the Borough and bullied them into action. They're starting soon.'

Taking her arm he led her into the Blind Beggar. 'Does this mean what I think it means? You won't be needing the flat?'

'It does, Max, yeah. I'm sorry to mess you about but—'

'Don't be silly, I'm pleased for you. You'll have Emma-Rose back again. I know how badly you miss her.' He ordered their drinks and pulled out a bar stool for Jessie. 'You can use the flat until your house is ready, you know.

Why don't you do that? It must be cramped at your mother-in-law's.'

While she explained that Tom had already secured temporary accommodation for them she couldn't help feeling as if she was treading on eggshells. The last thing she wanted was to hurt Max's feelings but there seemed little point in beating about the bush. 'I didn't tell Tom about your offer.'

'Why should you? He's found somewhere and that's the important thing. Where is it? Not miles out in the country I hope.'

'No. But it's not that far from Victoria Park. A good fifteen minutes walk, but you know I like walking, that's its only saving grace. It's a two-up two-down dump. No bathroom and the lavatory's in the backyard and that backs on to the railway yard. So all day and all night trains are gonna be roaring past on their way to Liverpool Street station.'

'But you'll be able to make it a decent place to live?'

'Not really. But Emmie and Dolly are gonna help me scrub it from top to bottom. We shouldn't be there for no more than three weeks, at the most.'

Gazing at her with that adoring look he couldn't disguise made Jessie feel warm and comfortable in his company. She had to be careful though, not to give any signs of what she really felt, what she'd always felt, that perhaps she should never have broken off their engagement. 'How's your dad,' she said, keeping things on the right level.

'Don't ask,' said Max, 'He's got a girlfriend. Purely platonic of course – according to Dad.'

'Oh come on, Max,' said Jessie, smiling at the thought of Leo kissing a woman with passion. 'He's too old for all that.'

'Don't you believe it.' Max went quiet and then taking Jessie by surprise asked if he could help in any way with regard to finding work for Tom. Reminding him of her husband's strong sense of pride, she thanked him but gave a definite no for the answer.

'He's still a bit jealous of you, Max, I don't wanna add insult to injury. No doubt by now he's heard how well you're doing.'

Max took her hand and squeezed it. 'I would never try and take a man's wife away from him, Jess, but should things go wrong...'

Placing her hand on his, she leaned forward and spoke quietly, intimately. 'Please God nothing will go wrong for me from now on, but you know that you would be the only person on my mind, if I needed a shoulder to cry on. You do know that, Max, don't you?'

'I'd like to think that...' his voice trailed off as he eyed someone familiar coming into the bar. It was Stanley – Tom's brother. Pulling his hand from Jessie's, Max straightened and indicated with his eyes that they had company. Turning round to face Stanley her heart sank, the expression on his face said it all. Giving Max a black look he did no more than turn around and walk out.

Things were worse than Jessie imagined, because, unknown to her, Stanley had seen her talking to Max outside and he'd seen her kiss him on the cheek. Now he believed his suspicions had been confirmed. Holding hands at the bar and enjoying a drink together meant only one thing as far as Stanley was concerned: Jessie was cheating on Tom and had probably been doing so while his brother had been fighting abroad.

'Do you think he'll say anything?' said Max, worried.

Ashamed at what her brother-in-law might be thinking, she shook her head. 'No, he's one of the best. One thing I do know though, he'll be upset by what he saw, or rather what he reads into it.'

'Not once you explain.'

'Explain? No, I can't do that. How can I? It'll sound like a trumped-up excuse. I'll just have to leave it be and he'll see that I'm not playing around. Poor devil, as if he hasn't got enough on 'is plate. He's the one whom you could 'ave helped on the work front, not now though.'

The light-hearted mood was now spoiled, there really was no more to be said. It seemed to Jessie that every time she took a step forward in life she took two or three steps backwards. She wondered if life would ever be what it once was. When she and Tom were first married, they were happy with not a care in the world, other than the rift between herself and her mother. Rose had not wanted Jessie to marry Tom in the first place and had been cold towards her during the weeks leading up to the wedding, after Jessie had told her she was pregnant.

–

Instead of going straight home to Bethnal Green after leaving Max, she made her way to her mother's house in Stepney. For some strange reason she wanted to be with her parents and since her father had died several years ago she had only Rose to turn to. Taking the chance that she could only be greeted with a cold shoulder, instead of a motherly hug, she wondered how she could win back her mother's love and favour. After all, life was better now than it had been during the war, and everyone was doing their best to make the most of things.

When Rose opened the door, Jessie was taken back by the look of surprise and pleasure on her mother's face. Instead of the cold welcome she had expected, she was greeted with open arms. 'You're the last person I expected to see. Come on in love out of the cold.'

'Is everything all right?' said Jessie, somewhat puzzled.

'All right? Hardly, Jessie.' Rose went straight into the kitchen and filled the kettle. 'I can't tell you how many poor souls in this street have been left war widows, not to mention those whose men *chose* not to come back to their wives and families.' She shook her head slowly as she put the kettle on the gas stove. 'I've not long been in, as it so happens. Ten minutes earlier and we would have missed each other.' She turned to Jessie and smiled. 'I'm glad we didn't.'

'Me too, Mum, I've missed you.'

'And I've missed you, you and my grandchildren. But there we are; things are not always as they should be.'

Drawing the conversation away from their differences, Rose went on to say that she'd been at a neighbour's house, trying to comfort the poor woman who'd been left with five children on her hands. 'Her husband survived the war, that much she does know. He'll have God to answer to is all I can say. After all we women have been through – keeping families together and suchlike – and then the man doesn't come home to his loved ones. It's disgraceful!'

'Tom's back…' said Jessie quietly.

'So I heard.'

'…and Stanley.'

'Yes, I know. Poor devil, how's he managing with only one arm? How's Emmie taking it?'

'You seem to be up on the news, Mum,' said Jessie, feeling her old self again.

'Dolly keeps me up to date.'

'Of course. She and Hannah arranged the welcome-home party. Anyway, Emmie would have been happy even if Stanley had come home in a wheelchair never mind minus an arm.'

'I dare say she would.' Rose sat down at the kitchen table and looked into her daughter's face. 'At least the cold air's put some colour back into your cheeks. How does Tom seem? Any more settled? Or is that too much to ask?'

Jessie detected a faint smile on her mother's lips and was fazed by her change in attitude. This was the first time she'd asked about Tom without frowning. 'I s'pose you could say that Tom's in a kind of shocked state, most of the men must be. All the changes…' She looked at her mother cautiously. Jessie then decided to mention the very thing that had caused them to fall out last time they were together: her having placed Emma-Rose in a children's home. 'We went to see Emma-Rose.'

'Well I should think that *would* have been the first thing he'd want to do.'

'Even Tom admitted she was being well looked after and had been safer there. But he wants her back home straight away.'

'Does he now? Well, maybe this will teach him to be patient. It'll take weeks, Jessie, what with all the offi-cialdom and paperwork not to mention no place of your own to live in.'

'Tom's found a two-up two-down which'll do fine, for a couple of weeks anyway, while he fixes our place.'

'Couple of weeks! Stop dreaming, Jessie, months more like, it's in a right state. The tenants in my attic are moving out in a couple of weeks' time. If you like you can tell the authorities at the children's home that you'll be moving in here. That might speed things up a bit.'

'But I just told you, Mum, Tom's *found* a place.'

'Let's hope history doesn't repeat itself, *again*.'

'What's that supposed to mean?'

'How many times in the past has Tom found you somewhere right to live which has turned out to be wrong? All your thoughts and energy should be on that poor child. If you moved in here you could have her home within days. Many a night I've cried thinking of what she might be going through. You can't trust anyone nowadays, Jessie.'

Ignoring her mum's criticism, Jessie said, 'If the attic rooms are not being let, and you feel lonely, why don't you ask Hannah if she wants to move in?'

'I didn't say I was lonely. She doesn't want to in any case. Your twin sister never wanted to live-in with us, Jessie. I expect she blames me for giving her up when she was a baby, as if I had any choice. God knows this war was bad enough but the last one' – she shook her head gravely – 'and the aftermath of that… it's a wonder I could manage to keep, feed and clothe *one* of you never mind two. But Hannah will never see it that way.' Rose lowered her head, saddened by the memory. 'I had no choice at the time. Your father and I *had* to give her up. But, after all is said and done, she found us in the end and I'm more than happy about that.' Rose stared out, thinking. 'Never in a million years would we have handed over one of our babies if we had had a choice.'

'Same as I never had a choice, Mum, with Emma—'

'Rubbish, that *was* different. You could have brought her to me to look after. Poor child. Get her out, Jessie, get her out as soon as you can and bring her home. Haven't we all suffered enough heartache?'

'But she *likes* it there. It's not as bad as you'd have it.'

'She's probably too frightened to tell you how she really feels. She'd have them to answer to once you'd gone home.' Rose was gazing out of the window now, her thoughts drifting back to the painful past.

'Is that what it was like for you?' said Jessie, treading carefully.

'I should think it was; I can't remember it all. I just remember the feeling, the emptiness. You never lose that – the pain of wanting your mother so badly.'

Placing a hand on her mother's arm, Jessie asked, 'If something's wrong, Mum, you *can* tell me.'

Averting her eyes, Rose murmured, 'It's my age, I expect. Creeping up on me too quickly…'

'Come on. You're in your fifties; that's not old. You're tired of course you are. It's been really hard for you – for all of us.'

'I never in a million years thought it would all turn out like this.' Still Rose wouldn't look at her. 'Me and your father did love each other and we had such plans for our children. We would have moved out of the East End you know. To the countryside. We used to talk about our children going to a village school in Kent or Essex and then on to grammar school and good jobs at the end of it all. Dreams. That's what they were and we had no idea at the time. There's our Alfie – a mobster. Stephen's not right – and we both know what that means. You behaved like a tart before you were married, and Dolly's—'

'Stop! You stop right there, Mum. I did *not* behave like a tart.'

'Of course you did. Tom bedded you after you'd only known each other for a few weeks. What would you call *that*? Hardly the behaviour of a decent young lady from a decent family.'

Had it not been for the forlorn expression on her mother's face, Jessie would have stormed out there and then. Something was troubling her mum. Something had upset her. 'Come on,' said Jessie, trying her best, 'the past is past. Like I said, you're bound to feel down. Thousands of mothers and wives must be at their lowest ever; look at Emmie and what she's got to cope with: her eldest son dead; Tom disillusioned with his lot... and now Stanley permanently disabled. At least none of us were killed or harmed in the war. We're all alive and kicking.'

'Yes, and at least Emmie's got you and our Billy and no doubt she'll see more of Emma-Rose once she's back home. She's got Tom and she's also got you. Whereas mine have all gone, flown the nest. Dolly's hardly ever in and now Stephen wants to move out as well.'

At last Rose had got if off her chest – Stephen wanted to move out; her youngest, her baby. Her lad who would rather have been born a girl. 'He's twenty, Mum. You can't blame 'im for wanting to be independent.'

'Stuff and nonsense, twenty's no age, whoever heard of such a thing? Moving out and for all the wrong reasons. There's plenty of space here. I don't interfere, I don't even say anything about the life he leads. It's mixing with that theatrical lot that's what it is. They've put ideas into his head. I wish he'd gone to war with the rest of the lads his age. He'd have gone out a boy and returned a man.'

'Or maybe he wouldn't 'ave returned at all? Don't wish that on him, he was needed back here. Someone had to keep the machines running, plenty of men didn't go. Us women couldn't cope all by ourselves.'

'I never said I wanted him to go to war! I just don't want him to leave home!' She thumped her fist on the table. 'His place is here with me!'

Realising that she would get nowhere with her mother in this mood, Jessie changed tactics. 'Look, Mum, I'm gonna 'ave to go soon. I shouldn't really 'ave been gone this long. Tom'll be wondering where I've got to. The reason I came was because I wanted to—'

'Yes, why *did you* come?' snapped Rose, interrupting. 'To tell me that you're going to emigrate? Nothing would surprise me.'

Taking a deep breath, Jessie kept calm. 'Don't be daft, I'm not going anywhere. I came, Mum, because I want you to come with me to speak to the people at Ongar. You're better than me at that kind of thing. I would like you to explain that the time is now right for Emma-Rose to come home.'

Rose went quiet and Jessie thought she saw a faint smile on her lips. 'Why didn't you say so in the first place? Of course I'll come with you.'

'Good.' Jessie feigned a sigh of relief. 'That's a weight off my mind. We'll go together, just you and me, who knows, maybe they'll let us fetch her 'ome with us.'

Slowly raising her eyes to meet Jessie's, Rose asked if she really meant it. 'Of course I do,' said Jessie, 'you're my mum and I want you with me when I go and get your granddaughter. It's only natural that I'd want that.'

'Is it?' Pressing her lips together, Rose reached for her handkerchief. Too proud to cry she dabbed her eyes. 'Don't fret, Jessie, we'll get her out of there, you and me.'

'And stop worrying over Stephen, he's the most sensible one out of the lot of us. Yes, he is keeping arms length with all the family, but I can understand that. One day he'll be ready to say what he truly feels and the way he wants to live.'

'I'm hoping he'll grow out of all that, Jessie. He's beginning to act and think more like a young man now. I know his voice hasn't broken properly yet, but it soon will, and when it does he'll be as normal as your brother, Alfie.'

'Maybe,' said Jessie, unconvinced. 'All I know is that you'll be very proud of him one day. He's a good actor and he's got a cracking voice as well, not to mention his good looks. Be thankful he's *not* like our Alfie, Mum, that sod thinks he's King Spit.'

A smile spread across Rose's face. 'His father would be amused by the way he struts about – as if he owns the East End.'

'I'm not so sure, but the point is that your family's all right. Or as Charlie would say, onwards and upwards.'

'Charlie,' chuckled Rose. 'How is the old codger?'

'Top of the tree, he's always asking after you, so is Emmie. Maybe it's time you got in touch and mixed with your old friends again?'

'We'll see,' said Rose, wondering how they would all take to Ted, her new friend. Smiling to herself, Rose thought about him when he first came to her door looking for antiques to buy. On his first try Ted had noticed that she'd been shedding a tear – her red-rimmed, puffy eyes gave her away. She had opened the door only because she believed him to be the postman with a package she'd ordered for her shop. When she saw a man in his fifties, with silver hair and blue eyes, smiling as if he knew her, she had to admit to herself that she welcomed the intrusion. He was smart, clean and had the air of a true gentleman.

Well practised at his trade, he used his charm to get her listening. He had talked quietly about people hoarding furniture they no longer had use for or even wanted. He had touched a chord – Rose was in the mood for change. Most of her furniture had come from men like himself, who bought and sold second-hand furniture. When Rose had married twenty-five years ago, all of her furniture had been second-hand and old-fashioned. But as Ted, who was only interested in antiques, had told her, when eyeing the grandfather clock in the hallway, she had taken care and lavished love as well as polish. His familiar manner had been welcome company into her lonely life. She told him she would think about selling some bits and that he may call again. Two days later he was back and surprising herself, Rose invited him in for a cup of tea. On his third visit she told him she'd decided not to sell any of her home for the time being. He shrugged and waved it off before asking if she'd like to go out with him for a drink. His sense of humour and easygoing ways had been like a breath of fresh air and in a rare moment of recklessness she had said yes. In fact, she was to go out with him that very evening but was feeling a little nervous.

'You go back a long way…' Jessie's voice broke into her thoughts. 'Emmie and Charlie consider you a close friend as well as family.'

'Family?' said Rose, still preoccupied with her own thoughts.

'Well, you are now, Mum. You share the same grand-children don't forget.'

'So we do,' she said, 'so we do.' Suddenly Rose saw a way of making less of this meeting she'd agreed to with her new friend. She was to meet Ted for a drink in the Old Lion Pub on the Mile End Road. If she could get Emmie and Charlie to join them, that would make it all seem less like a silly date. They were a shrewd couple and Emmie could read people like a book. If Ted wasn't all he seemed to be, she would spot the flaws straight away.

'I might walk back there with you now, Jessie,' said Rose, with an air of indifference. 'The fresh air might do me good.'

'Billy'd love that. They all would, Tom as well.'

'You don't have to say things just to try and cheer me up. I'm all right now.'

'Billy told Tom that you didn't come to see us and you weren't talking to me any more. Then he—'

'Well would you credit it, a child of his age taking notice.'

'And what's more, he's dropped the Rose off his sister's name. Insists on calling her Emmie.'

Rose sank back down into her chair. 'All right, Jessie, don't go too far, I'm not made of stone.'

'Well I'm sorry but it's true. You're his gran, his Granny Rose. Did you really think that Billy was just gonna forget you?'

'I suppose that is what I thought would happen, deep down, yes.' She became silent again, pensive. 'I just wish you hadn't put Emma-Rose in a home, Jessie. I don't think you have any idea how much that affected me.'

'I had no choice, the Welfare ordered it! We were cramped in a tiny room, she was better off there.'

Rose raised a hand to stop Jessie from going on. 'I can't help feeling what I feel, Jessie. I just can't help it. So let's get her out of that place as soon as we can.'

'All right,' said Jessie, 'we'll go tomorrow. You and me.'

'And Emmie,' said Rose, 'if we can't win them round, she will certainly.'

Minutes later, with her coat and hat on, Rose came back into the kitchen with some letters for Jessie. 'I meant to give these to Dolly for you, but forgot. None of them looked official so I wasn't too worried.' She handed them to Jessie who flipped through checking the backs to see who the senders were and was surprised and pleased to see one from Elmshill, the tiny Suffolk village where she'd been evacuated to, and another from her once saviour, Edna the transvestite who often had her reeling with laughter while bombs were dropping close-by. Edna's jokes were on the crude side but always funny. From the address it was clear that Jessie's friend was not living in rooms or a small flat as she would have expected, but in a house. This was the letter Jessie opened first. Skimming through, she read that Edna's partner of two years had said that he would like to meet Jessie having heard so much about her. This bit of news lifted her spirits. She would like to see Edna again.

–

By the time Jessie arrived at Emmie's with her mother in tow, Tom was in a sulky mood. Stanley was there and she hoped that he hadn't mentioned her meeting with Max – he hadn't. But seemingly he wasn't going to let her off the hook too easily. Instead of his usual cheery greeting he kept a serious face and nodded. 'All right, Jess?'

'Not too bad.' She turned to Tom and smiled. 'What's up with you?'

'Nothing.' He was surprised to see Rose with Jessie. 'You're a sight for sore eyes, Rose.'

'Hello, Tom,' said Rose, 'it's good to see you home and looking well.'

Scratching his head, he looked at her mischievously. 'You're still talking to me then?'

'Of course I am. Where's Emmie and Charlie?'

'Mum took Billy to a kid's tea party that Jessie'd forgot about, and Dad's gone to see a man about roof tiles. Everything all right, is it?'

'I think so. I don't suppose there's a chance of a cold drink? My throat's dry.' Rose dropped into an armchair and began to unlace her new boots. 'I should think it'll take ages to wear these in.'

Bemused by the change in his mother-in-law Tom looked to Jessie for an answer. 'So you went on to your Mum's then after the Welfare?'

She had lied about going to the Welfare and had to think quickly. If she had been found out, a double lie would make matters worse. She decided on evasion. 'I think I'll leave you and Mum to catch up, I'll put the kettle on. Come on, Stanley, keep me company in the kitchen.' It wasn't company she was seeking but the opportunity to put her brother-in-law straight as to why she had gone to see Max.

'Sorry, no can do, I should be elsewhere. Good to see you again, Mrs Warner, how's Dolly?'

'I thought you'd already seen her, Stanley, at the party,' said Rose, easing off one boot with her foot.

'Yeah but that was then and this is now. She blows with the wind, your Dolly, don't she?'

'Oh I'm not so sure, she's matured quite a bit since before the war. It's brought a change to all of us, I dare say.'

'Could be right,' he said, raising his eyebrows at Tom. 'Gotta go. Say hello to 'er for me then, won't you?' he said, leaving the room.

'Best if it came from you,' said Rose, 'she's still carrying a torch you know. I'd be pleased to see the pair of you walking out, most of her friends seem to be courting. Why don't you take her to the pictures, there are some good films showing these days.'

'Oh, so she's lonely then? Ah well, in that case I'll pop round and see 'er. If that's all right, Mrs Warner?'

'I said so, didn't I?' She became suspicious. 'You didn't get yourself married before the enemy captured you, did you?'

'Course I never. I just thought you might see me as the one-armed bandit.' He waited in the doorway for her response, enjoying the tease.

'It's the way *she* sees you that matters,' Rose looked up at him and smiled. 'I'm sure you've more strength in one arm than most men have in two put together.'

'Yeah?' This pleased Stanley. She was the first to have responded positively when he'd mentioned his missing limb, most people changed the subject and that made things worse. 'You could be right there. I might pop round then, see what kind of a welcome she gives me.'

'If you should come when she's out you can keep me company instead. Fill me in on what happened in that prisoner-of-war camp.'

Stanley wasn't the only one bewildered by the change in Rose; Tom could hardly believe it. Characteristically, he turned it to his advantage. Once they were alone and sitting comfortably, he told Rose he was thinking of starting up his own small business and asked if she'd be interested in investing some capital. She turned him down flat, saying that if he hadn't the faith to do it himself or with his brother then she couldn't possibly have confidence that his venture would be profitable. 'Come and talk to me once you're on the road, Tom,' was her answer, 'I might think differently then.'

'What about a small loan?' he said, boyishly, using his charm to win her round.

'No. "Neither a borrower nor lender be", that was my husband's motto and it's rubbed off on me over the years. There's no surer way of falling out with a relative or a friend when one or the other becomes the banker.'

She laid her head back and closed her eyes. 'There is something I *will* do, mind: help you and Jess with paid help to get your house back up to scratch. I'd be doing it for my grandchildren. You're old enough to take care of your own welfare but my grandchildren aren't. I should think that thirty pounds would help, meanwhile, in return, I should like you, Jessie, Billy *and* Emma-Rose to move in with me and Dolly. That's the deal – take it or leave it.'

'You've got me over a barrel, Rose,' he said. 'I'll have to think about it though.'

'I'm sure you will. I'll leave it to you to tell Jessie,' she said. 'You'll have to be firm with her and put your foot down. Ever since she ran that Westminster Women's Voluntary group, she thinks she's right about most things. Stubborn more likely.'

'Leave it to me,' he said, smiling, 'leave it to me.' *Things are looking up, Tom*, is what he thought, *things are looking up.* All he had to do was convince Jessie not to turn down the offer out of silly pride.

Later, once Rose had had a chat with Emmie by the fire, she felt much better about Ted. She half expected that her old friend would make fun of her, but no, Emmie was all for it and told Rose, that it was time she stopped being a damp squib. Rose surprised herself by talking non-stop about Ted: what he looked like, his easy manner, his sense of humour and more importantly how relaxed she was in his company.

'Well, it's done you the world of good already, Rose,' Emmie had said, 'so it can only get better. And don't you worry about Charlie making fun of you. We'll see you in the pub for a nice quiet drink.'

Rose had returned home happier than she had been in a while. She was looking forward to seeing Ted again and planned what she would wear that evening. She needn't have bothered because from the moment Ted walked into the saloon bar, Charlie had him laughing. He had hardly the time to give Rose the once-over. Luckily all four of them had a very enjoyable evening.

'He was all right,' said Charlie, on the way home.

'Mmm… nice nature.'

'Nice bank account as well if I'm not wrong.'

'I'm not so sure, Charlie. Let's wait and see. If he has got anyfing, it'll be stashed up a chimney stack to avoid the taxman.'

'Not for long, if young Alfie gets wind of it.' Laughing, they made their way back home, hoping that the next day Emmie, Rose and Jessie would be fetching home little Emma-Rose.

Chapter Five

Removing Emma-Rose had been easier than Jessie imagined. Once the authorities were satisfied that Jessie's mother's place was suitable, the necessary paperwork took just a few days and so the family were together for the build-up to Christmas. At last things seemed to be on the up. Tom and Stanley were making steadfast plans to start their own small business and Stanley had already approached the Borough with a deal that would give him and Tom enough work to see them through until spring.

The small contract he'd secured wasn't the best of work but, as he told Tom, there was no harm in small beginnings. Once the bombed houses had been repaired and furbished, people like Tom and Stanley went in as finishers, and since work had to be carried out with more speed than exactness, due to the thousands of buildings which had been hit, there was plenty of shoddy work that had to be fixed. Exterior paint work, for instance, had only had one top coat and sometimes not even that.

Jessie, Tom and the two kids had moved in with Rose and Christmas Day turned out to be one of the best ever, with Rose enjoying her children around her, together with her son-in-law, Tom, and grandchildren, Billy and Emma-Rose. Stanley had fallen head over heels in love with Dolly and it was by no means a love lost. After just one date they had gone everywhere together and this kind of lightning romance was not unusual, it was happening all over the place. Maybe it was the after-effects of a horrid war but true or false no one questioned it. Long courtships were out of fashion and the register offices had never been so busy.

After Christmas dinner, games, and a short nap, the family group walked through the East End to Emmie's house for high tea, enjoying the cold but sunny afternoon. Food rationing was still in operation, but Rose had managed to turn out a modest Christmas dinner and now at teatime, Emmie's table was laid with tasty dishes concocted from leftovers and whatever Emmie had managed to come by, with no questions asked. The Christmas cake was the centrepiece and looked as cheerful as those Emmie had iced before the war and rationing.

The special treat that Charlie had fetched home, courtesy of a 'good old contact', were bananas, a fruit which, apart from Alfie, none of them had yet had the pleasure of trying. Proud and a little tipsy, Alfie showed them how such unusual fruit should be eaten, resisting the strong urge to pull a practical joke and let Rose's friend, Ted, eat one with the peel still on.

Emma-Rose was being spoiled rotten and even Billy hardly left her side and asked Jessie several times if they were going to take her back to the home after Christmas. Try as she might, she couldn't quite convince him. Jessie was going to have to win his trust back too.

By late afternoon there was hardly an open eye in the house. Except for Jessie's twin, Hannah, they had all fallen asleep by the fire or found somewhere in the house to catnap. Instead of taking the obligatory fifteen-minute shuteye, Hannah went for a walk, a long walk. There had been several times when she thought she was ready for a particular visit but had lost her nerve at the last minute. Today was different. Today she *wanted* to go to her father's grave. With the war over and having spent Christmas Day with her real mother, she wanted to feel the presence of her real father too, in spirit if nothing else. Her father, whom she had never seen. His fatal accident in the docks had happened just a year or so before Hannah discovered her family and before she was brought back into the fold.

During a quiet moment on Christmas Eve, the twins' twenty-sixth birthday, Hannah had found and read one of Jessie's documented diaries which covered the time before and after they had found each other. It was the heading on one of the diaries which had intrigued her. 'I found my twin down Stepney Way'.

Moved by her sister's writings, Hannah was drawn back to the early days when she met up with Tom and met Jessie for the first time since they had been separated. Outside the People's Palace in the Mile End Road, Oswald Mosley had made a brief appearance to a large gathering. Hannah could remember it all and for the first and only time had been thankful for it. She might otherwise have never known the truth about her real parents or her blood brothers and sisters. Hannah had also found the page where Jessie had written a few heart-rending lines: 'Today is the worst day of my life. Dad has been killed. I want to go with him. God forgive me.'

Finding it all too much, Hannah had closed the diary and wept.

Now, with her coat, hat and scarf wrapped round her she was ready to face something she'd been putting off for too long. She would go to Bow cemetery to see her father's grave.

As she walked through the East End of London, she was shocked by the devastation – the bombed houses and wrecked buildings – and realised how cosseted she had been living at Bletchley Park for the duration of the war. Working as a code breaker for the War Office at Station X had been arduous but nothing compared to what her twin Jessie had gone through during the Blitz. Leaving the beautiful estate in Buckinghamshire for a one-bedroomed flat in Walthamstow had been something that she had had to adjust to, but now the reality of people having to get their lives back together made her realise how lucky she was. Compared to what she was seeing, Walthamstow was, to her, like a large country village. Guilt swept through her as she arrived at the cemetery gates.

Walking through the grounds, Hannah could hardly believe her eyes. Family members were tending their loved ones' graves as if they were tiny gardens. There were fresh flowers in pots and vases against the white and black marble headstones, but mostly home-made wreaths of holly and ivy decorated with red bows. With the sun shining in between the clouds, the scene was more uplifting than sad.

In a daze she drifted in and around the gravestones, glancing at each one in a vague hope to find the name of her father, Robert Warner. It seemed an impossible task.

'If you're looking for someone's grave, maybe I could 'elp' – the voice of a young man pierced her thoughts – 'help you find whoever you're searching for?'

Hannah looked at the handsome young man and managed a faint smile. With his black hair and dark blue eyes and wearing a smart navy serge suit and trilby, he reminded her of a film star. 'Thank you… I'm… well I'm looking for my father's grave. He died 1937… I think.'

'You think?' There was a moment of silence before he added, 'The church door's unlocked if you need to sit down?' He spoke without showing any emotion.

'Thank you,' said Hannah, 'it's all a bit…'

'Emotional?'

'Yes. Yes I think that's what it is.' Allowing him to take her by the arm, she walked slowly along the path. 'Did *you* come to visit a relative?' she asked, feeling silly at having used the word visit.

'A relative and a friend,' he said.

'It's very peaceful here… strange… the living and the dead… together. And yet, I don't feel sad. Doesn't that sound strange?'

'Most people feel the same.' He was taken by her slight accent which Hannah had picked up from her German foster mother.

'Do they? It's hard to believe.'

They sat together quietly at the back of the church.

'My name's David,' he said softly, 'what's yours?'

'Hannah.' She had warmed to this stranger.

David slowly turned his head to face her. He was stirred by her innocence and honesty. 'This your first time then… in a church, I mean?'

'Yes.'

'You must 'ave been christened?'

'Maybe; but then I wouldn't remember, would I?' she said, a small smile on her face. 'Do you remember your christening?'

'No.' He was smiling back at her. 'You know the cemetery warden reckons he knows where everyone is buried here. All he needs is a name to begin with.'

'How could the warden know that? There are hundreds of gravestones.'

'Well, let's test him.'

'What if he doesn't pass the test? We would embarrass him.'

'Teach him not to lie in the fixture.' He had a twinkle in his eye.

Stopping herself from laughing, Hannah tried to avoid his dark blue searching eyes. 'You shouldn't make fun in a church.'

'I know. Come on. Let's find him.' Once again she allowed him to take her arm and lead her back outside. 'You see,' he said, looking across the cemetery at the man who was showing someone to a gravestone. 'He loves it. You don't need me now. What did you say your father's name was?'

'I didn't. Why do you want to know?' She was disappointed that he was going to leave.

'He might turn out to be *my* father as well. *He* was a bit of a lad; I wouldn't want you for a sister.'

'Why not?' A tone of ire crept into her voice.

'Because I'd like to see you again… as a friend. I don't see any rings on your finger.'

Suddenly shy, she murmured, 'No. I'm not involved with anyone. My father's name was Robert – Robert Warner.'

Caught off guard, his unperturbed manner changed instantly. He turned and pointed. 'Follow that pathway over there and it's the third from the end.'

'How do you – If that's meant to be a joke, I don't find it amusing.'

'What a small world. Robert wasn't my father, but he was my boss… down the docks. I come every now and then to pay my respects. When he was alive he never mentioned you, Hannah. Why was that?'

'Did he mention my sister?'

'Jessie or Dolly?'

Hannah could not believe what she was hearing. 'It doesn't matter which one.' She was beginning to feel frightened of what was happening here. 'It can't be true, David? This is too much of a coincidence.'

'Do you want me to show you where it is – or the warden?'

'The warden.' Enough was enough, she could feel the hair on the back of her neck stand up.

'I'll be in the pub over the road. If you want to join me, I'll buy you a drink. You look as if you could do with one.' He turned away and strolled effortlessly towards the entrance gate, leaving Hannah flabbergasted. One thing she knew for certain was that she *would* go into the pub to find out more.

The warden was only too pleased to show Hannah to Robert's grave. The only trouble was that he didn't ever seem to stop talking, but she didn't mind. Even though he was a bit of a nosy parker. He wanted to know if David was family as well, since he seemed to visit regularly and kept the grave tidy.

'Course, he goes to see his dad's an' all when he comes but to give 'im is due, he never does one without the other. I respect that,' he said, lighting a roll-up. 'If he *is* a friend that is, and not family?' He obviously wanted to know.

'David is a family friend,' she said, hoping to end it there.

'I thought as much.' He winked knowingly at her. 'He sheds a tear by 'is dad's grave but not at Mr Warner's, I don't miss a trick. He's a nice bloke though. Now you're bound to 'ave a reaction this being your first time. All first timers do.' He stopped in his tracks to clarify his presumptions. ''Cos I 'aven't seen you 'ere before, 'ave I?'

'No. My mother visits—'

'Oh I know. Lovely woman, Mrs Warner. But there! You would know that, wouldn't you? Her being your mum and that. Right, 'ere we are then. I'll leave you to 'ave a little chat with your dad. I make a point of making myself scarce at the right moment if you get my drift.'

'I do, thank you. Thank you very much.'

'My pleasure,' he said, doffing his cap. 'Yes... I can see it now. You've got your mother's lovely eyes. Tell your dad that Ed showed the way. Gotta keep 'em 'appy, treat them all the same I do. No favouritism.' He walked away wondering why she had not been before.

Hannah stood by the grave and gazed at her father's headstone. Shuddering at the thought of him six feet under, she went icy cold.

Recalling the photographs that Rose had shown her when Robert was full of life and smiling did go some way to help her relax. She knew now that this visit was not something that she would repeat too often. In the church it had been different, calm and comforting.

Tracing her finger across the white marble headstone, she spoke in a matter-of-fact voice, 'Hello, Dad, I'm your *other* daughter, the one you had to part with. I don't bear a grudge any more, I understand. Maybe I will come again. Happy Christmas.'

As she turned to walk away, she saw the warden watching her and when he gave her a thumbs-up sign she couldn't help smiling. It was all rather bizarre. She couldn't say that the visit had helped her feel any closer to the father she'd never known, but equally, it had done no harm.

Preoccupied with thoughts of what her life might have been like, had she not have been split from her twin sister in the first place, Hannah approached the pub and David as he stood outside, waiting for her.

'You all right?' His voice was quiet and not without compassion.

She simply nodded at him as he opened the door for her. 'It's not such a bad place, is it?' she said.

'As cemeteries go, I s'pose not.'

Once they were settled at a small table with their drinks Hannah asked about her father, what he was like to work with and if he seemed as happy a man, as the family had led her to believe. 'I'm not looking for gossip just—'

'There isn't any.'

'No, I didn't think for one minute there would be. And you wouldn't come here, if you hadn't admired him so much, and you wouldn't admire someone who wasn't decent.'

David sipped his beer but kept his eyes on her face. 'Thanks. Now then, tell me about you.'

'The family secret?'

'If you like.'

'My parents had twins but could only just afford to feed and clothe one of us. I was fostered by my mother's brother and his German wife from the age of one year. I only found out about my real family some nineteen years later. My childhood friend, who had become more like a brother to me, met up with my sister Jessie and… well, the rest is history.'

'Good old Tom. Without knowing what he was doing, he brought you together?'

'Something like that, yes. So you know *Tom* as well?'

'He was a docker, wasn't he? Haven't seen him since before the war when he went AWOL, mind you.'

'He wasn't away on leave for long,' she said, 'that was only for a short while. He was stationed in North Africa, now he's back home.'

'All in one piece?'

'Yes, but his brother Johnnie was killed.'

'I know. I heard.'

'And Stanley lost an arm.'

'Not a leg as well, I hope?'

Again she found herself smiling at his witty sense of humour. 'No, he's fine. He and Tom are working on Jessie's bombed house.'

'And you?' David drank some more of his beer and waited.

'I came through without a mark as you can see.'

'Be thankful for that. Not everyone got through the Blitz.'

'I wasn't in London. I was working away from home.'

'Where was that?'

'I'm not at liberty to tell you,' she said earnestly, enjoying *her* chance to be evasive.

'Top secret, eh…? Fair enough. So… you not promised to anyone,' he said, looking at her left hand.

'Listen, David, it's time I was going. If you want to, you know how to find me.' She leaned forward, brushed a kiss across his cheek and thanked him for being her knight in a black overcoat and walked away.

'Hannah!'

Half turning, she eyed him with caution. There was a certain urgency in his voice. An urgency akin to the feeling in her own chest. She didn't want to leave. 'Yes?'

'Happy Christmas.'

On her way to Emmie's, Hannah tried to push the face of David from her mind and wondered if she would ever be able to speak freely about Station X at Bletchley Park. Certainly not for the present nor the foreseen future. To coin one of Emmie's phrases – it was still very much 'a hot potato'.

As code-breakers of the Enigma cipher machine used by the Germans, Hannah, like the others at Bletchley Park, was sworn to secrecy but had been assured that one day, in many years to come, the wartime work of the team of code-breakers would be celebrated worldwide. It was debatable whether the public would ever be told of the German and Polish code-breakers working as British agents. These brave men risked their lives in their efforts to bring down Hider, and in the process tens of thousands of lives were saved.

With thoughts of her years spent at Bletchley Park and all that had gone on there, Hannah was reminded of her foster mother, Gerta, and wondered what had become of her since she had been deported to her homeland. A German, living in the East End and an ardent member of the Blackshirts, she had blatantly waved the flag for Oswald Mosley and dragged Hannah into it against her will.

By the time Hannah arrived back at Emmie's, she was sorry to see that her mother, Rose, Dolly and the boys, had left. But it was Emmie and Charlie that Hannah wanted to be with on this Christmas night. They had been like parents to her throughout her childhood and teens when she was Tom's best friend.

Pleased that it was Jessie who opened the door to her, Hannah took her by the arm and pulled her outside. Then, in a hushed voice, told her where she'd been.

'You didn't say where you were going or even that you were going out! I've been worried.'

'I didn't want a fuss being made of it,' said Hannah. 'Why were you worried? I'm a big girl now. Same age as you, actually.' She smiled at her twin sister.

'But people don't just go out without saying on Christmas Day and then not come back for hours. No one I know does that. Not on Christmas Day.'

'Oh shut up, Jessie. Sometimes I wonder if you know me at all.' Taking Jessie's hand, Hannah looked into her face. 'I've been to the cemetery. At last. I've done it. And I enjoyed going.'

'I would 'ave come with you, you know that,' said Jessie, disappointed.

'I wanted to go by myself. I *had* to. I don't know why but I just did. I went into the church and then I stood quietly by his grave. The holly wreaths look lovely.' She pulled Jessie into the quiet kitchen. Leaning on the closed door satisfied that she could talk openly, she laid a hand on her heart. 'I've never felt like this before, Jessie. Never.'

There was a quiet moment before Jessie asked, 'Dad didn't show 'imself as a ghost, did he?'

'Of course not. You know I don't believe in all that. I met someone at the cemetery. He had just come from Dad's grave. He used to work for him at the docks and goes every now and then to pay his respects.' She sat back down on the bed and looked into her sister's face. 'Oh, Jessie, I think I've fallen in love. Love at first sight…'

Keeping her head down, Jessie was laughing quietly.

'Don't make fun of me. I'm being serious. I've never felt like this before. What if I never see him again? What then?'

'Well, who was he? Must have been special if he's done this to you.'

'It was just that… I felt as if I could trust him. You know, really trust him.'

'Well, that's worth a lot, Han, believe me. What's his name?'

'David. I don't even know his second name.'

'Don't ring any bells with me. Mum might know 'im though.'

'No! Don't say a word, in case I never see him again. I'd feel such a fool.'

'You'll see 'im again,' said Jessie smiling. 'Now give me a big hug for Christmas.'

Hugging and giggling like schoolgirls, neither of them heard the approaching footsteps. The sudden crashing of the door as Tom pushed it open startled them both. 'Jessie. In the sitting room. *Now!*'

'Pardon?' Jessie had never seen him so angry. 'What's wrong?'

'Tom? What's happened?' Seeing Tom in one of these moods worried Hannah. She had known him for practically all her life and had seen him explode before.

'Mind your own business, Hannah.' White-faced and grinding his teeth, Tom stood his ground. 'Move yourself, Jessie!'

'Don't you speak to her like that, you've had too much beer, Tom!'

'Shut up, Hannah!'

'All right, all right,' said Jessie, worried. 'Come on, Hannah and—'

'*No.* You come into the front room by yerself, Jessie. *Now, I said!*'

'All right, Tom, I will. Keep your hair on.' She eased her way past him, telling Hannah she would be straight back.

'In Mother's front room,' snapped Tom. 'It's just you, me and Stanley. I've sent the kids upstairs to the box room to play. Dad's still in bed and Mum's gone to join 'im.'

Her heart sinking, Jessie knew what had happened. Once inside she caught Stanley's eye. His expression was one of apology and despair. 'I'm sorry, Jess, I shouldn't 'ave drunk so much. My tongue just wagged.'

She heard the door shut and turned to see Tom leaning against it, arms folded. 'Well?'

'Well *what?*'

'Did Stanley see you and Max kissing at the Mile End Gate and then holding hands in the Blind Beggar? Yes or no?'

'It's not what you think—'

'YES OR NO!'

'Yes!'

'Not 'olding hands, Tom, just you know… touching,' said Stanley, trying his best to ease things.

'It's all right, Stan,' said Jessie, 'it's not your fault. Thanks for trying to…'

'You'd best go for a walk, Stanley,' said Tom.

'Oh come on,' objected Stanley.

'You'd best leave us,' said Jessie, squeezing Stanley's shoulder. 'Stop worrying. I'll explain it all. It'll be all right.'

'Call me if you need me, Jessie,' said Stanley, glowering at Tom.

Once they were alone, Jessie showed her rage.

84

'How dare you accuse me and in front of the others! You rotten lousy sod – it's Christmas! The first Christmas after the war. The *first* Christmas we've all been together for years!'

'Finished?' said Tom, as cool as a cucumber.

'You push me any further, Tom, and it might be. I've had a basinful of your selfish ways. You've not even asked why I went to see Max, I s'pose that's not really important to you, is it? Max helped me when I was desperate and when you were on the run. Helped me, Tom, nothing else but that! You don't 'ave a clue as to what I really went through during that bloody war!'

'Oh and I s'pose I've 'ad an easy time of it. Up to my neck in muck and bullets while you were 'aving a cosy time with yer old boyfriend. Don't forget, you was in *his* bed before you crawled into mine.'

'That's because I met Max before you. I was *engaged* to 'im, Tom. We'd been courting for three years!'

'Yep,' said Tom, not wishing to hear all of that, 'you must 'ave been in your seventh heaven while I was on the front line fighting for my life. Did you sleep with 'im, Jess?' Her anger rose as she dared him with her eyes not to ask again. He simply glared back at her. 'Gonna leave me and take my kids, were you? Shame really, wasn't it, that I came back when I did, spoiled your little plans. A sordid love nest in a flat above an East End shop. Not much on offer really, was there? Still, he's a Jew after all. I thought you'd 'ave done better than that, Jess. All them rich Yanks hanging around? You must 'ave bin desperate, even the army wouldn't take 'im, war or no war they wouldn't 'ave 'im. But you would, wouldn't you, like a shot, you was in there.'

'That's enough. We're in your mother's house, don't forget.'

'No, *you're* in my mother's house.' He stepped closer to her, more furious by the second.

'I'm leaving you, Jess,' he said, his face so close to hers it was almost touching. Grabbing her by the hair, he looked menacing. 'But I'll be back, one day, to get my kids. Don't ever think that that Jew will take my kids from me 'cos he *won't*.'

'Leaving me, again? Well, what else could we all expect, eh, Tom? No one's gonna be that shocked, are they? Where will you go – Scotland? To see the nurse you bedded while you were supposed to be convalescing?'

'There are plenty of places I can go. And the nurse was looking after my knee, Jess, it did receive a bullet at Dunkirk, don't forget.'

'Oh, I won't forget, Tom. I'll never forget your toing and froing to Scotland. The genuine visits or the times you went AWOL. Maybe you should have bedded down properly with your nurse. She'd 'ave hidden you away from the authorities.'

'What is all this? Dragging all that stuff up. Why now, eh?'

'Why? You ask *me* why? Well to coin one of your mothers sayings: "Don't tar me with the same brush!" *I* never slept with another man! Not Max, not one of the Dutch sailors; and certainly not one of the Yanks.'

'Yeah? Well I think there's no smoke without fire and you seem to be smouldering. Good luck to you, Jess – you're gonna need it. Thank your lucky stars it's Christmas. That's why I haven't knocked you black and blue.'

Jessie could do nothing but gaze at the closed door after he'd slammed it behind him. Sinking down on to the settee, she was at a loss as to what she should do, she was so angry. Whatever the reason, whatever the mood, this was not the way a normal husband would behave. But she'd seen something of this before. Before the war when she had dared to dance with another man, be it a relative at a family do or a stranger in a dance hall. To Tom, she was his property but he was never hers. Never. He had been coming and going since war was declared and not always to fight for his country. In fact, hardly ever to fight for his country after Dunkirk and before North Africa. So what was she supposed to do now – beg him to forgive her for something she hadn't done?

Giving him a few minutes to calm down, she waited to see if he would come back into the room and let her explain the way things really were and the real reason for meeting up with Max. When he did open the sitting-room door, he had on his overcoat.

'Tom, give me a chance to explain. Don't just march out of here the way you've done before. I don't like it! I'm always left with this anger that I can't do anything with!'

'No need to explain, Jess. It's all crystal clear.'

'This is *silly*—'

'It might be a lot of things, Jessie, but silly it's not. I'll play second fiddle to no one where my own wife's concerned. He's welcome to you. Second 'and goods, Jess, that's what you are, shop soiled. And I'll tell you this much, if ever I do weaken because of my kids, I'll repeat the same words over and over, *the Mile End Gate, Tom, the Mile End Gate*, 'cos that's where you've probably bin meeting up with 'im all this time, right through the war.'

'You're wrong. He offered us a flat to stay in till our house was ready and—'

'You should 'ave married 'im in the first place, Jess. It's what your mother would 'ave wanted. But you've got 'is sister to thank for that, ain't yer? She squeezed you out before you could say synagogue. They're Jews, Jess, they stick together. You didn't really think they were gonna let a Christian into their family without a fight, did you? Think about it. You saw the diamond ring in the window, but it never actually reached your finger, did it?' With that, he strode out of the house and out of her life.

Chapter Six

Convinced that Jessie had slept with Max, Tom went to his favourite drinking club which he knew would be open, Christmas night or not. He needed to think things through, and didn't give a second thought as to how Jessie might be feeling or how she and the children would get back to her mother's house in the cold and dark.

Stanley, without having to be asked, had stepped in and walked her back, chatting about Tom and how he would see reason once he'd come to his senses. Jessie was not persuaded. She had seen him in all kinds of moods but never like this. To ease Stanley's mind, she agreed with him and offered her own opinion that it would soon blow over and he'd be at her mother's house, full of apologies.

Unable to settle himself in the drinking club, Tom made his way back to his parents' house. He was still seething and still convinced that Jessie had had an affair and that her family probably knew and gave it the thumbs up, except for Hannah. She was probably his best friend and would never let Max assume his role as partner to Jessie. Yes, thought Tom, Jessie's mother would have given it her approval, strait-laced or not. She had never liked him and, if he was honest, he had never liked her. Rose Warner was a snob.

Passing his and Jessie's house which he, Stanley and his dad had been working on, Tom cursed under his breath, it all seemed to fit. The house which had been bought out of the compensation money, given after Jessie's dad's tragic accident in the docks, was in Jessie's name for one reason and one reason only – so that he couldn't make any claims should the marriage go wrong. In his present mood he had forgotten or ignored the fact that *he* had been the one who had insisted that, should Jessie use her portion of the money to buy a house for them to live in, then it had to be in *her name*. She at the time had not wanted it.

Thankful that there was a light coming from the living-room window of Emmie and Charlie's front room, he pushed the key into the lock and hoped that they were both up. Right then he needed his family and, even more so, he needed Johnnie, his elder brother, but Johnnie was dead and that was that.

Relaxing by the fire and listening to carols on the wireless, neither Emmie nor Charlie heard him come in, and it wasn't until he entered the room holding a cup of tea that they realised he had returned. 'What are *you* doing 'ere?' said Emmie, secretly pleased to see him. She hadn't wanted Jessie and her grandchildren to move out but had seen the sense in them going to Rose's place.

'I want a straight answer from both of you,' said Tom, standing in the doorway. 'No covering up, no lies, and no tears. I've seen enough of them in the past few years to last me a lifetime.'

Giving Charlie a look, which spoke volumes, Emmie took the lead, which was just as well because Tom's dad was too tired and too boozy to think clearly let alone advise should Tom need advice. It was, after all, Christmas Day, and if Charlie couldn't have a few drinks at that special time of year, he would be dull company. That was his way of seeing it. 'Fair enough, son,' said Emmie, 'get if off your chest. What's up?'

'Has Jessie been seeing Max while I've bin away?'

'Oh not that again.'

'*Has* she?'

'I expect so,' said Emmie casually, unaware of the possible consequences. 'As a friend though, Tom, nothing else. She's the mother of your two children, don't forget.'

'Yeah, is she though?' A new thought was taking root in his mind.

'Silly bugger. You've only got to look at our Emma to see who she takes after, blonde hair and blue eyes or not. You weren't around for her to mimic but she reminds us of you all the same, don't she, Charlie?' Emmie was playing it down. In truth, she felt like giving her son a dressing down for saying such things, but had to take into account what many husbands back from war must have wondered – and in many cases were right.

'You might 'ave brought *us* a cup of tea in, Tom. Still, you always did think of yourself first.' Charlie wasn't as dim as he made out. 'I thought I 'eard a bit of a commotion when me and your mother was 'aving a nap. Had a row, did yer? Lost your temper *and* sense again?'

He chose to ignore his dad's sarcasm. 'Did he ever come round 'ere, then, Mum?'

'No, Tom, not that I can remember.' Emmie thought about it. 'No, the lad never came here.'

'Well, there you are then, if it was innocent he would have. Probably jumped into my bed when I jumped out.'

'What *are* you talking about, son?' Now Charlie *was* getting worried.

'Whitehead Street, the little place that Jessie was in after our place was bombed. When I was on the run, I went there… yeah… it all fits now. The military police stormed in but I was out the window in a flash. How did they know I was there, eh? Answer me that. But Max knew, oh yeah he knew because I sent the bastard round to get Jessie from 'er mother's place and tell 'er I was waiting there. It was Christmas *then* as it 'appens. You always said God works in mysterious ways, Mum.'

'That's right, Tom, it's all coming back to me now. Lovely little house that was, we all worked on it together didn't we, Charlie? Jessie never stopped, bless 'er, even found some paint didn't we to freshen it up once we'd scrubbed away the layers of grime. It stunk when we first went in, but then it would do, it must 'ave bin left empty for years. Landlord was waiting for it to be bombed, I expect. All them 'ouses are coming down… I didn't tell you that, did I? Gonna build brand new council 'ouses, about time as well, bloody damp them places. Jessie kept the fire going though. Our Billy would 'ave bin all right there.'

'What d'yer mean, *would* have?'

Emmie's chuckle was loaded with anger. 'What, you think the landlord was gonna let 'er stay on there, rent free after the police 'ad been crawling all over it and it came out about you being a deserter?'

'I never deserted, I went AWOL for a bit that's all.'

His casual dismissal of something that had caused Jessie and Billy's life to be in turmoil was more than she could take. Leaning forward, her face almost meeting his, she was seething. 'Yeah, and your little holiday left Jessie homeless and pregnant. She was like a bloody nomad and we 'ad no idea where she was. Pushed Billy in the pram from pillar to post until she found a place in Westminster.

Six months, Tom, six months! That's how long we had to sit biting our nails wondering where the poor cow was.'

'I wasn't to know that, was I?'

'No, and do you know why? Because we – me and your dad – didn't 'ave a clue as to where you were. *That's* why!'

'Westminster, eh? Bloody la-di-da – she always was a bit of a snob.'

'Oh yeah, that's why she went to a place where she'd be a fish out of water. Still, it was a lovely big house and she 'ad company. Wives with children who had also been made homeless. Lovely place and she was doing all right there, was Jess, until a bloody great bomb fell and flattened it, with Jessie and Billy in the basement. That's when we found out where she was. When the police came round to tell us she and others like her were trapped.

'But don't you worry about that, Tom, we coped. Thankful that the fire brigade and God knows what other services got them out alive – all of them – except for the poor woman whose house it was. She went up from the basement to fetch her cats and copped the lot.'

'Why are you telling me all this?' Tom sat back in his chair and lit a cigarette. 'Worse things 'appened abroad. She's still 'ere, Mother, and so is Billy, if you want horror stories I've got plenty.'

'I'm sure you 'ave, son, I'm sure you 'ave. And to be honest I don't *know* why I went into all of that, the last thing I want is to dig it up.' Fed up with him Emmie sank back into her chair and concentrated on her favourite carol, 'Silent Night'.

'Seems like I was the enemy then. Causing Jessie to lose 'er house and all that went on afterwards, never mind Max 'aving turned me in.'

'Hold on, Tom, you don't know that's what 'appened,' said Charlie, taking up where Emmie had left off. 'Max's all right. His mother died, you know... broke 'is heart it did.'

'What're you talking about, Dad? You've never met the bloke.'

'Never met 'im? Course I bloody met 'im. Without 'is help we wouldn't've bin able to do half the things we did, he helped put food on many a table, I'll tell yer.'

'Oh right, so that's what he did while we were out there fighting, played the benefactor.'

'No, but he did put himself at risk with the law. He worked the black market, ask Jessie's brother, Alfie.'

Emmie knew that Charlie had said too much. There was no harm in his words but she knew her son would see all that he was saying in a different light to the way it was cast. 'Go and pour us a cup of tea, Tom, there's a good lad.'

'I ain't got time for that, Mum.' With that he left the room and went upstairs to where he still had some clothes stored. Determined to leave the house as soon as possible so he could find a cheap lodging room for the night, he reached under the bed for a suitcase. As he dragged it out, the kitbag, belonging to the soldier who had thrown himself in front of the train, came with it.

Pushing it back with his toe, he couldn't help but wonder what was in it. From the day he arrived home, happy to be back in the fold, he hadn't given the bag a second thought; but now, he was curious.

Nothing could have surprised him more when he opened it to find, not a pathetic bundle of clothing and personal bits and pieces, but cardboard files and envelopes clearly marked as to their contents: *Bank. Personal Identity.*

Family History. Legal. Properties: Grafton Way. High House.
There was also a bunch of keys and at the very bottom, a
linen soap bag, containing all the things he'd said the army
had let him have as a keepsake.

Intrigued by the sparse contents and the meticulous
handwriting on the labels, he decided to take the lot with
him and read them once he was settled in somewhere.
Taking a leaf out of the dead man's book and making
space for the files, Tom packed economically. One of
everything: shirt, jumper, socks, long johns, tie, and a
pair of pyjamas. That done, he avoided looking round
the room for the last time – this was not the moment
for sentiment. His children and his wife had fared well
without him so he had no reason to feel guilty about
leaving. To his mind, he was doing them a favour and
giving himself a new start.

A photograph of a smiling Billy and Emma-Rose
caught his attention. Snatching it from the dressing table,
he slipped it into his bag. Jessie would be furious that he'd
taken it but she had his children in the flesh, all he would
have was a sepia image.

Startled by the slamming of the street door, Emmie
and Charlie stared at each other. 'Where's he gone now?'
said Charlie. He had been under the impression that his
son just wanted to be left alone for a while to cool off.
Rushing to the door and wrenching it open, Emmie was
just in time to see the back of her son before he turned
the comer. The suitcase in his hand made her heart sink.

'See, I told yer!' yelled Charlie from the living room.
'He's gone to make amends. Half a pint too many that's
all it was.'

Coming into the room, Emmie slowly shook her head.
'No, I don't think so. He's not gone to Rose Warner's

'cause he's carrying that old suitcase of yours. I've got a terrible feeling, Charlie. Right deep inside me.'

'Don't be daft, woman, course he's carrying a suitcase. Taking the rest of 'is things to—'

'No, that won't be it, he took all he needed before. I should know, I washed, ironed and packed it for 'im.' She sat on the edge of the settee, choked. 'He's walked out. That's what he's done, Charlie. He's gone and walked out of our lives… again.'

Filled with a sense of betrayal by his entire family, Tom hadn't really thought things through. This was Christmas night and a very cold one with snow predicted. Wherever he was headed, with no public transport running, he was going to have to walk, like it or not. His free hand deep in his overcoat pocket, he hunched his shoulders and made his way through the darkness with just the glow from the streetlamps and the star-studded sky for company.

Making his way towards Bow where he knew there were plenty of lodging houses, he ran Jessie's story through his mind and couldn't begin to believe that she was innocent. It all made sense to him now. For all the problems of post-war Britain and the food shortages, she looked well, too well; Max must have seen to that. 'Can't blame you, I s'pose,' he murmured, 'any woman would 'ave been tempted. He's not Clark Gable but 'is pockets are lined with silk.'

With so many thoughts running through his head, he arrived in Bow before he knew it, but only to see that in every window of every lodging house there was a sign: No Vacancies. Taking a rest in a bus shelter, he told himself how stupid he was to expect any landlady to take in a traveller on Christmas night. 'No room at the inn, Tom,' he chuckled. 'No room at the bloody inn.'

Grateful for the shelter, the lamplight and the wooden slatted seat, he lit a cigarette and wished he'd popped a bottle of ale into his pocket. In a way, he felt kind of privileged having the streets to himself, but deep down he was miserable. He needed some company, to hear voices or laughter to confirm that this situation was real – that he wasn't dreaming. So, this is what it had come to. This was the reality and not the dream that had kept him going throughout the war. All he could think about now was how his family had deceived him, even his mum and dad. He was convinced that they must have known what had been going on.

Feeling the cold round his neck, he opened his suitcase and found his woollen scarf. He also spotted those mysterious files and folders and the bunch of labelled keys on the brass ring. He then opened the file marked *Properties*. High House had an address in Suffolk and Grafton Way off Fitzroy Square was in London, W1. Now he knew where he was headed, but it was a good two-hour walk away.

He knew exactly where Fitzroy Square was; as a twelve-year-old, he had been a delivery boy for Gamages store in Holborn, and the Square had been on his rounds. It was a long shot but at least it was somewhere to aim for. If there was no such house in Grafton Way, he would sleep in a doorway, which would compare favourably to those times of trying to slumber in between air raids on the beaches of Dunkirk.

Striding as if he were on a mission, Tom made his way through the East End into Holborn, and on to Tottenham

Court Road where, if his memory served him right, he would find Grafton Way on the left-hand side. His memory had served him perfectly. The West End of London, even that late on a Christmas night, was filled with the Yuletide spirit. Coloured lights and partygoers on their way home and singing, and, of course, there were the overly happy tramps who always fared well at that time of the year.

The intrigue of no lights shining in the tall Regency house in Grafton Way fuelled the daring sensation in the pit of his stomach. Taking the keys from his pocket, he tried three of them before he found the one which fitted the front door. Instinctively, his hand found the entrance hall light switch. He flicked it down while closing the door with his foot and then stood in awe of what lay before him.

The cut glass chandelier brought the place alive and Tom could not believe his eyes. A lavish Persian rug lay on the marble inlaid floor and ornate framed oil paintings hung on the richly patterned red and gold wallpaper. Opening a mahogany panelled door, he found a grand room which had been used as an office-cum-library with papers piled high in every corner. From the thick layer of dust everywhere it was clear that this house had not been lived in for quite a few years and possibly the duration of the war. Not only dusty, it was cold and damp and he had a feeling that there would be no electric fires in any of the rooms. He was right. Either side of the carved wooden fireplace there were two huge copper buckets, one full of coal and the other half filled. Not since North Africa had Tom experienced such an adrenaline surge. He was both thrilled and terrified. What if there were people asleep upstairs? What if this house didn't belong to the dead man? What if someone upstairs was arming himself ready to attack the intruder? What...?

The sensation of fearing for his life, once again, was making him giddy and his heart was thumping madly. Switching on every light as he made his way upstairs, Tom trumped up a story in case the owner were to suddenly pounce. He would say that the man whose kitbag he had landed had fought alongside him, and when they were demobbed, his mate had handed him the keys to his house, should he ever need to use them. But as it turned out, he didn't need to make up a story – the house was empty.

On the first floor Tom found what he could only assume to be the dead man's study. It was smaller than the rest of the rooms in the house and the most inviting. The black ornate fireplace was set with kindling and coal and was begging to be lit. That done, he went down into the basement to find the kitchen which was part of the servants' quarters and apart from the thick dust, it was tidy and clean. The red pammet tiled floor however was covered with mice droppings. To his relief, the larder had been cleared of perishable food but there were numerous canned delicacies, sweet and savoury.

Later, with his legs stretched in front of the fire, Tom enjoyed corned beef and cold baked beans washed down with an excellent bottle of red wine which he had taken from the well-stocked cellar. Smiling to himself he was playing knight for a night. Tomorrow, he would leave the place as if he hadn't been, and go on his way. Lifting his glass and wishing himself a merry Christmas, he thought seriously of going back home the next day and sorting things out.

The next day, however, which started at 11 a.m, when he woke up to sun streaming in through a gap in the blue velvet curtains of his chosen bedroom, made him rethink his strategy – why not stay right where he was?

When going through the dead man's spacious and immaculately kept wardrobes, before he crawled, fairly drunk, into the big feather bed, Tom had found, tucked away, a linen bag identical to the one in which the stranger kept his soap and sundries. Instead of finding shaving soap and brushes in this one, to his great pleasure, he found two thick wads of white five-pound notes.

After his third cup of tea with condensed milk and his fourth cigarette, Tom sat back in his chair in the study, enjoying the warmth of the fire. He was deeply engrossed in the files found in the kitbag. From the one marked *Personal Identity* he discovered that the man's name was Archibald John Thomas, born to the late Iris Jane Thomas, spinster and once orphan. Iris Jane had been founder of a private, exclusive, House of Assignation in Mayfair – a top-notch brothel. The further Tom read, the more intrigued he became.

'Well,' said Tom, having found and read a little green snakeskin diary and address book, 'you might 'ave bin a lone bastard, my old mate, but you were never lonely.' There was a list of women's names with stars marked in pencil next to them.

Tom deduced that Miss Nancy was a much-favoured companion for she merited six stars whereas Fat Annie only had one. Then there was a small, detailed piece on each of his staff – all female, naturally. Cook was rotund, rosy and reliable but never to be touched. The housemaids were pretty and frivolous and best left virgins. The two scullery maids – both chosen because they said they were Catholics – were as bright as a new sixpenny bit. They, according to Archibald John Thomas, should be sent to a convent and would make the finest of nuns to be touched only by God.

'Well, you may have been a fruit cake, Archie, but you certainly made the most of it. And what a way to end it all. Why jump in front of a train after you've spent years fighting the enemy to save your own skin? That's what I call a dark sense of humour.'

Leaning back, Tom's mind began to work overtime. If he was careful and clever and took it easy, he *could* change his lifestyle. Everything that a man wishing to be someone else could want was in Archibald's files.

'You bloody well planned it this way, Archie mate,' murmured Tom as it sank in. 'You planned to top yerself one way or another and leave the kitbag as a surprise gift should anyone with a half a brain find it. But you didn't leave it to chance did you…? No, you picked me. I 'appened to be in the same compartment on the same train coming from the same place.' Believing this to be the hand of destiny, Tom couldn't stop himself from smiling and laughing. 'You old bastard. This is what you wanted. You'd 'ad your fill of this bloody world for whatever reason and dumped your lot on me. Well, cheers, mate – I'll do it justice.'

Drawing deep on his cigarette, Tom thought it through. 'Archibald John Thomas. So your mother 'ad a sense of humour as well.' With that he threw back his head and roared with laughter and then remembered Archibald's statement on the train – *Easy Street, blown to pieces.* What he'd meant by it Tom had no idea, but he wasn't going to dwell on it. From now on, he would take the man's place and live like a king. He would change the way he looked; he would *become* Archibald John Thomas. Tom Smith would disappear – permanently.

As far as he could make out, no one was going to miss Archibald, and according to what he had seen in the files, the man never entertained his lady friends at home. Where he went with them to fulfil his lust was anyone's guess. If he played his cards carefully, Tom felt sure he could get away with it. All he had to do was practise Archibald's signature. Once he had gone through the man's papers in the filing cabinet in his study and knew everything there was to know, he would pay a visit to the house in the Suffolk village, to which he had keys. He hoped that High House would be just as thick with dust as this one.

Chapter Seven

Although Jessie had not heard from Tom during the three weeks since he had gone, her anger at him for deserting her, after all she'd been through, was now clouded by worry and isolation. She needed to know his whereabouts and the frustration of not knowing was getting her down. He hadn't even taken the trouble to send a postcard to any of his family.

Having moved back in with her mother made things worse. She felt as if she was going backwards and her confidence seemed to be slipping away. But there was a ray of light. The dear woman she had stayed with, when evacuated from London with Billy, had written her a lovely letter. In it, Alice Davey had told her all the news and written a postscript saying that should she wish to visit for a week or so, she was more than welcome. She also mentioned that there were two old, attached cottages for sale in the village which, although in need of attention, would make a lovely home for a young family.

In her reply to Alice, Jessie had said that she and her two children might take her up on the offer of a break away from London. She couldn't think of anything better than to go with Billy and Emma-Rose out into that lovely unspoiled village away from the East End with all its wreckage. Her mind was slowly turning to other things and another way of life. Perhaps she should sell and move on to start fresh. It was Emma-Rose who drew her away from slipping into a despairing mood, where she often went, when the situation of life for ever without Tom looked like becoming a permanent reality.

'Na-Na-Nanny wants you, M-mummy.' Concentrating so she might say the next sentence without stammering, Emma-Rose held up her little finger, something that Charlie had shown her, saying it would help. Emma didn't actually have a speech impediment, she was simply in too much of a hurry to get her words out. Before she had time to say anything else, Billy was there.

'Mummy, *quick*! Nan's—'

'No, no, no… let *me* tell!' cried Emma.

Jessie didn't wait to hear more. She rushed upstairs and into the parlour where Rose with her eyes closed was resting in her armchair. Jessie gazed at her, frightened. 'Mum?' There was no response. Seeing a small bottle of medicinal brandy on a shelf, she poured some into a glass.

Kneeling before her, the glass to her mother's lips, Jessie spoke in a quiet caring voice. 'Just sip it, you'll be all right in a minute. Don't be alarmed.'

Rose showed no resistance to drinking brandy at that time of day and, surprising Jessie, drank the whole lot in one go. Shuddering from it, she took a deep breath. 'That's better. Where's Emma-Rose?'

'She's downstairs in the kitchen,' said Jessie. 'Why?'

'I just want her to know I'm all right.'

'Did you doze off and have a horrible dream, is that what happened?'

'No, I was awake. One minute talking to Emma-Rose and then she started to talk about one of the children living at that place in Ongar. Said she cried all the time because she missed her mum. It was the look on Emma's face, the same look that she had when we arrived at that place to fetch her home with us, scared in case we left her there again.'

'But it doesn't matter now, does it? She's back here with us and we'll never be split up again, I promise. Wherever I go, my children'll be with me.'

'That look…' said Rose, miles away. 'It spoke volumes. Expressed the sadness that she was feeling inside.'

Clenching her free hand into a fist, Jessie could feel her nails biting into her flesh. 'Mum, please… Emma's all right now, she's with us again, and—'

'I'm not crying for Emma, Jessie. I'm thinking of another little girl who stood and watched as her mother walked away without looking back. She loved her mum more than anything in the world and she missed her. I can still hear her sobbing now…'

Jessie put an arm round her mother and began to rock her as though she were a child. 'It's all right, Mum. I think you must 'ave fallen asleep and woke up in the middle of a bad dream and—'

'I *didn't* fall asleep.' Drying her eyes, Rose sank back in her chair. 'I can't explain it, Jessie. Except to say that I remember what it felt like, crying and sobbing into your pillow in case you were heard and told off. I was back in that room, Jessie, I was back there, looking at the bed, looking at the little girl who was me, and wanting to tell her that it was going to be all right. Because it was in the end; I did grow up and I met your father and we had our lovely children. I want to tell her that, Jessie, but I can't.'

It was sinking in now. Rose was talking about herself, when she was left in a home as a small child. 'Who says you can't? If you remember the room and you say you can see yourself as a little girl, well then?'

Rose gazed up at Jessie, her eyes full of question. 'Well then… what?'

'Talk to her. Tell her that everything is going to be all right and it's all right for 'er to cry. There's nothing wrong with 'aving a cry, Mum, is there?'

'No. I must say I did feel better afterwards.' Rose smiled and shook her head. 'How can I as a grown woman talk to myself as a child? I'll be certified if I start doing such things.'

'Who's gonna know? People pray to God and we can't see Him, can we? You should do whatever makes you feel comfortable.'

'Lay the ghost? Maybe I will,' she said.

'And if we find out where you were placed, then—'

'I wasn't there for long, Jessie.'

'So what?'

'No. The memory can't hold things for ever. I'll be all right, especially if I go on with this crying; I'll wash it out of my mind for good.'

Struggling to keep her emotions in check, Jessie said, 'We'll do whatever makes you feel right and if ever you want to, we'll find out where you were and go back.'

'No. My name might be scrawled on something, the bed I slept on might still be there.' Rubbing her face, Rose sighed heavily. 'It's been festering for too long, just as well it came out. I hope I haven't frightened the children?'

'I think they're enjoying it. Granny's not as hard as she makes out.'

Rose heaved a sigh of relief. 'Good, I'm too set in my ways.' She went quiet again. 'It must have been terrible for my poor mother. It wasn't her fault she was alone and without any money. Your grandfather has a lot to answer for.'

There was a loud rapping on the street door. 'I expect that'll be Dolly; lost her key again.'

It was Billy who opened the front door. Grinning up at Dolly and Stanley, and bursting to tell all he'd overheard, he said, 'I know something you don't, Aunt Dolly.'

'Oh, do you now? Well, let us in then and I might listen to yer.'

'I might *not* tell…'

'I don't care what you do. Get out the way.' She eased her way past him, amused as ever by the skinny waif…

'All right, mate?' said Stanley, tousling Billy's hair. 'You found me a new arm yet?'

'I 'aven't looked.' He spun around and called after Dolly. 'You mustn't go in Gran's parlour!'

Dolly eyed him with caution. 'Why not?'

'It's a secret.' He waved her to him whispering urgently, 'Quick, before Emma comes up!'

Sighing she moved closer 'Go on then, trouble, spit it out.'

'Gran…' he said, eyes wide, '…and don't say I'm fibbing, Aunt Dolly…'

'Oh get on with it, Billy!'

'…Gran was in a children's home as well!' His dramatic delivery brought exactly the response he had hoped for. Dolly was rendered speechless. Her eyes questioned him and he was thrilled that she wanted to know more.

'And *she* cried when her mum left her as well!'

'Billy, stop it. You shouldn't 'ave been listening.'

'I heard Gran talking to Mum about it just now. I'm not fibbing.' The sound of the parlour door opening stopped him short.

'Go downstairs, Billy, there's a good boy. And no more eavesdropping,' said Jessie.

'See?' said Billy, splaying his hands. 'They're gonna tell *you* the secret now, Aunt Dolly.' On that note he ran off to tell Emma what he'd heard.

'What brought all this about?' said Dolly, hesitantly.

'I don't know. Mum's bottled up too much for too long. It's done 'er good though, talking about it. Go on, in you go, she's not finished yet.'

The second telling was much easier for Rose. The more she talked the more she remembered and the more she remembered the more she relaxed. When she had finished, she turned to Stanley, 'Have you heard from our Tom?'

'Nah not a word,' said Stanley, embarrassed. 'He's probably still sulking.'

'A grown man with two children should be past sulking. He'll have me to answer to when he does show his face.'

Rising from her chair, she touched Dolly on the arm. 'It's all right. I wasn't at the children's home for long.'

'Right,' said Dolly, brightly. 'So that's all right then. How about a nice cup of tea? Jess, put the kettle on and fetch me and Stan a cup of tea up, if you don't mind. He's gonna try and fix that old gramophone that's been stuck up in the attic.'

Rose had long since given up telling Dolly what to do and what not to do. She simply had to trust that nothing untoward would happen in Dolly's bedroom. She was fed up arguing. Dolly always won in any case, telling Rose that she should trust her more. Stanley *was* going to try and fix the gramophone, this was true, but he was also looking forward to another cuddle on Dolly's bed. Since Stanley first called to see Dolly, the pair of them were inseparable and were happy to wear their hearts on their sleeves for all to see.

While she made the tea, Jessie mulled over the idea of a family outing with Max. He had suggested such a trip more than once ever since he'd purchased his second-hand motor car. And now that Tom had run out on her, again, she could see no reason to refuse the invitation. Her mind was gradually being made up. She would from now on take up Max's offers, be it a night out or a day trip. She would also tell him that he was welcome to visit her at her mother's house as often as he liked. She needed the company of a friend from time to time and in Max's company she was always relaxed. That close friendship had never left her. From the day that Max's sister, Moira, had maliciously caused them to break off their engagement, Jessie still saw him as her close friend. A religious fanatic, Moira could not accept Jessie marrying into their family.

Deep in thought, Jessie didn't hear Billy and Emma creep into the room.

'Gran's all right now, Mum. She's smiling again,' said Billy, wondering why Jessie looked serious.

Uplifted by the sight of her two children, she held out her arms to them. 'Of course Gran's all right, she'll always be all right.'

'Was she upset because she was in a children's home once?'

'Yes, Billy, she was. But you mustn't ask too many questions over it. Just wait and see if your Gran starts to tell you nice stories about it, because I'm sure she will, now that she's remembered bits of it.'

'Did Gran lose 'er fingamy then?'

'Her what?'

Billy tapped his head. 'You know, her fingamy!'

'You mean her memory? Well no, not altogether, just *that* part of her life. She was only six or seven; she just forgot that's all and now it's all come back to 'er.'

'Emma will forget as well, then?'

With a child on each knee, Jessie cuddled them, knowing that she would always have them to love. 'It was all a long time ago, Billy. For Gran, I mean. I expect Emma would forget in time, if we don't take her back now and then, to visit.'

'B-b-but you won't leave me?'

'No, course not, Emma, and I'll tell you something else: very soon we're gonna 'ave our own house back – all shipshape and ready to move in. Tomorrow, I'm going round the town hall and tell 'em to get a move on.'

In her resolute mood, Jessie lost no time in finding her way through the bureaucratic machine at the town hall and had, within a week or so, received written confirmation that work on her house would commence within a fortnight. There had been an oversight in her case and it would now be put right.

Gradually, things were getting back to normal. Despite the death and destruction, the East End was rising from the ashes. But when the King and Queen and the two Princesses on a state visit drove through the ravaged East End, the papers reported the Royal comment that 'East London could never be the same again. Old landmarks had gone and thousands of houses were awaiting repair.'

By early March 1946, Jessie was getting her life in shape. She had moved back into 13 Grant Street and was happy with the new decor – cream gloss paint on all the woodwork and light flowery wallpaper in, each room and in the passage. The kitchen had been painted apple green and all of the windows had been replaced. Her mood of optimism of a country recovering was shared by thousands. Even though there was much to do *and* much to forget, the post-war depression was at last beginning to lift. The hopes and dreams of better things to come was voiced daily by the politicians. The message was getting through and it was working.

And yet, during all this time Jessie had not heard one word from Tom. What had happened to him? Where was he? She decided to go to the police station and report him as a missing person – she had to find out… she wanted the truth.

The duty-sergeant was well-acquainted with Tom Smith. It was a shock for Jessie to learn just how many times he had gone AWOL and how many times he had managed to slip through the net. Now, it would appear, he had become a local hero. Once again, Jessie was reminded that there was a part of Tom's life that she knew nothing about, she felt as if she was married to a stranger.

'You'd be cleverer than most women, Mrs Smith, if you could keep up with him,' were the words which would remain with her for a long time.

She felt so frustrated and at a loss as to her next move. As she walked aimlessly through the back streets, Jessie began to wonder if she and her children would be better off without him? Had the time finally arrived to start a new life?

Instead of going straight back to Emmie and Charlie's house where the children were being minded, she went to Max's flat above the delicatessen hoping to find him in. Having no joy, she scribbled a simple note on the back of a scrap of paper. 'The spare room is small but it's yours if you want to move in with us. I'm going to have to take in a lodger. Jessie.' She realised this would distress her mother and upset Tom's parents, but she now had to think ahead. The extra money from the rent would save her having to set out at dawn each morning, as she had been doing, to join the small team of cleaners at the London hospital. As a temporary measure it was fine, but this wasn't what she wanted. Until the children were both at school, she wanted to be there for them. Later in life, she would go back to her secretarial work.

Having dropped the note through the letterbox, Jessie felt a tiny flush of excitement. She was inviting another man to live with her, albeit an old family friend. Max had never pushed her or made any improper sexual advances whatsoever and Jessie had never encouraged him. But now with this note, she was clearly giving him a message – she was ready to spend more time with him. As she walked away, she heard Max's door open. Turning round, she saw an unshaven, tired man peering at her through red-rimmed eyes.

'He'll be back around six. I'll give 'im your note.'

Before he could close the door, Jessie was there, asking if she could possibly have a glass of water. The man stepped aside allowing her to go in. 'I didn't know that Max had a lodger,' she said, coaxing information.

'Oh well…' was his tired reply, as he scratched his cheek. 'I'm not a lodger. Just stopping for a bit that's all. Actually, I was just gonna make a cup of tea, would you like a cuppa?'

'Thanks. I could do with a break,' she said, going into the living room and dropping into an armchair. Jessie sank her head back into a cushion and imagined Max and herself by the fireside, in Grant Street – her home. All the emotions she had felt in the past, when they were practically engaged to be married, came flooding back.

'I didn't know if you wanted sugar,' the man's quiet voice brought Jessie from her daydreaming. 'So I've brought the bag and a spoon. I found a tray in the cupboard under the sink...'

'Sugar's a must,' she said yawning. 'Sorry... I nearly dozed off.'

'It's what you should do, I mean... sleep if you're tired. Best medicine that is... sleep.'

Jessie watched as the man, who looked so weary, poured a little milk from a bottle into her cup. His hand was trembling. 'Hope it's not too strong. I was brought up on strong brew.'

'What's your name?' said Jessie, relaxed.

'Derek. It looks a bit strong, you might want a drop of water in it.'

'No, it's fine, that's how I like my tea.'

Sitting in the other armchair, Derek fell silent. He was considering whether he should offer her a biscuit, there was a packet of digestives in the cupboard. If Jessie was a good friend of his benefactor, it would be impolite not to offer her one. On the other hand, if she wasn't, it could be seen as him taking liberties.

'He's got some biscuits,' he finally murmured. 'But—'

'I know. Max always keeps biscuits, he dips them in his tea. My mother had a fit when I did that.'

'Did she? I thought everyone dipped. It's what biscuits are for. You've known him a while then?'

'We're old mates.'

'Ah.' He raised an eyebrow as he glanced at her. 'Lovely man he is. Max makes me feel right at 'ome, but I'll be moving on soon. Mustn't take advantage. I'm not a scrounger.'

'Have you been back long from the war?' said Jessie. He looked as if he had seen active service.

'Oh, yeah. Too long. Be all right in a year or so.'

'Course you will. Where'd they ship you off to then?'

A faraway look filled his eyes and Jessie was reminded of when Tom came home after the horror of Dunkirk. 'I enjoyed the army *before* the war, it was good, orderly, if you know what I mean. Made you feel decent about yerself: regular pay and food, smart uniform. Couldn't ask for more than that. Got a lot of respect in that uniform. People admire a uniformed man,' he said.

'Then war broke out. I was sent to North Africa and was captured at Tobruk, then shipped off to a filthy Italian prison camp. Had to fight for my food, against men like myself, and other types as well – posh blokes with good manners. That's what it came to, you know, we were reduced to fighting like animals for food. Horrible it were. Then I was transferred to a German camp. I didn't mind that so much, it was a lot better organised. I settled there, but looked forward to when it was all over. I knew we'd win the war,' he said. 'It kept me going that. Thinking positive like that.'

He sipped at his tea. Jessie knew there was more coming and didn't mind. She felt too relaxed to mind anything. 'I couldn't wait to get home and see my cousin again, she had been like a mother to me. But I came 'ome to find a strange family living in our little 'ouse, shocked me that did. My cousin had moved out. I expect she was killed soon after, I dunno really, I reckon that's what must 'ave 'appened.'

Jessie was moved by his sad account and asked if he'd tried to find her.

'No, I didn't want to do that. You never really know, do you? She might not 'ave wanted me to find 'er. You can't tell.' A short silence fell between them.

'And then you met Max,' said Jessie, smiling and trying to lift things.

'No. It all went downhill then. I wasn't the only one who wasted my gratuity on drink, mind.' Trying to lighten things, he laughed quietly. 'Them park benches are not very comfortable. At least I never ended up in the loony bin like some poor sods. Thank God for the likes of Max.' Derek sat up. 'Speak of the devil...'

Jessie couldn't hear anything. 'I don't think—'

'Oh that's 'im all right. I recognise 'is soft-shoe shuffle. The downstairs door'll slam shut any second.' It did and Jessie had to smile at this skinny, unshaven man.

'Out there you 'ad to rely on sounds. I reckon I could 'ear a pin drop in a crowded room.'

'The sirens back here at home would have sent you mad then,' said Jessie, distracted. She couldn't wait to see Max's face when he walked in. He would be surprised to see her there.

'It's funny you should say that because, no, loud noises don't affect me. I've watched other blokes keel over, covering their ears, and all because of a steam train passing on the nearby tracks.'

Max *was* taken back to see Jessie sitting in his living room as comfortable as you like. 'Me and Derek 'ave been getting to know each other.'

'I can see that, Jessie. How long have you been here?'

'Not long.'

Derek checked the clock on the mantelshelf. 'Hour and 'alf.'

'Don't be daft. Twenty minutes more like,' said Jessie.

'See. That proves I've not bin boring the young lady, eh, Max?'

'I should think you could keep her entertained for hours.' Wanting Jessie to himself, Max declined the offer of a cup of tea and tossed some tobacco at his house guest. 'Don't smoke it all at once.'

Derek's blue eyes came alive as he gave Max a thumbs up sign. 'May an angel kiss your feet,' he said.

Unable to resist letting that slip by, Max gave Jessie an endearing smile. 'Think *you* could manage to do that, Jess? Kiss my feet.' She didn't answer.

Leaving the contented Derek to himself, Max led Jessie out of the flat for Annie Brown's Tea Rooms, which was just one room and a small one at that. But as Annie Brown told her customers when they questioned the sign above her window: 'One day, cock, one day I'll extend out into that backyard, you see if I don't.'

'Shall I try and guess what's in the note,' said Max, holding open the door into the cosy place.

'If you like,' said Jessie, amused. 'Come on then, mind-reader. What did I write?'

'Tom's back and we can't see each other again,' he said, resigned to it.

'Well, you're not such a clever dick after all, are you? Tom's *not* back and I want you to move into my spare room.' She sat back in her chair wondering if she'd got it all wrong. What if Max wasn't as keen as she thought?

'Depends on how much the rent is,' he said.

'Ah well, it has been freshly wallpapered and painted, and there's a big demand for a room like that.'

'Room only or breakfast and evening meal?'

'All or nothing,' she said, unable to stop herself smiling.

'Two pounds ten shillings. That's my first and final offer. I'll need a small writing desk and chair. I like to work from home when I can.'

There was his answer – he liked to work from *home* when he could. Slipping her arm into his, she laid her head on his shoulder. 'What goes round comes round, eh, Max?'

'Yes. We could have passed like ships in the night, Jessie. I'm so happy you want me with you.'

'Me too, Max.' She kissed him gently on the cheek.

Strolling hand in hand, back to Jessie's house, they were both deep in thought. Jess wondering if she was doing the right thing and Max contemplating if he was setting himself up to be knocked down. Once was enough for any man to be broken-hearted, and Jessie had broken his before when she had left him for Tom.

By the time they arrived at Grant Street, Jessie was beginning to feel apprehensive. The light shining from her front room window was welcoming but she had to brace herself to face Emmie and Charlie who were looking after the children for her. She was going to have to be strong in the face of possible renunciation. To lose the loyalty of Emmie and Charlie would be worse in a way than being abandoned by her own mother. She couldn't have wished for more caring in-laws and more than that, she had come to love them dearly.

Taking the bull by the horns, she pushed open the door of the sitting room. 'Guess what? I've found myself a paying lodger for the spare room!'

Charlie's first reaction was negative. 'Can't say I like the sound of that Jessie. Can't trust strangers… not with a woman on 'er own…'

'Who said it was a man?' said Emmie, digging him in the ribs. 'Look on the bright side for once!' She then turned to Jessie. 'A nice schoolteacher, is she?'

'No. *He's* an accountant and willing to pay two pounds ten shillings a week, breakfast and evening meal thrown in.'

'Two pounds ten shilling!' Charlie could hardly believe. 'What's *he* after?'

Eyeing Max, Jessie gave him a look which said it all. Get in now, Max.

'A clean room,' said Max, 'home cooking and friendship. Not to mention the best neighbours a man could ask for.'

'Stone the crows,' murmured Charlie, 'it's you!'

'What do you think?' said Jessie taking the lead. 'Tom'd understand, wouldn't he? He'd realise that I can't manage on what I earn cleaning, wouldn't he?'

'Never you mind what *he* thinks,' said Emmie, 'I can't think of anyone better. I'll soon put 'im straight when he does think fit to show 'is face.' She turned to Max, 'The sooner you're in 'ere the better. She needs a bit of company and I'll sleep a lot easier knowing there's a man about the place to look after my daughter-in-law and grandchildren. Not to mention rent, which she could do with.'

'So you don't mind then?' said Jessie, relieved. 'People are bound to talk.'

'Let 'em. Sticks and stories break the bones,' said Emmie, decided.

'But names will never 'urt yer,' added Charlie, giving his stamp of approval. 'We'll 'ave a pint of ale on it, shall we?'

Slowly shaking her head, Emmie sighed. 'Any excuse. We'll 'ave a cup of tea Charlie, and no arguing.' Emmie squeezed Max's arm. 'I'm pleased about this. You've taken a weight off my mind. Any funny business mark you and I'll be in like a shot with my rolling pin.'

'She will an' all, Max,' said Charlie, 'she will an' all.'

'You don't have to worry about anything, either of you. We've all been friends for too long to spoil it. Besides, I wouldn't do something like that to Tom. He's got enough to cope with, I've seen what post-war depression can do to men. He'll be back once he's got used to the changes everywhere.'

'I should think you're right about that,' said Charlie, concern creeping into his voice. 'Course, once he does come 'ome, I don't know 'ow he'd feel with you living-in, son. He's a proud bugger at the best of times. Taking rent from a pal...'

'I wouldn't stay on once Tom's home,' said Max, showing no emotion.

'Wouldn't you? Oh. But someone else'd be renting them little rooms of yours, wouldn't they? You can't just chuck people out like that.'

'There's already someone living there, ex-soldier. He's been staying with me until he can find work.' A silence followed as both Emmie and Charlie thought the worst. It was Charlie who tried to put Max straight as to some of the scoundrels that use the war as an excuse and use soft-hearted blokes to live off. Soft-hearted wasn't the word running through Emmie's mind – fool was more in keeping – but she held her tongue. As far as she was concerned Max was old enough to think for himself and she'd never had doubts over his intelligence. Lifting the mood and changing the subject she asked Max when he would be fetching his things.

'No time like the present, if that's all right by you, Jessie?' said Max, carefully.

'Sooner the better. I could do with the extra cash to be honest; shoes for the kids, that sort of thing.'

Feeling uncomfortable about the situation, Charlie wondered if Max knew *why* Tom left home. If he did know, to Charlie's way of thinking, he would be wary as to what might happen when Jessie's husband did walk back in through that door. Another man might have waited and had a quiet word with Jessie, but not Charlie: 'I wouldn't like to be in your shoes mind you – when Tom does show 'is face.' He rubbed his chin, searching his brain for the best way of getting his message across. 'It's because of *you* he went in the first place.' Tact had never been his speciality.

Stunned by this remark, Max waited for him to break into laughter and say he'd been kidding. Scolding Charlie, with her eyes, Jessie gave a version which distorted the truth enough to take the sting out of the tail.

'Take no notice, Max,' she said, 'Tom's gone off looking for work in another part of the country and we all know what that means. He'll do 'is best to uproot me again – if he finds somewhere *he* fancies living. Well this time, *I'll* be staying put!' She had raised her voice deliberately to show Charlie she was nettled.

'If you want to fetch your things tomorrow, Max, that's fine by me.'

'OK,' said Max, 'if you're sure. Tomorrow evening, after work, once I've packed my things.'

'Good,' said Jessie, pushing her worry to the back of her mind. Whether he'd meant to or not, Charlie had sown the seed. If Tom did turn up again – out of the blue – he would be filled with rage and jealousy to find Max living there and would vent his anger with his fists. But, in her heart Jessie didn't believe that Tom would come back, at least, not for a very long time. She had had enough experience by now to know that he thought little of staying away without a word or trace.

Emmie, as ever, picked up on Jessie's anxiety and tried to get the mood back to the way it was when Max first arrived. 'Do you know what, Charlie... I think you're right. I think we should celebrate this business deal with a beer *after* our cup of tea. What d'yer reckon, Max? Shall we send the old codger out for some stout?'

'Never mind what Max thinks. It's about time you listened to me. I wouldn't 'ave suggested a drink to celebrate if it wasn't right and proper. Bloody tea...' He rolled his eyes at Max. 'I'll be back with the beer before you can say Jack Robinson,' he said as he left the room.

'Stop fretting, Jessie, anyone'd think we were planning to rob a bank from the look on your face.' Emmie smiled at her daughter-in-law.

'Eh? No... I was just thinking about Billy and Emma-Rose,' she said, changing the mood. 'They're quiet up there. They can't be in bed already?'

'They're not up there, that's why. Dolly came round and took 'em to the little fairground on the gypsy site. Should be back any minute,'

'By herself?' Jessie was worried that her sometimes absent-minded sister might just lose sight of one of them.

'No,' said Emmie, 'Stanley's gone as well. They needed the kids to go with 'em as a foil. My Stanley's always loved a fairground, I don't know about Dolly?'

'I do. She should 'ave known not to take them without asking me first. I would 'ave gone as well if she'd asked.'

'Well, you weren't in so she couldn't ask. She's not daft and nor is my Stanley. Anyway, all that about gypsies taking kids is a load of rubbish. I know some of the women on that site and they're no different from us.

'Now... this business of Johnnie's house,' said Emmie, reeling off her words. 'Being his next of kin, it came to *us* when he was killed. But that wasn't what me and Charlie wanted. We wanted to sign it over to our grandchildren, for when they come of age. And that's what we were, going to do.'

'Oh Emmie, you can't—'

'No let me finish! I want to get this over and done with. Now since our Stanley came back with that dreadful injury I've 'ad to think differently. So me and Charlie 'ave decided that Johnnie's youngest brother should have the house. But we have willed *our* place to the children.'

'Emmie, you don't have to do that. My kids are not your responsibility...'

'Oh yes they are. So long as I'm fit and able to be a good grandmother, that's what I shall be.'

'No,' said Jessie. 'You've done enough. If it wasn't for you pushing all of us to buy the block of four houses before the war, we would *all* be living in rented. By all accounts, they've gone up in value since then, as *you* said they would. And as for giving Johnnie's place to Stanley, I think that's a lovely idea.' She sipped her tea and studied Emmie who had now relaxed and looked contented.

'Anyway, if he and Dolly do get married, you'll be gifting my sister as well as your son. Johnnie liked Dolly, you know he did.'

'All's well that goes well,' said Max, easing back into the squashy cushion of the armchair. 'It's what Tom would want.'

'What Tom wants and what he gets is another thing,' said Charlie, coming into the room, after his five minutes walk to the pub and back. 'He's not too old to feel the sting of my belt. I never thought—'

'Have you told Stanley, about the house?' said Jessie, interrupting him to avoid any more talk on Tom. Disloyalty could only be taken so far; this was her husband after all.

'No,' said Emmie, 'but I intend to when he gets back. I wanted you to know first. I shall tell 'im that you flatly refused to let us sign it over to the kids – if that's all right?'

'Of course it is, that's a good idea. Stanley knows he can't sway me.'

'Now, *I've* got something to get off me chest. Once I've said it I won't say it again.' Charlie turned to Max. 'Promise me you'll keep an eye on that scrounger in your flat.'

'Oh Gawd,' said Emmie, ''is mind's bin working overtime on 'is little walk.' She was sometimes embarrassed at the way Charlie came out with things.

Before Max could defend Derek, Charlie raised a hand. A signal that he wanted no parley on the subject. 'Forewarned is forearmed,' he said, going into the kitchen to fetch some glasses. Looking to Jessie for moral support, Max received no more than a shrug and an uncertain smile.

Chapter Eight

By the summer of 1946, the Abercrombie survey had produced a Greater London Plan, recommending a ring of new towns in the Home Counties, where 300,000 Londoners could settle. Unlike many others, Emmie and Charlie were not thrilled at the prospect of leaving the place where they and generations before them had been born and bred. They were more than happy to have their family living in the same street. As far as Emmie was concerned, East Enders moving out spelt trouble and the beginning of the end for the East End. As for Charlie, as he had been heard to say many times, Grant Street was his street and when he left, it would be feet first in a pine box.

The long term designs of the Ministry of Planning were new towns for Britain, including two in Essex: Basildon and Harlow. As a stopgap measure for those made homeless, prefabricated houses as temporary places to live were being manufactured. To most, the promise of living in a prefab similar to the Government's showpiece was something of a dream come true.

This new mood of optimism reflected in other areas too: new schools and parklands were pledged. Hopes were high as Londoners believed what the politicians were indicating – the East End would, within a few years, be a worthy place again in which to live, work and play. Architects spoke of a new town in the East End which would follow, once the bomb-damaged Victorian terraced houses had been levelled to make space for blocks of flats.

To those who would never leave the East End, a high rise flat, which was also on the drawing board, was an exciting option. It was true that paddle-steamer trips down the Thames might never return once the riverside had been rebuilt, but this was not uppermost in the minds of those who had lost everything lock stock and barrel in the Blitz.

Stanley and Dolly, happily caught up in the post war mood of love in the air had surprised everyone with their lightning romance and shotgun marriage. They were living in Johnnie's house and looking forward very much to their new addition to the family which, so far, no one knew about. One more grandchild for next door to fuss over. As for Jessie, she couldn't have wished for a better tenant than Max. Apart from the rent, which had made a difference to Jessie's workload, he often came home with little treats for her, Billy and Emma-Rose. More importantly, he really did get on well with Charlie and enjoyed a beer with him now and again.

Having heard nothing from Tom, Emmie and Charlie had made a pact not to talk any more about where he might be or how he was faring. Bad news travelled fast, so if he was in any kind of trouble they would be the first to know. They held no grudge towards Max living in the same house as Jessie arid furthermore were comforted by it. He was a good, steady chap and in a way, a replacement father for their grandchildren.

It hadn't been easy for them to come to terms with a son forsaking his family, but a feeling of accepting the inevitable had taken over from grief. With Johnnie dead and Tom now 'missing', their parental love was lavished on Stanley. But Stanley, unbeknown to them, was discovering that to live in his dead brother's house, was distressful. There were too many memories.

Dolly, on the other hand, was happy and content living with the man she loved and being right next door to family was a bonus. Her new job, working in the local library as general cleaner and dogsbody, suited her down to the ground. Whenever she could, true to form and like all bookworms, she would curl up in a corner and read. Content with her lot, all she hoped now was that Stanley would settle to living in the house and that time would heal his pains. His eldest brother, Johnnie, had always spoiled him and now he was gone.

Sworn to secrecy, Dolly had promised never to let on to Emmie and Charlie of Stanley's intention of moving out. His questions to Jessie as to what it had been like living in a country village during her evacuation had not been simple conversation, but out of real interest. The Suffolk village of Elmshill sounded all right to Stanley. As for Dolly, if she had to go there then she would – so long as she was with Stanley she didn't really mind where they lived, especially now that she was going to have his baby.

When Rose arrived at Jessie's to discuss plans for her forthcoming marriage to Ted, Jessie was concentrating on the job in hand: working on a dress pattern for Emma-Rose. She felt very uncomfortable about the whole thing. She was still trying to come to terms with the fact that her mother was going to remarry.

'So what do you think then, Jessie? Am I too old to wear light colours?' said Rose, for the second time.

'Age shouldn't come into it, Mum.'

'That's what Dolly keeps telling me. She was the one who said I should wear cream and pale blue, but she follows trends and I don't want to be seen as mutton dressed as lamb.'

'Pale blue and cream – for you?'

'If *you* think it's too young as well, then say so. I'm here for your advice, I can't trust Dolly.'

Jessie glanced at the picture that Rose had cut out from a magazine of a model showing the latest style of a two-piece suit, a fitted jacket and pencil slim skirt to match. 'Are you showing me this for the colour of the costume or—'

'Both! I'll wear navy and white,' decided Rose, slipping the journal into her bag. 'It's only Stepney register office and it'll be over in minutes so why bother?'

'It's a special occasion. So if you wanna wear pale blue and cream, you wear it. Do what makes you feel good, Mum. Make the most of it.'

'My mind's made up, navy and white. I've brought the guest list to see what you think. I've invited my stepmother and half-brothers although I doubt any of them will come. *I'm* supposed to be the snob and yet they're the ones who snub me, I'm not really bothered if they turn up, just so long as my children are there to give their blessings; that's all I want. Ted hasn't got anyone other than a brother and he can't make it but it would have been nice to have met him.' Jessie could tell that Rose was uptight about the whole thing and even embarrassed to be discussing it. She spoke rapidly as if she wanted to get it out of the way as soon as possible and yet, there was a sparkle in her eyes and a glow in her cheeks – she had, at her age, fallen in love again!

'Didn't you say Ted's been married once before?'

'Yes, he's a widower. His wife passed away a few years after they were married. They had planned a family but her illness put a stop to that. He's been living by himself for years, poor man. I know what it's, like to be left suddenly like that. He'd vowed to her that he'd never remarry but...'

'Now that he's met you,' said Jessie, 'he wants to – after all this time?'

'Like me, he's finding life a bit lonely. We get on well, and have a lot in common and he's prepared to run the shop and give me a little bit more time to myself. Since your father was killed I seem to have been on a treadmill. I'm tired Jessie, all I seem to do is go back and forth to the shop, I'm entitled to enjoy some time off, surely?'

'Of course you are. We all knew you were doing too much but you couldn't be stopped. You missed Dad, so kept busy, it's understandable. Now you've met someone you think is right for you so...' she shrugged and went back to her pattern cutting.

'I should marry whether you like him or not. Is that it?'

'I never said I didn't like 'im. I'm just... I'm not sure, that's all.'

'About his motives?'

Surprised that Rose was aware of what she had been thinking, she looked at her, questioningly. 'So it's crossed your mind as well then?'

'Of course it has. I'm not a silly old woman blinded by a handsome man, Jessie. I know all there is to know about him and I can assure you that he is trustworthy.'

'So your life should get easier. Like I said, you did far too much after Dad died; now you can ease up a bit.'

Rose became thoughtful, 'I suppose I was trying to be both mother and father, which is why I was flabbergasted when you got yourself pregnant. Would you have done such a thing if your father had still been alive I ask myself. And there's another thing' – said Rose, before Jessie could get in – 'you could try and make conversation with Ted when you're in the same room. Try a bit harder for my sake if nothing else. I mean, Dolly and Hannah get on with him; the boys too for that matter. After all,' continued Rose, 'I've accepted Max moving in with you. Not that I didn't prefer him over Tom but nevertheless you didn't marry Max. I just hope it doesn't reach my neighbours' ears that Jessie Smith's living in sin.'

The sound of Jessie's children playing in Emmie's backyard drifted through the open window.

'I'm gonna forget you said that, Mum. You're all at sixes and sevens over what to get married in and God knows what else, let's leave it there. And yes, now, that it's really happening, I will make an effort with Ted. All right?'

'Don't you come all superior with me, Jessie, I'm no fool and I won't be put down!'

As ever, Jessie had talked her way into another clash with her mother. 'It's time I called the children in,' she said, running her fingers through her hair. 'They'd be upset if you left before they've seen you.'

'I wouldn't let that happen,' said Rose, rising from her chair. 'I intend to go in and see Emmie and Charlie and to invite them to… to the register office.' She couldn't bring herself to say wedding. 'Tell Max I'll see him next time round.'

Pushing her feelings to one side, Jessie nodded. 'Tell Emmie to fetch the children back in half an hour; it'll soon be time for tea and then bed.'

Collecting her handbag, Rose left the room, but before she left the house her parting words cut Jessie to the quick.

'The sooner you get a divorce from that no-good waster the better.'

Pleased to have Rose in their home, both Emmie and Charlie went overboard to make her welcome, while Billy and Emma were now upstairs bouncing on their grandparents' bed.

'Well all I can say, Rose, gal, is good luck to yer,' said Charlie. 'You're a lovely woman and what a waste it would 'ave bin if you'd stayed a lonely widow, eh, Emmie? You agree with me, don't yer?'

'Oh give it a rest, Charlie.' Emmie turned to Rose with a set look on her face. 'Now then, what're you gonna wear?'

'I don't know, Emmie, to be honest. I was set on powder blue and cream but Jessie thought that that was too young.'

'Powder blue? Whose idea was that?'

'Dolly's at first, then Ted agreed and that seemed to be that.'

'I might 'ave known.'

'It's Ted I feel sorry for,' said Charlie. 'Poor sod, coming into this family, too many women, that's the trouble. So where you gonna live, Rose, in your place or Ted's?'

'Ted's only got a flat, Charlie, that wouldn't suit Rose.'

'Well, to tell the truth we've been talking about moving, selling the business and moving out. But I'm not keen, I'd sooner Ted moved in with me.'

'That makes sense,' said Emmie, pleased. 'Too many people have set their sights on moving out.'

'I know. Hannah's living in Walthamstow and I wouldn't be surprised if she moves further afield. If we're not careful, families will be spread far and wide, mind you,

I wouldn't blame Jessie if she started to get ideas. What with the children and—'

'Oh, no,' said Emmie. 'Jessie's fine where she is.'

'I'm not saying that I want her to go. But I can't put pressure on my children now they're adults so I suppose I'm just preparing myself for what might happen, that's all.'

'So what kind of work is your Ted in – I don't remember you saying?'

'Oh, come on, Emmie, he's a tout and you know it. But he would love to get back into his proper trade again – restoring antique furniture. I might sell my little business and buy a different property, maybe a workshop out the back and saleroom in the front. He'd like that.'

Yes, thought Charlie, and so would any man. 'Don't like the sound of that, Rose, no – too risky; you could end up in debt. You'd 'ave to put money into the business and it could go bust with debts No, don't like the sound of it at all.'

'That's just what Ted said, Charlie. But I suggested we put it all in his name so, if there is a debt, he'll be the one who'll go to the debtors' prison. Not that I think for one minute it would come to that. I've been in business for too long to make silly mistakes. It took some persuading but Ted did finally agree with me.' She looked at them and shrugged, 'At the end of the day does it matter whose name the business will be in? We'll be man and wife by then.'

Surprised by the speed at which things were going, Emmie and Charlie went quiet. Each had things they would like to have said but each knew that they might say too much. Doubts about Ted were now creeping into their minds. 'You wouldn't put the property in his name though, Rose, surely?' said Emmie, braving it.

'Why not?' She let out a long sigh. 'I'm tired, Emmie. I've worked all my life, one way or another, and I'm tired. Be happy for me that someone like Ted's come along and is willing to take the load off my shoulders. I'll keep the books for him at first and once he's up and running I'll pass that over too.' She sighed again. 'What a relief it will be to stay at home and take up sewing again.'

Looking at each other, Emmie and Charlie remained silent. Knowing Rose as they did, they realised nothing could stop her from doing what she thought was for the best. It was risky, but then Rose was used to taking risks. Only time would tell if she had made the right decision.

–

Relaxing in a deckchair in Jessie's small garden and enjoying a glass of beer, Max was waiting for her to join him. The children were in bed and she was tidying up in the kitchen. All in all things had gone well and as far as he could tell, no one had guessed that he and Jessie were now lovers. In any case, if things had gone, as they ought to have done, Billy and Emma would be *his* children and Jessie *his* wife. But affairs of the heart didn't always go to plan and until there was a divorce, Max knew that he would have to settle for being seen as a paying tenant.

More important was the way they felt about each other. The love they once had and lost had grown again. Glancing down at a new rose bush that he had planted for Jessie in late spring, he found himself thinking about Tom and wondered where he might be and what he might be doing. He couldn't understand how a man could leave a lovely wife and two adorable children without a word. Either he was in trouble somewhere or suffering from post-war depression.

His mind turned to his lodger, poor Derek who had no family, no trade, no money, and no one to love or be loved by. Feeling guilty for not having been to visit him during the past couple of weeks, he made a promise to himself that he would go the very next day to make sure he was all right. Solitude, to Max's way of thinking, was the worst kind of state to slip into. Loneliness could be a killer in the long run.

'He's a funny lad, you know,' said Jessie, coming out into the garden and smiling.

'Who?'

'Billy. For all his bravado and cheek, he can't go to sleep without kissing our Emma goodnight. He wanted you to go up as well but I told 'im no, said you was too tired after working all day. And so you are, you look drawn.'

'You're right, I am tired. My eyes are tired from looking at figures all day. He won't mind, will he?'

'He's already asleep, Max. Once his busy little head hits that pillow, he's out like a light, So's Emma, thank God. What was you thinking about then?'

He didn't want her to know that he had been thinking about Tom. 'Your mother, mostly, and your sisters. Three marriages within months of each other, it must have something to do with the end of the war. Taking their chance on happiness under peaceful conditions.'

'Hannah's the one who shocked me. She only met David at Christmas.'

'How long was it between your meeting Tom and getting married?'

'Don't start all that again, anyway, it's different with Hannah, she's not compulsive or a silly cow like I was.'

'I'm not so sure about that, Jess. Gretna Green? I can't see you doing something as wild as that. Anyway, she looks radiant, they're both happy. Mind you, David must be feeling like a fish out of water in Walthamstow, he's a stock East Ender, all of his mates live round here.'

'Maybe they'll move back in. I don't know anything about 'im, it all happened overnight. What opportunity 'ave I had to talk to Hannah about it? None. She rushes in and rushes out, when she visits, which isn't often, all we ever say is hello and cheerio! I don't really know anything about David.'

'I do, recognised him straight away,' said Max, a touch smug.

'Recognised?'

'I've seen him around, that's all I meant, mostly at the boys' club. He's a keen boxing fan, keeps an eye out for talent and then passes it on.'

'Oh. So you know each other, then?'

'Not really. David likes to keep himself to himself, we don't mix in the same company, Jess.'

A sickening feeling swept through her. She knew some of the types who were involved in boxing. 'So what sort of company does David keep?'

'You don't want to know.'

'I do, Max. Stop mucking about, he's just married my sister!'

'You want names?' He looked at the ceiling, thoughtful. 'Let's see: Dodger Mullins, Timmy Hayes, Jimmy Spinks. Then there's John Lee known as the Southall Cannonball because of his fierce punch – now there's a man! And I should think his two grandsons will follow in his footsteps – two thirteen-year-old kids and brilliant on their feet: Ronnie and Reggie Kray. Reggie's the one who'll really make it in the ring. Good boxing's in the blood. If they put their mind to it they'll be up there with the top professionals.'

'Yeah, all right, Max. Might 'ave known it would all come back to boxing. So that's it then, that's where you know him from?'

'God you're predictable, Jessie, I knew you'd say that.' Max held back on the other types that David was associated with. Hardened East End professional criminals who held a veiled mystery which impressed. If asked, Max would have to admit that the men were quiet, polite and generous with their time and cash when it came to the youth clubs and the boxing championships. It was a way of life – their way. Some of these men ran the East End underworld and no one asked questions. It was taken for granted that the mohair suits and gold cuff-links were a sign of wealth and good brains; no questions asked.

'Did you ever box, Max,' said Jessie, 'when you was little, did your dad take you to the junior dubs?'

'No. It's in some families and not in others, I told you, boxing's in the blood. You'd best watch Charlie though, he'll have Billy inside a ring if you let him.'

'He bloody-well won't!'

Max closed his eyes and suppressed a grin; Jessie didn't know Charlie the way he did. When he'd taken his grandson, Billy, to a local fairground and to Stewart's boxing booth, the five-year-old was very enthusiastic, according to Charlie. On the way home and in a faraway mood, Billy had wanted to know if he would be able to box in a proper ring when *he* was thirteen, like the Kray twins had, Charlie had had to stifle his laughter and make him promise not to let on to Emmie or his mother exactly which attraction he had taken him to see before he went on the merry-go-round and tucked into candyfloss.

With no more talk of David and his dubious pals, both Jessie and Max were engrossed in their paperbacks when the door knocker went. Believing it to be Dolly popping in for some sugar or tea or something else she'd run out of, Jessie took a handwritten sign from behind the settee, which Max had made and carried it with her to the street door. The sign said simply: JESSIE'S CORNER SHOP, NO TICK.

No one could be more surprised than she was, when she opened the door to Edna, the friend she had not seen in a very long time. Stunned and bemused, Jessie was unable to take in her friend's new style.

'Bleeding 'ell, leave me out 'ere all day why don't yer,' said Edna, true to form. 'I s'pose it's my rig-out. Don't ask,' he said, pushing past her. 'Well, this is a fine little place you've got yerself into. Lucky cow.'

Following Edna into the front room, Jessie looked at Max and wondered what he would make of Edna. Max looked bemused to say the least.

'This your bloke?' He turned to Jessie and flicked the air. 'Take no notice of this bloody suit, Stuart insisted I wear it. I feel like a real butch. The tits 'ad to go as well as did my lovely ginger blond locks.'

'Max,' said Jessie pursing her lips so as not to smile. 'This is Edna.'

'No, it's not love, that 'ad to go as well, it's Eddie now. How are you, Max love, keeping you 'appy is she? Sexy cow.' Max's jaw dropped.

'At least he gave in on the make-up, I told him no messing, the eye shadow and lipstick stay or I go.' He sat next to Max on the settee and patted his leg. 'He's a white-collar worker, Max. They'd shove 'im right out the bleeding door if they caught on, mind you there're more queers in the city than in the slums, take my word for it.'

'Edna used to be a female impersonator,' said Jessie.

'Eddie, love, *Eddie*. At least it goes with this bloody suit, I feel like a tin soldier. There's a bottle in that shopping bag, Jess, get some glasses for Gawd's sake. Drop of rum'll do us all the world of good.'

Jessie wasn't out of the room five minutes before she heard Max and Eddie reeling with laughter. He had obviously told Max one of his dirty jokes and by the time Jessie was back in the room they were getting on like a house on fire. Max had simply gone with the flow, what could he say? Eddie was something else.

'How's your twin sister, Jessie love?' Eddie nudged Max and screwed up her nose. 'They don't make too many like that – thank Gawd. Posh girls are a bit too stiff for me as a rule, but she was all right once she got used to me. Her and that other one she worked with at that place they couldn't tell us about. Pair of bleeding spies if you ask me.'

He went through the motions of hitching the strap of his brassiere which he no longer wore. 'I thought she was a bit butch, that Helen,' he said, pushing his painted fingernails through his short hair. 'Still, you can't always tell, can you, Max. I mean, to look at me, you wouldn't think I was a woman, not in this bloody suit. Well, I'm not a woman *really, I* think I am but others don't. Got the wrong bits on the outside love, two dumplings and a saveloy instead of a meat pie.'

One hour later, the bottle of rum was empty and all three were drunk and happy. Max had never laughed so much, his sides were aching. 'I think I'm going to have to go to bed,' he said, pulling himself up from the armchair, on unsteady feet.

'Careful, cock,' said Eddie, 'two drunk left feet are worse than a pair of sober ones.' Now it was his turn to keel over with laughter. 'Do us both a favour, Max love, and go to bed. Don't fall over them peculiar plates of meat or I'll wet me knickers. Yeah, Jessie, love, I get away with that as well. No *way* will I wear men's pants – oh, the very thought of it.'

Laughing and swaying, Max left the room and Jessie had a feeling she would find him on top of the bed fully dressed and out like a light, Max was not a drinker. 'Poor bugger,' said Eddie, 'he's had a bit of a shock. Mind you, I do it on purpose, I just love it. Born to entertain, I am. I never asked for this bleeding gift, it was forced on me. He who knows best can do what He bleeding well likes. You wait till I get up there, He'll get a piece of my mind. God? Who *does* He think He is?'

'Well, you look happy enough, Ed, and to be honest your new look, now that I'm getting used to it, is more you. A suit instead of a frock, short hair, it suits yer. You're still the same old friend, you 'aven't really changed and that's the important thing.'

'So you like my quaff then?'

'Yeah, and the colour. You've tinted it chestnut, haven't you? It looks more you.'

'Why don't you say boring and be done with.'

'You're gonna 'ave to drop wearing make-up,' said Jessie, grinning. 'It don't go with the rest of you.'

'Oh, cheers. Remind me never to let you meet Stuart, the pair of you'll 'ave me in greasy dungarees and hobnail boots before I can say piddle on your pussy and watch it drown. Anyway, enough of all that. You look as if you've got over the wartime nightmare, and what a nightmare it was, eh? Remember that cow, Eileen Gatlin? Some landlady *she* was.'

'You're not s'posed to talk ill of the dead, Edna… sorry, *Eddie*.'

'Oh spare me, please, was that woman ever in the land of the living?' She glanced at Jessie's face, trying to read her mind. 'I 'ope you're not gonna tell me you feel guilty?'

'No, but I'm sorry it 'appened, of course I am. Who wouldn't be? I know I only slapped the bitch's face and with good reason.'

'You 'ad enough soddin reason to push 'er over a cliff, Jessie love, and so did I.'

'She polished that passage floor every day except Sundays. I slipped on that rag mat more than once and with Billy in my arms.'

'I skidded enough times but never broke a leg, worse luck, I would 'ave sued the cow. House-proud to the point of no return. Bloody nutcase and rolling in money, I never did find where she 'id it. Wouldn't 'ave bin in a bank count on that. Her greedy daughter must 'ave 'ad all the floorboards up after the funeral. Looking for it. Well, it's bin lovely seeing you again, Jess, and if you don't mind I'll come back soon.'

'You'd better – I miss you and your jokes.'

'I bet you do.' Eddie stood up ready to leave. 'It's lovely all this… flowers in the back garden and jam making in the kitchen, but don't get lost in it, love, will yer?'

'When're you gonna fetch Stuart to meet me?' said Jessie, ignoring his well-meant advice.

'Oh, not yet, cock, he'd accuse me of telling pork pies. How was I to know that the woman who took on all that was chucked at 'er during the Blitz, would turn into a soppy soft housewife. No, get that old fighting spirit back first, love.'

'What are you talking about? I've not changed.'

'I never said you 'ad. Your mettle's slipped down into your shoes, that's all. If it 'adn't, you'd move heaven and earth to find Tom, now tell me I'm wrong.'

'You're wrong. I've 'ad it up to here with 'im. I don't give a monkey's what he's doing or who he's shacked up with. How many times did he drag me away from where I was safe during the war to dump me in a hellhole? And why did he do it – for my sake or for baby Billy's? No, it was for Tom's sake – selfish bastard. And now he's walked out on his wife and two kids, right after a world war. Not to mention going AWOL again and again. Not to mention a lot of things, actually,' she said, downhearted.

'Yeah, there was a time I did 'ave to use every ounce of guts, spirit and energy, even though I was aching from top to toe, cold and damp, hungry and tired. I pushed my baby in the pram from pillar to post to find a roof to put over our 'eads, I slept in wet shelters, filthy bug-ridden halfway houses. I was taken in and turned out and all the while it was raining bombs. I should think I did need to pull on my inner strength!'

Leaning back, Jessie smiled. 'I'll settle for this uneventful life any day, it took me long enough to get it.'

Winking at her, Eddie said, 'I knew it was in there somewhere, hang on to it, Jessie love, and don't dare go all soft on us. You've got a lot more to do before you put on a bleeding shawl and sit in a rocking chair. There's *still* poor bastards out there who are going through what you suffered. You know you'd like to 'elp 'em, Jessie love and deep down you want to. Don't bother to see me out, love.' With that, Eddie kissed her on the cheek and was gone.

Sod it, thought Jessie. Sod it, sod it! Eddie was right. Her 'fight for right' was far from dead, it had just taken a back seat, now Eddie had reminded her. 'Sod you, Edna!' she yelled at the closed front door. 'You and your new look! You're not Eddie, you're Edna, my friend Edna! She wouldn't be told what to wear by any man, *you're* the one who's turned soft!'

The sound of the letterbox opening stopped her. 'That a girl, Jessie love!' laughed Eddie through the tiny space. 'That's my girl!'

'And tell your bloke that I'll visit you whenever I like and I'll bring Billy and Emma-Rose with me as well. I might 'ave lost an 'usband but I'm not gonna let go of a good friend, tell 'im that from me!'

Eddie's laughter could still be heard as he walked away, happy that his soulmate still accepted him. At one time, they had been like a couple of girls, talking and laughing for hours, he couldn't see that it was going to be any different, not now, or ever.

Chapter Nine

Wrapped in her own thoughts, Jessie hadn't heard her sister coming in through the back door, and when she caught a glimpse of her reflection in the small mirror above the kitchen sink, she turned round, startled. 'Dolly! I wish you wouldn't *do* that. I've a good mind to get Charlie to fix that broken fence.'

'Sorry,' said Dolly. 'Next time I'll cough to let you know it's me. Blimey, Jess, you been frying fish again, this place stinks.'

'What d'you want?' Jessie was in no mood for Dolly and her baiting.

'Still, *Jews* round here, like a bit of fish don't they?' smiled Dolly before popping a cigarette into her mouth. 'Mind you, so do I give it to me wrapped in newspaper with piping 'ot chips and—'

'Dolly,' said Jessie, defensively, 'don't call 'em Jews in such a derogatory way – it's insulting. Max is Jewish and proud of it.'

'Oh dear, who's got fleas in her knickers… someone upset you, 'ave they?'

'Not yet.' She narrowed her eyes at her sister. 'Pull the other one, you're in a mood, Jess. I should know.'

'Is that right? Well as it 'appens I was thinking about Hannah my *nice* sister who doesn't try and upset me. Tea or Camp coffee?'

'Tea, ta. What about Hannah?'

'I 'aven't seen 'er for ages. I know she's only just married but you'd think she'd come to visit more often. When she does I never get her to myself, they're like Siamese twins, her and David.'

'Just as well you and Hannah weren't Siamese – otherwise *you'd* be stuck with 'im as well. I know you don't like 'im.' Dolly tossed her hair back and filled the kettle. 'I don't know why you don't. I think he's lovely. Perhaps you're jealous, that's probably what it is.'

'Who said I never liked him?'

'Well, do yer?'

'He's all right, bit distant. Max gets on with him so it must be me, I don't know what I've done.'

'Oh for Gawd's sake,' said Dolly, sighing, 'you always take things so personally, Jess, I doubt he gives you a second thought. Who's picking up Billy from school?'

'Charlie. Anyway, why ain't you at work today?'

''Cos I'm pregnant. And do you know what' – she said, turning to face Jessie and loving the look of shock on her face – 'I've not bin sick *once*. Can you believe that, not once. Well, I'm not being done out of a day off here and there, so I'm gonna say I was sick, brought all me breakfast up, is what I'll tell my boss.'

'Dolly, are you being serious?'

'Look at that flat tummy, I'm three months, don't show do it. That's 'cos I'm wearing a corset, I ain't walking round like a bleeding orange on legs before I 'ave to. Got any biscuits?' She opened one of Jessie's cupboards and peered in. 'I've got a craving for custard creams.'

Dropping into her favourite kitchen chair, Jessie gazed at her sister, a smile spreading across her face. 'You dark horse, three months gone and not a word, or *have* you told everyone else before me?'

'No, it's my business what I do with my fanny.'

'Very nice, I must say. Stop showing off you're so crude at times it's not funny.'

'Crude? I'm being honest, Jess, I know the way people's minds work, same as mine I s'pose. Whenever one of the girls at the factory says she's pregnant, I get this horrible vision of 'em on a delivery bed, looking up at the midwife, legs wide open, all sweaty and panting... So if that's what 'appens in my imagination it must be the same for everyone else. Jesus, Jess, is this all you've got – tea biscuits? I thought Max made a fortune, accountants usually do.'

'He's not an accountant, he's a bookkeeper. Is Stanley pleased?'

'Course he is!' Emma-Rose calling from upstairs stopped the conversation exactly where Dolly wanted it to stop. 'Shh! Don't say anything. See, my little Emma knew 'er Auntie Doll was in, shall I go up?'

'Any point in my saying no?'

'No.' Dolly hadn't got further than the bottom of the staircase when her shrill voice pierced through the house. 'Emma! What d'yer think? Your favourite Auntie is gonna 'ave a baby!'

A few silent moments passed before Emma called back. 'Can, can, can I 'ave one as well, Auntie Dolly?' Wondering what Jessie would make of that, Dolly, laughing quietly, climbed the stairs, 'I don't fink you're quite old enough yet, sweet'eart!'

'I'm four now!'

'Never! Blooming 'eck!'

There was no point in trying to stop Dolly when she was in one of these moods and Jessie knew better than to try. Besides, she was too taken with the news to care that much. She tried to imagine Dolly coping with pregnancy and childbirth.

Knowing the usual routine of Dolly going up to see her niece, either before she went to sleep, or when she'd woken up, Jessie knew she would be up there for a while, lying next to her and chatting ten to the dozen. What they would be talking about right then was anyone's guess, Dolly had at last found a snared listener. The difference was that she had managed, by simplifying things, to get her niece wanting to know more, probably about Dolly's favourite subject – the history of London.

'Billy said they put kids in chimney pots in the old days?' The look of worry on Emma-Rose's face melted Dolly's heart, she had obviously been waiting to ask Dolly if it was true. 'I wouldn't like that,' said Emma, shaking her head. 'Billy would. Let 'im go in a chimney pot, eh?'

'Did Billy say *why* boys went up chimneys? I bet he never.'

Her nose screwed up and still shaking her head, Emma said, 'Little girls never went up, did they?'

'The little boys went up to sweep the chimneys, wiv their special chimney brushes, to clean 'em, and that's why they were called chimney sweeps. Have you ever looked up *your* chimney?'

'Will, will, will there be a boy up there, will there, Auntie Dolly?'

'Course not, unless Billy's up there and got stuck.'

'No,' giggled Emma, 'no, he's at school.'

'Course he is, but the point is, they sent skinny little waifs like 'im up, 'cos chimneys are very narrow and they were the only ones who could fit and squeeze 'emselves up there and they got paid for it.'

'Hundreds of pounds?'

'No, a penny and a crust of bread.'

'A penny's not very much… can I have a story now?'

'I reckon you can,' said Dolly, pinching Emma's pillow. 'Move over a bit more and make room for me, I'm bigger'n you. Right, let me think… I know, yeah, you'll like this one.'

'Is it one that, that, that happened?'

'All my stories are, you know that.'

'Mummy said it, Auntie Dolly. I didn't say it.'

'Quiet and listen and take no notice of what yer muvver tells yer. She's got no imagination. Right, here we go: There was once a place called the work 'ouse in Whitechapel near the hospital that we took Billy to when he 'ad to 'ave a stitch in 'is leg—'

'Two. It was *two* Auntie Dolly.'

'And it was a very dark grim place and freezing cold and everyone 'ad to sleep on long wooden benches, side by side and nose to toes. There wasn't any windows and the candles only got lit on Sunday nights, and all they got to eat was cold, stodgy porridge and mouldy bread, and in the mornings they 'ad to work very 'ard and smash half-a-ton of stone with an 'ammer. Nobody wanted to go into a work 'ouse 'cos they feared it with their very life. Some ran away but they always got caught and taken back and then it was worse and they would 'ave to starve for three days and nights as a punishment. And the blisters on their 'ands from all that smashing of stone would rub and smart and water and become *so* painful they couldn't—'

'*Stop it*, Auntie Dolly!' said Emma, close to tears. 'I didn't *want* that one.'

'Ah, but you will once I get to the good bit,' said Dolly, enjoying herself. 'And then one day there was a little girl who was so freezing cold and had no shoes and no coat and shivered all day long. This little girl had never, ever, sat in a warm bath by the fire like some lucky little girls, and her name was Emma.'

'*Stop it*, Auntie Dolly!'

'Her name was… Emma-*nuesta*.' She looked sideways at her niece. 'Do yer still want me to stop?'

'No,' said Emma-Rose, sulkily.

'And one freezing cold morning, before most people were out of bed, Emma-*nuesta* was using all of 'er strength, as she struggled to ring the work 'ouse bell, with 'er fingers so freezing cold and numb that they nearly snapped off. And they might 'ave but… then… who should 'appen to come along, but a man called Doctor Barnardo! "Little girl," he said, "why are you not tucked up snug in your mother's bed?"

'"P-p-p-please sir, I don't 'ave a muvver, I'm an orphan," said the thin pale-faced waif, who 'ad blue eyes and straggly, curly, blonde hair just like you.'

'Will he get 'er a muvver, Auntie Dolly? Will he?'

'I should say so! Dr Barnardo? The man was a god! He rescued hundreds and hundreds of poor children from the work 'ouses and others who slept in the streets, courtyards and alleys. They wore rags and 'ad to beg for food. Yes, Dr Barnardo was a kind and wonderful man who built nice 'ouses so the very, very poor children could live there and be warm and fed and just like one big family. And do you know what? He was really s'posed to go to China, to be a missionary but instead of that he stayed in the East End and went out 'imself in search of kids who were sleeping rough and dying of starvation and cold. *And* he saved every single one he found, and he made the Government do something about the poverty. You remember what that word means – poverty?'

'Poor, very, very poor. What sort of china, Auntie Dolly?'

'It's a country, sweetheart, right across the other side of the world. Right! Story over.'

'But, but but what happened to Emma?'

'Emma-*nuesta*, you mean? Oh, she lived 'appily ever after and wore nice clean clothes and was never, never 'ungry again. And do you know what? She 'ad an old black and white panda as well.'

Emma clutched her panda tighter. 'Not mine. Wasn't mine?'

'No, but it could 'ave bin *your* panda's granny. And do you know that panda looks just like the one in the story, just like *you* look like Granddad Charlie.'

'I don't! I don't look like 'im. Billy swears like Granddad though.'

'You should ask Granddad about Dr Barnardo. *He* was a cheeky, scruffy, little boy once and probably got a clip round the ear from the doctor for 'is cheek, 'cos Granddad says naughty words sometimes.'

'I know. Calls me a *blooming* angel!'

'No?'

'He does.'

'Well then, he's a naughty boy and Dr Barnardo wouldn't 'ave 'ad none of that. He wouldn't stand for swearing.'

'Will he come 'ere, Dr Bravado?'

'Afraid not sweetheart, he went up to heaven in 1905.'

'I don't know what you *mean*, Auntie Dolly!' The curled lip was back as was the threat of tears.

'Come on, time for milk and a biscuit. Billy'll be in from school any minute and I don't wanna be here then 'cause he drives me mad with 'is rabbiting on about sums and all that rubbish.'

'But, but, but you haven't asked me *questions*.'

'Oh Gawd, what do I let myself in for? Right, what's the name of the king of England?'

Making the most of her time alone, Jessie had been thinking about Hannah and David. They were happy and had a good social life, nightclubs, restaurants and always out dancing. She had to admit that she was feeling like a frump and was a touch jealous.

'I gave smelly knickers something to do so I could 'ave ten minutes peace,' said Dolly, coming in and flopping down on to a chair. 'She's crayoning a picture of what she thinks the kid in the story I told 'er looks like.'

'That was clever. So… my little sister is gonna be a mum, eh,' said Jessie. 'What does Stanley think?'

'You've already asked me that, Jess. He's over the moon. And talking of Stanley, I'm gonna tell you something that you've gotta keep stum about.'

'Go on then, Drama Lil, spit it out.'

'He wants to get out of London, move out to the countryside.'

'Don't we all at times. It'll pass, we all fancy ourselves in a country cottage with roses round the door.'

'It's more serious than that. Stanley wants to sell the 'ouse and buy somefing cheap that needs doin' up, I was finking about that letter you got from Alice Davey. You know, about the two terraced cottages?'

Jessie hesitated. Alice had told her about the bargain offer because she wanted *Jessie* to move to Elmshill.

'What would Stanley do for work?' To Jessie, Elmshill was *her* find, *her* lovely village, that by luck or fate she had evacuated to during the war. Had it not been for Tom tearing her away when he did, for his own reasons, her life might have been very different now.

'No worse than what he's doing for work now. He can't manage his old job at the bell foundry and never in a million years will he settle for being tea boy and odd-job man. If we make the move, at least we'll 'ave some money left over to live on while Stan learns a new trade. And before you ask, yes he can manage very well, one arm or not. He wants to carry on working with metal but learn 'ow to work wrought iron and stuff like that. Country crafts, he calls it.'

'What makes you think you'll make money by selling one house and buying two?'

'Stanley's guvnor's looking for a small place to buy for 'is sister who's a war widow. That's what started this off, got 'im thinking. He'll get more for the one than the price of the two cottages.'

'Sounds like you've worked it all out. You of all people wanting to leave London.'

'Well, I don't really, I'll be doing it for Stan, we 'ave to do somefing. It's perked Stanley up, anyway, went to find out about an artificial limb yesterday.' She cast her eyes down. 'He liked Suffolk when he was stationed there for army training.'

'Well,' said Jessie, 'sounds to me like we'll all 'ave to go on a day's outing to Suffolk.'

'Ah, Jess, would yer, could yer arrange that for us? We really do need a bit of moral support, especially now that I'm pregnant.'

'I know Dolly, Emmie and Charlie'll be only too pleased to have the kids for a whole day. I'll drop Alice a postcard, once I've had a word with Max.'

–

As Jessie had predicted, Max had no qualms about driving to Suffolk, especially since Dolly and Stanley were joining them. He felt that this was the beginning of him being accepted as one of the family.

Leaving Billy and Emma with their grandparents, the family group left very early on a sunny September morning and headed North. Stanley insisted on being the map reader, which Max agreed to even though he knew the route, having been to Bury St Edmunds twice before. Once as a boy on a day's outing with his family, and again, just before the war, when he bought his second-hand motor car and became a lone day-tripper.

'It should take about two and a half hours,' said Max, beginning to chart the day, 'by then we'll be ready for lunch. I telephoned the hotel yesterday and booked us a table for one o'clock.'

'Hotel?' said Dolly. 'We ain't stopping overnight, Max, are we?'

'No, of course we're not, I couldn't afford their prices. But we will be eating in their restaurant, my treat, you'll love it. I remember when my parents took us to the Cherub Hotel for afternoon tea.'

'Sounds all right to me,' said Dolly. 'What d'yer reckon Stanley, good enough for the likes of us is it?'

'Yeah, I'm not fussed,' he said, preoccupied with his map. 'Do you know your way to Epping, Max?'

'I do.'

'Good, 'cos that's where we're 'eading. From there you wanna pick up the…' he peered more closely at the map. ''Ow you supposed to read these things? Look at the print – if you can see it! Anyway, there'll be road signs,' he said, pushing the map into the side pocket of the car door.

'Epping, Newmarket, then Bury St Edmunds – piece of cake. That's what I mean, Doll. See… them Romans… they knew what they was doing. Wish I knew where they buried their dead, treasure must be down there somewhere, eh, Max? 'Cos you know, a lot of Romans settled there in Suffolk and Norfolk, and the Celts before 'em, ain't that right, Doll?'

'More or less.' Dolly wanted to drop the subject, *her* subject. She loved Stanley to bits but he did have a tendency to overdo the little he'd picked up from reading her library books and sometimes got his times and places wrong. 'Is it posh then, Max? This hotel?'

'Well, no posher than some of ours.'

'What, in the East End Max?' said Stanley, grinning. 'Gotta be joking, ain't yer?'

'Not *in* it,' said Max, slowing down for the traffic lights. 'But the West End's not that many miles away and given time, certain parts of the East End will be back on the map.'

'Yeah,' grinned Stanley, 'I can just see 'em queuing up to live in Aldgate, Whitechapel and Brick Lane. Slumming it with the rest of us.'

'Some parts of the East End like Beaumont Square in Stepney are in prime positions – close to the heart of London. And once the new central line underground is up and running, Bethnal Green will be seen differently as well, you'll see,' he said, steering round a cyclist.

'Landlords are not daft, they'll hang on to every bit of property until it happens.'

'They'll be hanging on for a long bloody time then, won't they?' said Stanley. 'You should buy as much as you can while you can, Max.'

'I will, depending on finances.'

'I'll sell you *mine* if you like, buy mine and knock through to Jessie's, then you *would* 'ave something. Good investment that'd be.'

'Shut up, Stanley, Max can do his own thinking. Ain't that right, Max?' said Dolly.

'I s'pose it is, but Stanley's got a point. It never occurred to me to knock through…'

'I'm pleased to hear it,' said Jessie. 'I like my little house the way it is, thank you.'

And so the banter continued until the three passengers fell asleep, whether out of boredom or travel weariness, Max didn't care. He was enjoying the quiet drive with time to ponder over what Stanley had casually suggested. Again, as happened so many times when Max began to try and plan a future, Tom came to mind.

The only way forward that he could see, was for Jessie to be free of Tom. Only when that happened could Max and Jessie be truly together.

–

High House, where Tom was living in comfort and style, was located on the outskirts of a small, quiet village in Suffolk only a few miles from Bury St Edmunds. Today, he had an appointment with his personal tailor and later that afternoon he would be visiting the young teacher, who worked as a private tutor. Tom had many lady friends, but this one was particularly sweet.

Now a gentleman of means, living in the grand house once owned by the real Archibald John Thomas – a recluse who kept himself to himself – Tom was enjoying life to the full. High House was his private domain which he had come to love; his Tudor home. Never in his wildest dreams had he imagined Lady Luck would smile on him so generously. From every window he had a view of the beautiful gardens which were looked after by a local young man who lived for his work.

Inside the oak-beamed rooms, everything was spic and span. The pammet tiled floors gleamed and the furniture shone – thanks to his daily help. The house was in excellent condition. Most of the antique furniture was elaborately carved, black oak, against the greyish-blue walls; timber beams and lush red curtains helped create a place fit for a prince, and Tom had been more than ready to assume that role. Having managed to dupe the bank by written request – with a forged signature – to have Archibald John Thomas's account transferred to a branch in Norwich, where he would not have been personally known or recognised by the bank manager or staff, Tom had actually pulled off his well-laid plan of adopting the man's persona.

He could easily afford to have live-in staff but he guarded his solitude jealously. Instead, the domestic help came daily, and he kept out of the way.

Carefully tying a knot in his silk tie, Tom felt so smug. Things couldn't be better. He had everything money could buy *and* looks that attracted bored, rich housewives as well as voluptuous country girls.

Catching sight of the photograph of Billy holding Emma-Rose as a baby, he felt the old familiar pull to the heartstrings but rose above it. Once he'd locked the heavy oak door of the house, he made his way towards his motor car ready for his trip into town. After his fitting with the tailor and his visit to his lady friend, he would drop in on Colonel Brewster, whom he knew to be away on a business trip, leaving his attractive wife to herself in their rambling country mansion.

By now, Tom had stopped trying to fathom why upper-class women found his cockney accent attractive or why his evasive manner stimulated them. It hadn't taken him long to realise that this teasing game was safer than any concocted story he might have come up with, as to who he was, or how he made his fortune. When one of the women, excited by his elusive ways, inferred that he might be a senior official in the Secret Service, he deliberately protested too much and it worked. He slipped into high society with ease. Going to the races at Newmarket was his passion and having been brought up in a gambling family, he was adept at picking a winner, using his brother Johnnie's system which had given *him* a good return at the greyhound stadiums in days gone by.

Archibald John Thomas, it would appear, from the snippets of information Tom had picked up at the very start of his new life, had hardly spent time at High House and when he did, he'd kept himself to himself and wasn't much seen by the village people, if at all. Tom slipped into the role like a duck to water, the life of luxury suited him down to the ground. How long it would last was anyone's guess, but he was wily enough to hide enough revenue away in a secret place, should the day come when he might have to make a moonlight escape.

'Blimey,' said Dolly as Max pulled up in Bury St Edmunds outside the Cherub Hotel, 'it's a bit posh, innit? Can't we go to a small cafe?'

'Certainly not. This is our day out and we're making the most of it. You can sit outside and eat fish and chips from newspaper if you want to, but we're having lunch in style,' said Max, enjoying himself.

'Fish and chips... like coals to Newcastle, innit?' she said, admiring the surroundings. The area was steeped in history and some of the architecture surpassed what she had seen in London. Gazing at a row of grand Georgian houses which lined the east of the Angel Hill, she could tell instantly, from her years of learning, that behind the façade of each one would be older timber-framed town houses. She imagined Charles Dickens wandering round the town in the same way as he wandered round London. Breaking into her thoughts, Max asked if she really did feel uncomfortable about having lunch in the hotel, but she wasn't listening.

'Nah, it's all right,' said Stanley, peering at the palatial entrance. 'We're all the same under the skin and we're suited up, what d'yer reckon, Jess? You've gone a bit quiet.'

'I'm too hungry to care and stiff from sitting in one position for too long. Come on. I can't wait to see Elmshill again.'

'And I can't wait to see them cottages,' said Dolly.

Laughing and in a good mood they walked up the steps leading into the hotel and paused. Outside in the square which faced the entrance gates into the Abbey ruins was a different matter, this was market day in Bury and the square was bustling with locals who had come in mostly by horse and cart or bus from surrounding villages. Here you would be hard-pressed to sense the aftermath of a country having been at war.

Tom had been leaning on his car, enjoying a smoke and also studying the row of Georgian houses which Dolly had been so taken with. He had heard that one of them was up for sale. Looking from the houses to the hotel he couldn't believe his eyes. Max Cohen had been looking in his direction! Max Cohen in Bury St Edmunds with Jessie, his brother Stanley and his sister-in-law, Dolly! His first thoughts had been to rush over but, with practised poise, he got back into his car, hoping that he hadn't been spotted.

Tom had been in and out of Bury St Edmunds practically every other day since he'd arrived and had come to think of it as his town. And there, in broad daylight, had been Jessie smiling and linking arms with her old sweetheart. Anger, resentment and a deep feeling of betrayal swept through him, he couldn't believe it of Stanley, his brother. Did his family believe him to be dead? Or, he wondered, had Max managed to worm his way into his shoes?

Checking in his mirror, anxious that he might be recognised should they spot him, Tom was satisfied. His hair, now dyed black to match his moustache and expensive clothes, put his mind at rest. Getting out of the car he made his way towards the entrance of the hotel, striding with confidence to befit a man of his standing. Once inside the hotel foyer he saw that the family group were heading towards the restaurant. He went to the reception desk. Fortunately, Claud, a man of discretion whom he had come to trust, was on duty.

'Good evening, Archie,' he said, smiling. 'Reservation for dinner or a room?'

'Neither. A little bit of business between the two of us is what I'm after. First off, the people at the table by the main window, are they booked in for the night?'

'Friends of yours, are they?' said Claud, a mischievous look on his face.

'Never you mind.'

Chuckling, Claud ran his finger down the list and shook his head. 'No, table for four and that's all.'

'Good. Right...' Tom looked the man in the eye. 'This is what I want you to fix. If you 'aven't got an address, get one. Then 'ave a letter sent out telling them they've won an overnight stay because they're the... say the five-hundredth customer since VE Day. Something like that – use your imagination. Reserve a family suite to take two adults and two children for one night: evening meal, breakfast and lunch. Can you do that?'

Claud let out a low uneasy whistle. 'Oh, I couldn't do that. Against company rules that kind of thing, I wouldn't want to lose my job. I'm sure there's a way round it, though.' He tapped his pencil, concentrating. 'Why don't you simply make the booking and pay in advance. In their name not yours.'

'And then what?'

'Well... I'm sure you could persuade one of your lady friends to type up a letter for you.'

'Oh right, and make it sound as if it's from a wealthy eccentric who might 'ave a few shares in the hotel?'

'What a thing to say!' said Claud, laughing. 'I don't know where you get your ideas from Archie. You'll be asking if you can use some of the hotel stationery next.'

'Well, can I?'

'Be more than my life's worth. Next thing you'll be thinking of getting a lady friend to use a fictitious Lord somebody-or-other's letterheading.'

'Well, she'd hardly gonna get hold of something like that, is she?'

'No,' said Claud leaning forward, 'but knowing you you'll have her typing an impressive heading. Honestly, you kill me at times, that you do!'

'What if I asked for the address of your guests in there?'

'Couldn't do it.'

'Thought as much. Just as well I've already got it then, isn't it? One of the ladies is an old friend of mine.'

'Ah, but you haven't let me finish,' said Claud, seeing his nice big tip slipping away. 'I might have turned round to check my key rack and you might have taken a crafty peek at today's booking page. Turning a blind eye and keeping my mouth shut about all you've been saying could cost me my job you know,' he said, raising his eyes to meet Tom's and giving him a look which said it all. It would cost him for Claud to forget all he'd asked of him.

'Yeah all right, I've got the gist.' He shoved a five-pound note in the man's top pocket. 'I'll arrange to deal with the correspondence. You just make sure that when my guests arrive and ask questions about their benefactor, you say you cannot divulge the information. And don't go blabbing to your fancy woman either. I know you've got something going with that cracking little receptionist when she's on duty. And who can blame you, Claud? She comes on to you like a bee to honey, lucky bastard!'

Glowing and unable to contain a broad smile, Claud leaned forward and whispered, 'She does, doesn't she? It's that obvious, is it?'

'No, but nothing passes *me* by, they say it takes one to see one,' he said, giving a nudge and a wink.

'Pair of rascals, eh?' Claud hadn't actually touched the girl in question, but it was enough for him just to have the reputation.

Tom pushed a twenty-pound note into Claud's hand. 'That should cover the family room and meals for an overnight stay, and remember... not a word.'

Shaking hands, the men wished each other well and Tom felt on top of things, until Claud pulled him forward and spoke into his ear. 'They've both got wedding rings on you know and the one I should think you've got your sights set on, looks more likely to go for a swim.' He was referring to Dolly. 'The other one looks too married to the Jewish chap to want to go dancing... if you get my drift.'

Claud couldn't know how close he came to receiving a hefty punch on the jaw, but Tom took it like a man and gave a wink before turning away. Once outside, he swore and cursed under his breath. On the way back to High House he schemed ways of getting back at Jessie and taking the children from her, if only for a day. He would use his teacher girlfriend to do more than send a letter. Smiling to himself, he conceived a plan and would lay it well. He would show his children the best day of their lives and then when he took them back to the hotel, to a distraught mother and Max, the drip, they could judge for themselves whether they wanted to come and stay with him at High House for weekends and holidays or stay for ever cooped up in Jessie's rabbit hutch.

'You're in for a shock, Jessie, if you really believed I'd disappear from your life and give up my family to that drip,' he murmured to himself. 'They say that revenge is sweet.' Laughing, he put his foot down and took the bends in the lane as if he were on a racing track. As he pulled into his private grounds, where he could really think things through, he could see nothing wrong with wanting to get his own back.

After a glass of his best port with some cheese and bread, Tom relaxed in an armchair and dozed. This afternoon nap was something he had begun to get used to. The two women who had been expecting his call would be disappointed but like his best port, they would keep and be all the better for it. Drifting off, he dreamed of his nurse in Scotland, it seemed such a long time ago…

–

'Well, I'll go to my Aunt Mary's. You *do* look well, Jessie, that you do!' Alice's happy, round face, was a lovely welcome. Glad to be back in Elmshill, where the scent of blackberries and honeysuckle floated through on the warm breeze, Jessie hugged her motherly friend.

'And so do you look well, Alice. Sunny as ever. How's Jack?'

'He's all right,' she said, dropping her smile. 'Had a drop too much cider and serve him right. Now, come you in and take me as you find me, I've bin that busy Jessie and I don't mind saying so.'

Going into the cottage Jessie introduced her family. 'We won't stop long, Alice,' said Max, glancing at his wristwatch.

'Well, I should be disappointed if you didn't,' she said. 'I've bin looking forward to seeing Jessie again and I shan't say no more than that. You must do as suits you.'

Jessie gave Max a scolding look. He hadn't meant to offend, the very opposite in fact, but as Jessie had learned, you had to give country people time. Time to weigh up a newcomer and to Alice, that's what Max was.

Turning to Jessie, Alice said, 'Jack let me down and I shan't let him forget it. But never mind that.' She turned her attention to Dolly. 'Well now, if you aren't the sister I heard so much about. Oh, she did tell me some rum stories when me and her sat round the fireside.'

'Well, you don't wanna believe all she says. Goody-two-shoes. I s'pose she said she never did anyfing wrong when we were kids?'

'She told me all about *you*,' said Alice, a saucy grin on her face. 'And my, my, don't you look a picture, straight out of one of them magazines.'

'Ta very much,' said Dolly, lapping it up. 'No one's ever said that to me before. Hear that Stanley – I look like a model. I keep telling him but he won't listen. I love yer 'ouse, Alice,' she continued, glancing round the room. 'I just love it. Are the two cottages just like this?'

Taken with Dolly, Alice found herself in a teasing mood, the side of her personality that her brother Jack saw most of. ''*Course* they aren't like *mine*! You can't hev *two* palaces in one little village.'

'Oh,' said Dolly, not sure how to take her.

'Now you jes make yourselves at home while I fetch in the tea and cake,' said Alice, deliberately leaving Dolly wondering. 'And if that brother of mine *do* come down while I'm in the kitchen take no heed to what he say. He talk so much rubbish when he's had one over the top, that he do.'

'I'll come and give an 'and,' said Dolly, 'if that's all right?'

'As you like my dear, though I can manage. But a little bit of company out there would be very nice. You come on through.'

Following Alice, Dolly fired questions at her, reeled them off. Wanted to know how often the bus ran into Diss and how far it was walking distance to the local shop and post office and if a doctor or nurse lived in the village. Jessie could hear her from the sitting room and hoped she wouldn't talk too much or say something that might sound offensive. She looked across to Stanley and shrugged, 'I think you'll have your work cut out trying to *stop* Dolly from pulling up her roots. She's put 'em down here already by the sound of it.'

'Yeah,' said Stanley scratching his chin, thoughtful. 'I can't say I blame 'er,' he added, looking round the lovely old, beamed room. 'Nah… can't blame 'er, Jess. I feel as if I've walked into a bit of the past myself.' He admired the old cottage armchair he sat in. 'Yeah, I could settle in 'ere all right, it's lovely. What d'yer reckon, Max?'

'What about in the winter?' was his down-to-earth response.

'Oh, leave off. Ain't bin 'ere for five minutes and you're putting a damper on it. Loosen up a bit, do *you* good to live this sort of life.' He leaned forward and whispered, 'I can't wait to meet brother Jack.'

Coming into the room with a tray of freshly baked buns and jam tarts, Dolly almost had tears in her eyes. 'You should see the back garden, Stan. And there're all kinds of chickens out there and ducks and—'

'In the *garden*?' said Max, amazed.

'Yeah, but not in it exactly, sort of penned off in a kind of separate bit. And you'll never guess what…' There was a brief silence as they waited, 'They' ve only got two peacocks that's all, I've never seen anyfing so beautiful. Alice's gonna give me a few feathers to take 'ome.'

Following Dolly in, Alice called up the winding staircase to her brother. 'Jack! If you want some tea best you come down, I en't fetching it up. Jack!'

'I *heard* you, woman! No need to wake the neighbours in the next village!'

'I doubt they're asleep at this time of day, most are out there, working the land.' Alice shook her head and smiled at Max. 'Lazy Jack by name and lazy Jack by nature. I shouldn't like to be without him, mind.' She placed the pot of tea on an oak trolley and wheeled it across to where they were sitting.

'Pour the tea for me, would you, Dolly? We haven't got long and I should like to sit down and tell you what I know about the cottages.'

Happy to oblige, Dolly did as she was asked as if she'd been born to serve and all the time listening intently to Alice.

'They hev bin let go a little, I will say that, but when I was a child, The Lilacs were the prettiest little houses in the villages.' Her eyes glazed over as she remembered.

'They had a well in the front garden, and do you know, I made a wish every time I passed or went in to collect our boots.' Alice turned to Jessie. 'Just like *your* mother, Tilly Hilldrop ran a little shoe and boot-mending service from The Lilacs.

'Arnold, her husband, used one of his outbuildings to cobble. Oooh, it did smell lovely in there, fresh cut leather. I could hev spent hours watching him carving the shape of a sole out of a small sheet. Well, he were a craftsman, that he was. And do you know, that woman, she needed only

164

four hours sleep a night, right up to the day she passed away. And look well on it? I should think she did.'

Alice took her cup of tea from Dolly and leaned back. 'Arnold, rest his soul, died peacefully, in his sleep, which was a blessing. She followed soon after, it couldn't hev bin more than three months on. To be truthful, I believe she died from a broken heart, they didn't hev no children you see, just each other.'

'How long ago was that?' asked Max.

'I should say it must be seven or eight years now. It was a few years before war broke out that I *do* know.'

'And you know what follow a funeral,' said Jack, making a show of the effort it took for him to struggle down the stairs, 'blooming rows! Every cousin you could think of crawled out of the woodwork. There was a brother who survived the First World War but *he* didn't want to know.'

'No. He lives in London you see, did all right for himself. So, no, Jack's right,' said Alice, 'he weren't interested in them cottages. There wasn't an official will you see… well not as such. But the vicar *did* find, tucked away in a drawer, a written piece, which could be used as the last will and testament. They wanted all they owned to go to their only niece. They hadn't seen hide nor hair of the lass but remembered her in their will and I think that was right and proper. Don't you think so, Jessie?'

'I do, Alice, yeah,' said Jessie, longing to see The Lilacs.

'I do believe the niece is now a woman in her fifties, and settled in Devon somewhere, so she's leaving it to the solicitor to sell off her inheritance.'

'Did they live in one or use both cottages?'

'Lived in one, Jessie, and rented the other out to an old boy from Thetford, who kept himself to himself, before *he* went. They didn't bother to rent out after that.' She paused. 'I dare say you could make one lovely house out of them, but I shouldn't like to see that happen,' she said, shaking her head. 'But there, things change and we must go along with it.'

'We wasn't thinking of doing that. Me and Stanley want to live in one while we fix up the other, then we'll do up the other one and rent it out to a local,' said Dolly.

'I don't suppose there's electric laid on?' said Max.

'No. But they got by just as well with oil lamps and candles bless their hearts. They turned down electric lines going into their house, frightened you see, well we *all* were! I wouldn't like to be without it now, mind.'

Stanley eyed the haphazard cables which were looped round and against the walls. 'You've 'ad no trouble with fuses blowing then?'

'Not really, hev we, Jack?'

'I can't say we have and then again I can't say we hevn't, I'm always fixing something or the other. Sometime I think she put it wrong so I *hev* to put it right.'

'Daft old bugger,' said Alice.

Once tea was finished, Jack, bad leg or not, showed Dolly, Stanley and Max round their house and garden and the bit of land out the back. He was proud of his home and proud that he and his sister owned it. Their mother had bought it, for the sum of twenty pounds, in 1920, after she'd been made a widow, and immediately sold off an attached field which she had no need for.

While Jack was playing the landowner and tour guide, Jessie filled Alice in on her life after she left Elmshill, and Alice brought Jessie up to date on the village news since then.

'Rupert still asks after you, you know, whenever I see him, he wants to know if I've heard from you.' A lovely smile spread across her face. 'You won his heart, Jessie, that's what happened. Wouldn't it be lovely,' she said, dreamily, 'if you were to get a divorce and marry our Rupert. Oooh... that would please me. But there, we jes hev to wait and see what the future hold.'

'I've not heard from Tom since he walked out. He must be alive or I would 'ave heard, wouldn't I?'

'I should think you would, Jessie. I should think you would hev heard. Max seems a nice chap mind.'

'He's been a brick, faithful right up to the day. We were engaged once you know, way back.'

'So you said.' Alice leaned back and looked at Jessie as if she were reading her like a book. 'What if your sister do buy them cottages, Jessie, and she settle down? Shall we be seeing much of you and your children?'

'I hope so, Alice. I love it here, you know I do. If I could put an old caravan somewhere... you'd see a great deal of me.'

'But you wouldn't want to leave London?'

'No, my roots are there. Besides, since all the troubles I don't like to plan further than a week or so. Don't know why; I just don't trust fate any more, too much 'as happened to me, too many times, and sometimes overnight. Honest to God, Alice, overnight I've been shot down in flames.'

'Well, you're not alone there, Jessie. We're all a bit afraid and we're all lacking a bit of confidence. That'll change though,' she said, resolute. 'It always has done in the past. We can learn a lot from history, you know.'

The excited voice of Dolly as she came in from the back garden was a well-timed interruption for Jessie. Thinking of what used to be had lowered her spirits.

'I can't believe this place! All you can 'ear out there are birds and the smell! Oooh, that smell… it's better than Mr Martin's flower-stall down the Waste. Well, come on, Jess! Up off your arse. We're off to see the cottages.'

'Oh, I say,' said Alice, chuckling. 'If she en't going to fit in I'm a brown teapot.'

'Fit in?' said Dolly. 'I belong 'ere! Reckon I must 'ave lived 'ere in one of my other lives. I was probably a local before you was, Alice.'

'Well, if you say so,' she said, glancing at Jack, who was enjoying a good belly laugh. 'If you say so.'

At first glance, Jessie had reservations about The Lilacs. There was a great deal of work to do and she wasn't sure that Stanley, as keen and eager as he was, could do as much as he imagined. Keeping her thoughts to herself had been the right thing, because when she caught a glimpse of Stanley, at the back of the overgrown garden, using the stump of his injured arm, her heart went out to him. He was managing as if he'd always been disabled, and it brought a lump to her throat. He never looked happier, pulling at overgrown shrubs to make a clearance.

Feeling his eyes on her, he turned and waved her over. 'Come and 'ave a look at these outbuildings, Jess! I could turn 'em into a guest room for when you come down and visit!'

He's glowing, thought Jessie. Stanley, with everything that had happened to him and his family, could still be overjoyed by an old brick outbuilding. Making her way towards him, she beat down tall nettles with a stick to make her own pathway, which led towards an overgrown bluey-pink hydrangea. This bush reminded her of her dad's back garden in Stepney. On closer inspection she could see that it was in dire need of pruning and that some fertiliser would not go amiss. 'Are there any old pots in there, Stan?'

'Stacks!'

'Good. I'm going to take a few cuttings off this shrub. The soil looks good enough to use.'

Walking towards her and laughing, Stanley held his nose and pointed around to the back of the brick outbuilding. 'There's a pile of manure round there. I don't think it's horse-shit but it don't 'alf pen and ink.'

Looking round the garden Jessie made a quick calculation of how long it would take *her* to get it in shape, with maybe some local paid help. 'Tell you what, I'll come up with the kids for a week's holiday and work on the garden, I can stop with Alice. That will be a present from me, how does that sound?'

'Bloody marvellous, Jess. When d'yer reckon that'll be?'

Laughing, she told him to hold his horses. He had, after all, to sell his house before he could buy this one. But Stanley had worked that out for himself and wasn't going to waste any time. He would strike while the iron was hot and play a game with his guvnor. Tell him there was someone else interested and use his gift of the gab to do a lightning deal and hopefully, a profitable one.

'Well,' said Jessie, 'let's hope it does work out. Meanwhile, I'm gonna take a cutting off the hydrangea, for my backyard, and then we'll go otherwise we'll be 'ere till midnight.'

'So,' said Stanley, putting his arm round her waist. 'What d'yer reckon, Jess?'

She looked into his freckly open face and grinned. 'It's got your name on, that tree.'

'Nah. Straight up?'

'Yeah. Someone's carved STAN in the trunk of that one.' She pointed to a very old apple tree.

'Oh, right… I'll go an' 'ave a butcher's. See, Jess, this place 'as bin waiting for me and Dolly.'

'Maybe, but have you done your sums properly, Stan?'

'Course I have! We'll come out with enough change to keep us going while I work on it. I wish that brother of mine'd turn up, between the two of us we'd soon get cracking.'

Jessie ignored the reference to Tom. 'What about work? I doubt there's much going out this way.'

'Stop worrying, Jess. I'm gonna make it 'appen.' He paused for a minute and then said, 'You know what I reckon? I reckon that in ten years' time – when the country's really on the up – them blokes who make their money in the City will give anything for a weekend place up 'ere.'

His mind was now one-tracked. 'I wouldn't mind betting there're a few places like this going for a song. Think I'll 'ave a little chat with Max.' He smiled and winked at her. 'Onward and upwards, Jess, eh?'

Dolly's voice broke through the heavenly quiet. 'Glass of lemonade you two?'

'Just coming!' Jessie called back.

'You go on, I've got a little bit of carving to do.' Jessie looked across at the apple tree and as Stanley sauntered off, she knew exactly what he was going to do: add Dolly's name to his.

She could understand their enthusiasm. Jessie had fallen in love with the cottages too. They weren't much different from Alice and Jack's house, the only difference being that the Daveys had the lovely fen for their front view while The Lilacs had open landscape. Dolly and Stan would be living at the top road in Elmshill while Alice lived in the bottom road, Fen Lane.

–

On their journey back to London the conversation was non-stop as to what could be done to turn the cottages into lovely homes, even Max was caught up in it. He suggested going half-and-half with Stanley and keeping one for himself, but Stanley knew he was on to something really good and this bit of luck was just what he needed. He didn't lose the opportunity to point out that they should perhaps look to see if there were others going cheap. Max didn't reject the idea out of hand.

It was ten o'clock by the time they pulled into Grant Street and they were all dog tired, even though, with the exception of Max, they had each snatched another doze on the way home.

Dolly, more awake than the others, suggested they go into Jessie's for a cup of cocoa. She couldn't wait to tell the babysitters, Emmie and Charlie, about their find.

Expecting them both to be dozing with the wireless still on, they crept into the front room only to find them wide awake in a silent room. It wasn't only Jessie who picked up on the atmosphere – Stanley frowned at her. Something was wrong.

'Kids get off to sleep all right?' said Jessie, knowing the worry on their faces had nothing to do with their grandchildren. It would have been an entirely different mood if either Billy or Emma-Rose had been taken ill or had had an accident. They would have been pacing the floor, red-eyed.

'Good as gold,' said Emmie, expressionless. 'You'd best sit down, Max,' said Charlie at last. 'The police 'ave bin round.'

It wouldn't have made any difference which way Charlie had presented the news, it came as a shock to all of them. Max simply gazed at him, waiting for more until he finally broke the silence. 'Something's happened to Dad?' he spoke with a husky choked voice.

'No, son. Nothing like that,' said Charlie. The room became quiet again.

'Thank God.' Max pulled out his pristine white handkerchief and wiped his eyes. 'Silly of me to think the worst. Mum's death was such a shock that I just thought the worst had happened again.'

'Nothing wrong with shedding a few tears, son,' said Charlie. 'Do us all a bit of good to 'ave a cry now and then, ain't that right, Emmie?'

'Course it is. Trouble with you men is you're too soft to let go.'

'That's a bit Irish, innit?' said Charlie, scratching his bald head.

'No,' said Max, 'I know what she means.' He took a good deep breath and then waited for the news.

'It don't seem as bad now,' said Charlie, 'even though it is.'

'Oh for Gawd's sake, Dad, tell him will yer!' yelled Stanley. 'Talk about making a play of it!'

'It's your lodger, Max...'

'What about him, he hasn't done something silly, has he?' Max was thinking of suicide.

'Topped 'imself you mean? No... more's the pity. He's gone and so's all your furniture – cleaned out the lot.'

Max didn't believe it. 'There must be a mistake. He wouldn't—'

'He would *and* he has,' said Emmie. 'Did you 'ave any money tucked away?'

A horrid silence hung in the room. 'Some.'

'Where was it hidden?'

'Emmie, he wouldn't do that to me, I gave him a fresh start in life. He was... he wouldn't...'

'*Did* you?'

'Well, yes, of course I did. Most of my clients prefer to pay cash. I know I shouldn't have...'

'Max, we don't give a toss *why* you had it hidden. Good luck if you saved some from the taxman, I say, but was it somewhere he couldn't get at it?'

'I keep it under the floorboards in my bedroom.' Max was doing his best not to sound worried. 'There was a rug over the boards, a small armchair on the rug and some books deliberately stacked round the chair and a pile of old newspapers.'

'Well, there's no chair, nor rug any more. Nothing. Anything that wasn't nailed down has gone, I should bloody know, I went straight round there to see for myself,' said Charlie. 'The place is empty. The bastard even took your cooker. He took the lot – or to be more accurate – he sold the lot to a dealer. A removal van was seen outside by one of the waitresses in the cafe opposite, she thought you were moving out for good.'

Staring down at the floor, Max was shattered. He'd been had for a fool but that wasn't the worst of it, he believed genuinely that he was doing good for Derek and all the time his lodger was probably planning to take him for everything. 'So why did the police come round?'

'Your dad had popped into his deli for something or other and saw that the door to your flat was ajar, he went upstairs and got the shock that you was in for. Then he phoned the police and sent them to Jessie's thinking you'd be in. To tell you the truth, Max, my heart nearly jumped out of my chest when I saw that police car outside Jessie's. I thought they'd come with worse news about my Tom. I thought they'd come to tell 'er that he was dead and that's the truth. I think I'm still in shock to be honest, Charlie as well if he would but admit it.'

'Shock? Daft cow. I *know* Tom's all right, I can feel it in me bones.'

'Well, I suppose I'd best go to the flat,' said Max, disheartened.

'I'll come with yer,' said Stanley, patting his friend on the back. 'It might not be as bad as all that. A few bits of furniture? Could be worse, I s'pose, at least the sponger's gone now. Bloody good job an' all, took you for a mug, Max. You gonna 'ave to swallow that bit mate, he saw you coming.' Stanley was trying to get Max to respond, to let off some steam.

'He seemed so genuine,' said Max, shaking his head.

'Course he did. Played on your sympathy. He knew you was a soft touch and… oh sod 'im. Come on. Let's go an' check the flat out.'

Once alone with Emmie and Charlie, Jessie allowed her feelings to surface. 'Why does it happen to good people? People who are genuine and kind and who *want to* help others who're not so fortunate. Why does it always 'appen to people like Max?'

'It 'appens to anyone who's got anything to thieve, if they've not got their wits about them. Remember, Jessie, this is the East End, where men and women are desperate, still trying to recover from the effects of the Blitz. If *you* couldn't feed your kids, you'd no doubt do the same if the chance came up.'

'I wouldn't, Emmie. You're wrong there.'

'You would. Any mother would,' said Emmie. 'Would you let our Billy and Emma starve to death rather than take from them who're not *really* gonna miss it? Not really gonna go hungry because of it. Not really any more deserving of it than any other poor devil whose luck's run out.'

'Oi!' Charlie gave Emmie a slap on the bottom which was not meant to be playful. 'You don't know what you're talking about woman! That scrounging bastard would 'ave done the same thing to Max whether he was broke or not. "Poor devil"? Is that what you think of someone who'd do a thing like this? What if he'd slipped in through Jessie's back window and took the rent money out of a tin, would you still 'ave sympathy for 'im?'

'She don't pay rent, Charlie. She owns the 'ouse,' said Emmie, without humour.

'And what if she didn't, what then? Bastards like that scrounger are not to know whether she bloody well owns it or not. Nor would they care. If there's something to be nicked, they'll nick it. I've seen the vilest of the vile steal from a dead man's pocket. Thieves are thieves and 'is type is the lowest of the low, so don't let me 'ear you calling that man a "poor devil whose luck's run out." If I saw 'im now I'd kill the swine!'

'Yeah all right, Charlie,' said Emmie, cowering, 'shh, don't wake the kids up.'

'And while we're at it I'll tell you something else: Max is worth two of our Tom!' Catching his breath, Charlie turned to Jessie. 'You'll be all right won't you, Jess, love? Dolly, you'll stop with 'er til Max gets back, will yer?'

Dolly, pale and shocked by the turn of events, simply nodded at Charlie.

'Good. Come on, Emmie. Time you was in bed.' Emmie bade them goodnight and smiled at Charlie as she left the room.

'You can tell us in the morning, all about your trip, eh, Doll?' said Charlie. 'I could see you was excited when you first got back. Night, night, Jess.'

'Night, Charlie.' Once Jessie heard the sound of the street door closing behind him, she looked at Dolly and each of them started to laugh quietly and before the laughter got out of hand, Jessie grabbed a cushion for herself and threw one to her sister so they could each muffle their hysteria just in case they were heard next door.

'See?' said Dolly, wiping her eyes. 'Men are such crafty sods,' she said, still chuckling. 'Not often Charlie gets the upper hand with Emmie.'

'Not often she lets him,' said Jessie. 'Oh God,' she sighed, slumping back in her armchair. 'Whatever's going to happen next, eh? Poor old Max.'

Dolly was laughing again. 'I'm sorry, Jess, but the thought of 'im down on 'is 'ands and knees looking for 'is booty.'

'Shh… you'll wake the kids.'

'Sorry, Jess, I just can't 'elp it. Picturing Max on his knees with 'is two left feet sticking up in the air and Stanley with 'is good arm searching under the floor-boards…'

The two sisters collapsed into each other's arms, laughing uncontrollably.

–

In contrast, the flat above the delicatessen was all doom and gloom. The floorboard over the secret hiding place hadn't even been put back into position and Max's bedroom had been stripped curtains included. His husky voice in the now empty echoing room was chilling to his own ears.

'I can't believe this has happened,' was all he said before he went into the kitchen to get a glass of water. The only glass that had been left behind was one which had his special toothbrush in. Rinsing it, he began to feel light-headed and looked round the bare kitchen for his chair. There was nothing to sit on.

'You all right?' asked Stanley from the doorway.

'I think so.' He managed a faint smile. 'It would be nice if he'd left at least one chair for me.'

'Come on. We'll go down the pub, I think we both need a drink.'

'Give me a minute,' said Max, leaning on the sink and sipping water. 'You haven't asked,' he said.

'I don't have to, Max. Forget it. The money's gone, there's nothing you can do.'

'What a fool,' he said. 'I've been taken for a first-class idiot.'

Stanley wanted to agree with him but from the look on Max's face, he knew this was one of those times to keep his mouth shut and his thoughts to himself.

'Well, you've still got the flat. Let it unfurnished, least that way you get a bit of revenue from it. Put an advert in the paper, plenty of businessmen who live out in the suburbs would take this. Somewhere to bring their bit on the side.'

'In the East End? I don't think so.'

'You'd be surprised, mate… you'd be surprised. Do all the rooms with white wash.'

'Make it look like a hospital? You'll be telling me to put red lino down next – bloodstains on the floor.'

'As it 'appens, that'd look all right, you wanna get rid of this flowery wallpaper that's definite. And paint all this old wooden stuff black, red, white and black. Then chuck in some orange bric-a-brac, a bit of green, yeah that's what you wanna do – make it art deco.'

'Didn't know you were an expert on design and decorating.'

'Na… it's Dolly, innit? Drags me round the blooming art galleries. You get some good ideas though from modem painting an' that.' Leaving Max to think about it, Stanley went to explore the other rooms. There were a few minutes silence before he returned. 'Well, he left you something Max: a cupboard full of empty bottles – liked a drop of whisky didn't he?'

'Don't rub it in. Come on, I've had enough.' Max looked dead beat.

'I don't know 'ow much you 'ad under them floorboards and I don't wanna know but I'll tell you this much, the bloke's done you a favour by doing a runner now. Give us ten per cent and I'll get you a good rent from a toff for this place. What d'yer reckon?'

'Fine. Do what you think best. I'll get a decorator in and—'

'You what? Decorator? What d'yer think my right arm's for? You get the paint, I'll slap it on the walls and you can 'elp me at weekends. Yeah, two weeks and we'll 'ave put the rent up by a third.'

'Maybe I should get rid of it. Sell it off.'

'Over my dead body. It's buying time not selling, use your loaf. Come on, I'm all geared up to it now. Let's go for a beer on the way back.'

His arm round Max's shoulder, Stanley told him that this was the best thing that could have happened to him. 'You need to toughen up a bit, Max, you let people walk all over you. Be *mean*, Max. Be hard.'

Max couldn't help smiling at Stanley's advice. 'Point taken,' he said.

'Anyway, you must be insured.'

'Yes, but the only furniture I put in was utility stuff – cheap and plain. It won't come to much. I've lost a lot of cash though, Stanley, I can't put in a claim for that.'

'Funny that. I could 'ave sworn I saw some really good bits an' pieces in here – family heirlooms and that, antique stuff – that grandfather clock must 'ave bin worth a few bob.'

'What antique clock?'

'Then there was that lovely Jacobean dresser. Black oak… worth a lot of money you know. Yeah I think if we sat down and thought about it you'd 'ave a few hundred quid to come back,' said Stanley, with a gleam in his eye.

'No. I'm not going down that road, Stan. Too risky and it's not right.'

''Cos you know them insurance companies' – Stanley sucked air through his teeth – 'richest people in England, pots of money, got it made, ain't they? Yeah, you could get a bit of justice, Max. Your mate copped some notes for your stuff so you cop some from the rich. Touch of the Robin Hoods, know what I mean? Little bit of cunning and you can turn a bad day into…' he scratched his chin '…into an advantage.'

'Would I get away with it though?'

'Course you would. *I* wouldn't, but you… well… upright citizen, white-collar man?'

'I'll think about it,'

'Nah, mustn't do that. You've gotta think like a man whose lost 'is prized possessions. Act the part! What would you be like if you 'ad of 'ad decent stuff nicked? Up in arms, right?'

'I guess so… let me think about it, Stanley. Look, I'm really tired, I think I'll turn in.'

'Oh, shame that. I was looking forward to a pint. Not to worry; we can have a real, proper drink once your claim comes through. Champagne even.'

Chapter Ten

When the Labour Party won a forceful victory in the post-war elections, a new era was ushered in, with Clement Attlee as the leader of the new Labour Government. Pre-election promises made by Mr Attlee gave hope to everyone. Plans to nationalise the coal industry and railways were introduced; there was to be a National Health Service, a better deal on social security and towns and cities would be rebuilt, with the promise of decent housing for everyone, *and* full employment. Hopes were high and the mood favourable. Free medical service would be a godsend.

Britain was, however, chronically short of the basic materials; food and clothing. Rationing continued and the house-building programme was hampered by a shortage of timber. The reality was that the country was broke, as it had been since early in the war.

Like most people, Jessie was mindful of the reality and blessed the day, back in 1938, when Emmie pushed the family into buying three terraced houses in Grant Street, which were going for a knockdown price. Emmie's eldest, Johnnie the entrepreneur, bought his outright and Jessie paid for hers out of her portion of the compensation fund given to her mother, Rose, when Jessie's dad had been killed in the docks. Emmie and Charlie, through their son

Johnnie, secured a mortgage which he arranged for them at the bank.

The Smiths were, without doubt, one of the lucky few families in the East End, who were faring well under the circumstances.

Despite everything, the atmosphere in London was still one of hope for a prosperous future. The war over, everyone had had enough of doom, gloom and tragedies. Now, they were determined not to let governments, or the struggle for survival, get them down. They had been promised a 'new Jerusalem' and they would get one, come hell or high water.

Dolly was certainly in this mood. She and Stanley had made their decision and the wheels had been oiled. Soon they would be moving out into the countryside to their dream cottages in Elmshill. Breaking the news to Emmie and Charlie, however, was not going to be easy. Dolly's own mother, Rose, had already been told and could see nothing wrong with the move and gave it her stamp of approval. Dolly would now come into her share from the compensation fund. This, however, would not all be used to renovate the cottages. Most would be invested as a back-up, should things go wrong. Stanley wasn't as proud as his brother, Tom, but nevertheless, he was desperate to be independent and to show that he could be as good as any man, disability or not.

Having sworn Jessie to secrecy, Dolly invited her and Stanley's family round for Sunday tea, so she could tell them herself. This should have been a dead give-away, since she was not one for entertaining, Dolly's door was always open but no one expected anything more than a cup of tea and a biscuit. She was too homespun for high tea and all the paraphernalia that went with it.

Today was different. On this mild, sunny October day, she was also going to announce her other good news that she was going to become a mum. And Stanley was going to announce that he had found a buyer for his house and that he and Dolly would be moving on. Emmie and Charlie were going to need a little sugar to help the medicine go down, which is why Dolly had invited everyone to high tea. Even Hannah and David had written to say they would be there.

Wearing a red and green fitted frock which had been copied from a woman's fashion journal and made by Dolly the week before, she looked glamorous. Her new boned corset was working wonders; her dark hair pulled up with combs she appeared to have changed from a blithe young lady into a woman overnight. This change had not gone unnoticed by Stanley who couldn't take his eyes off her and was already wishing the afternoon away so that they could have a cuddle in bed. Dolly could read his mind.

'I know what you're thinking, Stanley Smith, but unless you get off your arse and 'elp me get the table ready, I'll be too bleeding worn out by the time I get to bed.'

'What? I was only remembering 'ow lovely it was last night in bed, that's all.'

'Well, that's all right then. Pass me them tomatoes.'

''Cos you know soon we ain't gonna be able to 'ave a little bit, Doll. You know...' He stretched his legs and rested them on a chair, '...so really...'

'Make the most of our time while we can?' she said, smiling.

'I wasn't gonna say that, I was only thinking of you and ow you should put your feet up and that.'

'Is that right? Well pass them bleedin' tomatoes then!'

Making hard work of it, Stanley heaved himself off of the Derbyshire chair which he'd wheedled from Charlie when his dad was in a good mood. This was the family chair which had been passed down from Emmie's grand-father. 'You'll 'ave me wearing the pinny soon.'

'No I won't, Stan, I would never do that. You wait till we're in our cottage. I'm gonna bake cakes and make jam.' She stopped slicing the cucumber, remembering the overgrown garden behind The Lilacs. 'That plum tree was full of fruit and so was the greengage.'

'Cor...' said Stanley, smelling the tomatoes which were still on a vine, 'these are the best yet. You'll 'ave to get Dad to show you 'ow to grow these, Doll.'

'No – you will.'

'Leave off. I'll 'ave enough to do knocking down walls and that. Fixing tiles, painting.'

'And the rest: plumbing, electrics, rubbing down all the beams...'

'Yeah all right, I know.' He placed the tomatoes on the kitchen table and sat down again. 'You won't frighten me off, Doll. I can't wait.'

'Mum used to bake bread you know,' said Dolly, still in her own dream world. 'I might do that as well. We could save money growing our own vegetables and fruit.' Her eyes lit up suddenly as she spun round to face him.

'We should buy a pig! Feed it with all the peelings and leftovers like they did at the brewery where your mum used to work. They kept a pig as a pet, but we wouldn't do that, we'd get a sow so she could 'ave little uns. Alice'd tell us what to do.'

'Yeah...' said Stanley, getting caught up in it. 'Pork chops, a roast, sausages, bacon, 'am. I think you've got a point there, love.'

Fired up, the happy couple came up with more ideas as if they were the first to think of them. Little did they realise that in remote villages such as Elmshill, most families had been doing for centuries what they were now thinking about.

If Stanley, as a seventeen-year-old, had seen into a crystal ball, on the day he swaggered home to his parents' house, several years ago, when Jessie was there with her fashionable sister, Dolly, he would never have believed the way it was going to turn out. He had been very much a free spirit and with his sunny looks the girls fell at his feet. Yet here he was, approaching his mid-twenties talking like a mature married man.

With the table laid 'fit for the gentry', as Dolly put it, the house shining like a pin and embellished with dahlias and chrysanthemums from her and Jessie's garden, she was ready for her visitors. Despite Dolly's appearance of being a bit of a scatterbrain, she was more than ready when the door knocker went. It was her mother Rose with her new husband, Ted.

Opening the door to them, Dolly, for the first time since she'd married, felt like a proper grown-up house-wife. Rose was proud of her and it showed in her eyes.

'Hello, Mum,' said Dolly, kissing her on the cheek. 'You're my very first guest.' She smiled at Ted and then stood aside to let them through. 'I like the look of them biscuit tins you're carrying, Mum. Been baking, 'ave yer?'

'Yes, Dolly, I have,' said Rose, placing the tin on the kitchen table, inwardly disappointed that her daughter was still using broad cockney. She hoped that the wartime trend would soon fizzle out. It had all started with the upper classes, who found themselves rubbing shoulders with cockneys in shelters and finding them to be, not just amusing, but attractive – and oh how they enjoyed their singing.

'I don't expect you had time to think about such things. So I—'

'Ah, but I did, Mum. I got Emmie on to it. She's made some butterfly cakes.'

'And…?'

'That's all. I thought it'd be enough.'

'Gracious no. There's a lemon sponge in the red tin and a tea-cake in the green one. I should think that'll be enough.' Rose looked round the clean and tidy kitchen. 'You *have* been busy. What about cups and saucers? Have you got plenty?'

'Twelve of each, Mum, you should know you gave us the tea service as a wedding present.'

'You mean you haven't broken any?' Rose couldn't believe how responsible Dolly had become.

'Course not. This is the first time they've bin out of the box.' The door knocker went again. 'Ah, I bet this is Emmie, she's bin so looking forward to this. To seeing you… and Ted.'

Rose looked at Ted as he stood awkwardly in the kitchen doorway. 'Take off your hat and coat You'll soon feel at home once—' Emmie's voice calling out from the passage stopped her.

'Where are you then Rose not in the kitchen I should hope!'

'I am, Emmie – but not working!'

Coming in, Emmie winked at her. 'I don't want madam to think we're gonna do all the toing and froing. She said yesterday we were to behave like proper guests, so I shall. Hello, Ted. How's life treating yer?'

'I'm very well… thanks…'

'Emmie,' said Emmie finishing his sentence for him. 'Don't tell me you've forgot or you're so polite as not to be on first names yet?'

'No, of course not.'

She gave him a certain look which Rose would see as a smile, he saw it as something else. Emmie's message was clear: I'm still not quite sure of you, Ted.

Soon after they had arrived, the house was full. Stephen was the only one who couldn't make it since he was rehearsing for a pantomime soon to be on at the London Palladium and Jessie's other brother, Alfie, was late. Other than that they were all there and cups of tea were being served by Stanley and Max. Together in the kitchen, their duty completed, the two of them were getting on as well as ever. They chatted about Elmshill and how they might go into partnership once Stanley was settled in the village and if he found any run-down properties that might be going for a song.

'I think Jessie's a bit envious, you know,' said Max.

'Bound to be. I'm telling you, Max, you've gotta get out of the smoke. I can just see you living in one of them big places, you know... a nice old rectory.'

'And what would I do for work? Farmers won't pay to have their accounts seen to.'

'You always 'ave to put a bloomin' damper on it, don't yer? Come on, better join 'em in there, Dolly'll wanna make 'er little speech straight away. She's letting me wait till we've 'ad our tea before I break the news. Mum's gonna go haywire.'

'Oi you two!' said Dolly, coming into the kitchen. 'Stop gossiping like a couple of fish wives. Get in there and socialise. No one's talking to David and Hannah's not

187

best pleased, face as long as a kite.' She picked up the sugar bowl. 'Forget your 'ead if it wasn't screwed on.'

'Don't start nagging me, Doll,' moaned Stanley. 'Jessie's in there. She'll soon break the ice.'

'She's talking to Ted, or listening I should say – he's a boring sod you know.'

Rolling his eyes, Stanley went into the living room and over to David and Hannah. 'How's tricks, Dave, mate?'

'Not so bad, Stan. You?'

'Well, it's this married lark, innit? Hannah tied you to 'er apron strings as well 'as she?'

Laughing, Hannah threw her head back. 'I don't believe that for one minute. *You* tied to apron strings?' She turned to David, 'Of Emmie's three sons, Stanley was the most canny; still is. But of course, being the baby of the family, he got away with murder; probably still does!'

'Spoiled me rotten, ruined me they did but what could I do? Hannah was just as bad. Gave me threepence every Friday once she started work, too cute, weren't I? They couldn't say no to anything I wanted.'

'It's true,' said Hannah, relaxing. 'My baby brother could have had anything that he wanted.'

'Brother?' David raised an eyebrow.

'Well… you know.'

'Yeah, brother. She *was* like a sister. I s'pose it was because we never 'ad one. She was always round our 'ouse, wasn't you, Han?'

'Yes. Emmie was looking out for me, someone had to. My foster mother was a very strange woman. But I had Emmie and Charlie and my three adopted brothers.'

'Your foster mother was *deranged*, Hannah. Anyway, how's business, Dave?'

'So so,' he said, evasively.

Timely, as far as David was concerned, Jessie arrived into their company. 'I can't believe my Billy at times, honest to God. He outsmarts even me I. tell you.'

'Why,' said Hannah, always pleased to hear of Billy's antics, 'what's he done now?'

'What he always does when he gets a bee in 'is bonnet, goes on and on and on. I've left 'im telling Charlie all about it.'

'About what?' said Hannah.

'We've won a prize!'

'Yeah, how come?' Stanley's face lit up.

Jessie went on to tell them that she had received a letter saying that theirs had been the one-thousandth booking for lunch and they had won an overnight stay with dinner, breakfast and lunch provided for two adults and two children.

'If it was a boarding house by the seaside, I would jump at it,' said Jessie, 'but taking Billy and Emma to the Cherub Hotel in Bury St Edmunds? I'd be on edge all the time.'

'Well, I wouldn't!' said Hannah. 'I'll go in your place.' She looked to David hopefully. 'Could you cope with playing the role of dad for a couple of days?'

'Not me,' he said, decisively.

'Dead right, not you!' said Stanley. 'Me and Dolly'll take 'em, Jess. Blimey, what a lark, eh, us lot staying overnight in that place.'

'Would you, Stan? Would you take 'em?' asked Jessie.

'Not much! Does Dolly know?'

'No, I've not said anything yet except to Billy – my big mistake!' She looked over to where he was sitting, next to his granddad, telling him all about it and showing his vexation over Jessie not wanting to go.

'Right,' said Stanley, seeing an opportunity to lighten his speech, which he was going to have to make, like it or not. 'Let's get this lot to attention.' He put his arm round Jessie's shoulders, 'Help me out if Mother starts to perform. I'm gonna break my bit of news about selling up. Then Dolly can come in with 'er bit.'

'Rather you than me,' said Jessie. 'Good luck.'

As wily as ever, Stanley deliberately dragged out his little speech. Boring them was a way of defusing the situation, he thought. He started by telling them about Jessie's good fortune and how she'd passed the prize over to him and Dolly.

Concluding, he said, 'And now I'm gonna tell you why it makes sense for me and Doll to go in Jessie's place. Mum. Dad. I've got some smashing news for you. Me and Dolly 'ave found a lovely little cottage that's going for a song. Handsome it is; roses all round the front door and vegetables in the back garden. So we're gonna sell our 'ouse and buy that one.'

'Over my dead body,' said Emmie.

'No listen, Mum. You've not 'eard the best bit. The bit that's made us think this way.' He turned to Dolly and grinned. 'Your turn, love.'

The room went silent as they waited to hear what she had to say. 'Gawd help us, anyone'd think it was a funeral!' She stood up and stroked away any creases that might have appeared on her nice new frock. 'Really and truly we shouldn't be drinking tea at a moment like this, but, since that's all we've got, it'll 'ave to do. So I'm gonna ask you all to be upstanding and raise your cups to Stanley. We are gonna toast *Stanley*!'

'What for?' said Charlie. 'It ain't 'is birthday!'

'No, it ain't,' said Dolly, giving Stanley the evil eye to get a move on.

'That's right,' said Stanley, 'it's not my birthday, but you was close, Dad – very close. Go on then, Doll. I can't blooming well toast myself, can I?' As usual, Stanley had managed with just a few words to lighten the mood. They were all smiling again.

Raising her cup even higher, she said, 'I would like to toast Stanley Smith, for making me… pregnant!'

'Our Stanley's starting 'is own family! Oh, I get it,' said Charlie, helping his son out, 'new house – new baby! That's why they've bin nosing round that little cottage in the country, Em.'

Everyone cheered and toasted the happy couple, except for Emmie who, begrudgingly, raised her cup, she didn't like this one bit. Stanley selling Johnnie's house, which they had not long ago signed over, seemed wrong. She felt as if she'd been double-crossed. Had he known then what his future intentions were? Surely he hadn't conned his old mum and dad… She needn't have signed it over to Stanley; she could have kept it and passed it on to the grandchildren.

With everyone else excited about *both* forthcoming events, Emmie slipped away into the kitchen, to be by herself. This wasn't how she imagined it would be, when her youngest son, her baby, announced that he was going to be a father. She should be thrilled. But Stanley saying that he was going to sell the house had put a damper on it. The fact that he would be living so far away with his family…

'Come on, Em,' said Jessie, who had seen her slip out of the front room. 'Johnnie would have given it the thumbs up.'

Slowly turning to face her daughter-in-law, Emmie sighed. 'Would he though? Maybe not. He might have wanted it to go to the children.'

'Don't be daft, course he wouldn't. His younger brother who spent time in a a prison camp and still can't bear to have it mentioned? His Stanley who survived it *all*; yeah Johnnie would have wanted this for Stanley.'

'Jessie, don't…'

'Emmie, it's got to be said. He hasn't done this deliberately. Stanley would never hurt you and Charlie. In his place, I would want to go away and make a new start. And believe me, where he'll be going, will be so good for 'im and definitely better for a new baby.'

'I s'pose you're right, you usually are, Jess.' Watery-eyed she looked at her. 'Come over 'ere, love, and give me a hug.'

'You silly old thing,' said Jessie, holding Emmie close. 'Fancy thinking that your little boy was going against you. 'Cos don't tell me you wasn't thinking that way, I *know* you. He loves you, and Charlie and he wants to make you proud of 'im. You can't ask for more than that.'

'No, I can't. And what about you, Jess? I can't tell you the nights I've lain awake wondering what you must be feeling like, with Tom walking out on you like that and no word.'

'It was lonely at first, if you want to know. Lonely and… well, just horrible. It was different during the war.'

'I can't say I really understand,' said Emmie, wiping her eyes. 'But you're all right now, eh? Now that Max is there to keep you company.'

'I am, Emmie. It might look—'

'Don't you care what it looks like! Billy and Emma-Rose think the world of Max and for that he gets my blessing. I just hope he doesn't get too hurt, that's all, once Tom's back and he has to go.'

Jessie was being drawn into something she didn't want to discuss. 'We'll get through that bit when the time comes – if it comes. I think he's made a new life for 'imself somewhere, probably in Scotland. Don't be shocked if he turns up one day with a new wife and baby to show off.'

'That's bigamy, he can't do a thing like that! He'd be breaking the law.'

Laughing warmly at Emmie, Jessie said, 'That's never bothered Tom in the past.'

Bursting into the kitchen, Dolly was beside herself. 'Jess, is it true? Me, Stanley and the kids 'ave won a prize?'

'No. I won a prize but I'm passing it over to you. You can 'ave Billy and Emma for two whole days. Come to think of it, that'll give me a holiday too, with them off my hands.'

'Well, I've got to get some practice in, ain't I?' She turned to Emmie. 'You are pleased for us, Em?'

'Course I am. It came as a bit of a shock, that's all. I s'pose we'll all 'ave a day out soon, and give this thatched cottage the once over.' She went to Dolly and gave her a big hug. 'Congratulations, love.' Pulling away from her, Emmie ran her hand over Dolly's stomach and then her buttocks. 'You've got one of them new corsets on!'

'Yeah, good innit?'

'Good! It's like a bloody clamp, go and take it off! You'll do damage to yerself and the baby,' Emmie shook her head, not pleased. 'You're gonna 'ave to change a bit, Dolly. Stop all this glamour lark and put your welfare in front of fashion. Not everyone can 'ave babies you know so don't take it for granted.'

'Sorry, Em, I wasn't thinking. But it can't 'urt the baby surely, I'm only four months gone.'

'Four months! Get upstairs now and get that off. Silly cow.'

Dolly backed out of the kitchen and ran upstairs to change.

'Bit hard on her, weren't you, Em?'

Smiling craftily, Emmie flapped a hand. 'I've bin dying to 'ave a go at your fashion mad sister, I enjoyed that.'

Going into the front room to join the party, Jessie saw that Alfie had arrived and was showing something to David, in secret. She lost no time in finding out what he was up to. 'What you got there then, Alfie?'

'Hello, sis. All right?'

'Fine. What was in your hand before you slipped it into your pocket?'

Splaying his arms and grinning, Alfie shook his head slowly, the face of innocence. 'Don't know what you're talking about.'

'Bloody liar. Show us or I'll raise me voice so they'll all hear. *Mum* included.'

'See what I mean, Dave. She still treats me like a kid.'

'I might want to buy one for Max,' she said, baiting him.

'True. I never thought of that, Jess.'

'Well, my money's as good as anyone else's, Alf.'

'All right,' he said, 'have it your way.' He reached into his jacket pocket and pulled out a gold coloured ballpoint pen. 'Five bob to you.'

'How much are you charging, David?'

'Half a crown.'

'I'll give you two shillings and not a penny more.'

'What's come over you? This could be bent gear.'

194

'Well, if you've got a spiv for a brother, you might as well make the most of it, right, David?'

'Couldn't agree more,' he said, beginning to relax in her company, 'But I don't think you should call your brother a spiv.'

'No? What about a Flash Harry then? After all, Alfie does make a living selling mysteriously acquired goods. *You* wouldn't do a thing like that would you?' she said, hoping to find out exactly what David did do for a living.

Alfie roared with laughter. 'Oh Jessie, you're living in a different world. Dave might not be a spiv, but he *is* a top-class fence.'

David coughed deliberately to stop Alfie saying any more.

'Ah well, that puts a different light on it,' said Jessie, 'he might 'ave something more interesting for me to see.' She looked into David's questioning face. 'I want to buy something nice for Max. Something really special.'

'Get in while she's in the right mood, Dave. Her purse 'as got mothballs, pound notes never see the light of day. Show 'er the watch.' He turned to Jessie. 'It's a sample, understand, so you can't 'ave it now, but Dave'll get one for yer. They're dear but top-notch.'

'Come on then, David,' said Jessie, pleased to have got this far. 'I won't tell Mum.'

Now it was David's turn to smile. 'Don't think it'd matter if you did.' He looked to Alfie for a sign that it was fine to tell her what they both knew. 'What's that supposed to mean?'

'Come on,, Jess,' said Alfie. 'Ted's a diamond. Don't start putting 'im down.'

'Alfie, what are you talking about – what is this? You telling me that my stepfather works in Loot Alley, as well?'

'Course he does he's an old veteran, eh, Dave?'

'He could teach us a thing or two.'

Fazed by the sudden revelation, Jessie's mind turned to Hannah. Wondering how she would feel, once she found out what her new husband was involved in, not to mention the new man in their mother's life. 'Well, there's one in the eye for me. I hope for your sake, David, that Hannah doesn't find out.'

Again, she found them laughing at her. It didn't take much coaxing to discover that Hannah was fully aware of what her husband did and she herself took small items into work to sell on to the girls. It seemed that there was a free market reasserting itself after the war-time controls. She wondered who else might be involved – Max, possibly? Surely not?

There was no need for her to ask because Max had slipped into their company and was shaking hands with David as if they were old pals. She felt like the odd one out with all these revelations. Her own mother, her very proper, churchgoing mother, had remarried, and to someone who walked on the wrong side of the law! Presuming that Hannah was aware of everything, she approached her twin sister and was even more thrown by what she heard.

'You know, Jessie,' she said, 'you really should try to break out of your mould. Things are different now. We've all changed since the war ended, and unless you really are as thick as you make out, you should think more about what people have been through.'

'I *know* what people have been through,' said Jessie, annoyed at her sister's high and mighty tone.

'I was going through it with them. That doesn't mean to say—'

'Oh, Jessie,' said Hannah, 'stop going on about it. If there's going to be a new Britain, as we keep hearing, then it has to be brought about by the people – our own people. The rich don't give a damn about us, so if we can buy a nice thing now and then because it's cheap, so what? What do you think Charlie was doing during the war? Black market, that's what. It was no more legal than what David, Alfie and Ted get away with now.' She held out her arm to show a lovely gold chain-link bracelet. 'Would you turn something like this down? It was a present from David and I don't *care* where it came from. Come on, Jess, it's about time *you* started to have a little fun. You take everything so seriously.'

'What about Max?' said Jessie, letting the last remark wash over her.

'What about him?'

'Well, am I gonna find out that he's been living a secret life as well?'

'No, but I'm sure that even Max wouldn't turn down something going cheap.'

'And Mum?'

'Well,' smiled Hannah, 'there's one in the eye for all of us. She knows and pretends not to. She's the blind, deaf and dumb, brass monkey, I think she's secretly enjoying it. Ted's good for her, he's pulling her into the twentieth century.'

'I can't believe that—'

'No, I don't suppose you can. Like I said, Jess, things are different now. Tell me, have you heard from Tom yet?'

'Nothing at all. Who knows whether he's dead or alive?'

'Of course he's alive otherwise we would have heard. I know Tom too well, but if he loses you to Max it's his own fault and he deserves to lose you.'

'So,' said Jessie, deliberately changing the subject, 'you and David must be very happy. We never see anything of you, so I expect you're so wrapped up in each other to bother with family.'

'Actually, yes.'

Lost for something to say, Jessie simply shrugged. 'Well, you could at least call in to see how Mum is now and then.'

'I could and I do, sometimes, when it suits *me*. Don't forget, Jessie, I was shunned for eighteen years. Where was my mother – or my father, come to that – when I most needed them? When my foster mother dragged me on her political marches? When she let me go without a hot meal because she was in one of her moods?'

'I thought you'd got over all of that.'

'Well yes, it would be nice if that had happened, Jessie. But you don't get over something like that *just* like that. Anyway, I don't bear a grudge, I visit Mum when I feel like it and not out of obligation.'

'Fair enough. I s'pose the same goes for me?'

'Yes. I'm sorry, I know you're my twin sister and I do feel close to you. If you're ever in trouble I want you to know I'll be there, otherwise, we are bound to lead different lives. We were apart for too long for it to be any different. I'm sorry that I can't pretend to be the grateful lost child welcomed home.'

'I can understand that,' said Jessie. 'And I do like your bracelet and your rings *and* your expensive suit. You look great.'

'Thank you.' She looked over Jessie's shoulder and gave David a signal that it was time for them to leave.

'See you soon, then, Jessie,' said David, squeezing her shoulder. 'Take care of yerself.'

Jessie wished them well and went into the kitchen. Hannah was enjoying life to the full and David was a mainstream fence in the East End. Hannah knew that and she didn't care, and Jessie could understand why. Life for Hannah, after the decoding centre at Bletchley Park during the war, had been dull by comparison. Now it had livened up again and Hannah welcomed it.

Later, once all but Jessie, Max and the children had gone, Dolly, as instructed by Stanley, went to have 'a rest' with him. Busy in the kitchen, clearing things away, Jessie was going over in her mind all that she had learned in the past couple of hours.

'A penny for them,' said Max, coming into the kitchen.

'Oh, I was just thinking about life in general and nothing in particular, that's all.'

'And Tom...'

'No. He was the furthest thing from my mind.' She folded the tea towel and sat down. 'I've wasted enough time trying to fathom Tom. He only really ever thought of 'imself. He's not even bothered about Billy and Emma nor his own mum and dad.'

'Well, that can happen I suppose, when...'

'You don't 'ave to defend 'im just because you feel guilty. I *want* you here with me, Max, and I invited you, don't forget.'

'Jessie,' he said, sitting down next to her and taking her hand. 'If you only knew how long I've waited to hear you say that.'

'You're one of the best, Max. And if Tom does come back, he won't be welcome. I've made my mind up – I want a divorce.'

'And then…?' said Max.

'Well, that's really up to you. Look, I know I've never said it before… well, not since we were seventeen and nearly engaged, but I do love you, Max.' She took his hands and held them tightly in her own. 'I'm just sorry I've taken so long to realise it.'

'It doesn't matter, Jess, I would have waited.'

So engrossed with each other, neither of them had heard Emmie coming in through the street door.

'I don't know why you're blushing,' said Emmie, going straight for the teapot. 'I wasn't born yesterday.'

'So you're not going to throw something at me then,' said Max, smiling shyly.

'If I had a good luck charm, I would. I can't say I'm surprised or that I blame either one of you. It's Tom's own fault, but he won't take it sitting down. I suppose you'll be wanting to make it all legal as soon as you can?'

Raising their eyebrows at each other, Jessie and Max went quiet. If they said yes, this would be the start of wheels being set in motion and once things were rolling there would only be one finishing line: the register office.

'How would you feel about that, Emmie?' said Max, taking the reins.

'That depends.'

'On?'

Pouring herself a cup of tea, she said, 'On whether you're gonna take my grandchildren away to some Godforsaken place in the country. Like Stanley intends to.'

'My roots are here and I think Jessie's are too,' he said.

'Good.'

Emmie slumped back in her chair and let out a sigh of relief. 'I can't tell you what a load you've taken from my mind. I've had sleepless nights, let me tell you. Tossing and turning, imagining just me and poor Charlie, on our own in the East End, with none of our family around us. Mind you. I don't think Stanley'll last five minutes in the outback of Norfolk.'

'Suffolk,' said Jessie. 'Which isn't *that* far from London.'

'It bloody well is and you know it. Suffolk? Silly bleeder. Can you see 'im carrot crunching? 'Cos I can't. He'll miss going to the dogs for a kick off. Still, a few quiet lectures from me might take the edge off it.'

'Well, whatever happens,' said Max, 'you can be sure that Stanley will turn the cottages into a lovely home.'

'You're not kidding,' said Jessie, 'look what he's done to this little place. Decorated, ripped out the old fireplace and made this kitchen modern – and with very little money.'

'I know,' said Emmie, 'he's made it really nice.' She gulped her tea in one go. 'I might 'ave known that'd be lukewarm by now. I'd best get back to Charlie, poor devil.'

'Why "poor devil",' said Max, 'he's not upset is he?'

'His memory's going, Max, and he's getting all het up over it – repeating himself over and over...'

'We all do that at times,' said Jessie, trying to ease Emmie's worry.

'No, this is different. He comes into the room, says something, goes out again and five minutes later comes back and says it again as if it was the first time. Take 'is Pye wireless set, it ain't working properly and three times he came in this morning and did exactly the same thing. Looked at it, scratched his head and said, "Blow me, I think that's going on the blink."'

She looked from Jessie to Max. 'Other times he just sits there happy as a sandboy, staring out at nothing. I ask what he's thinking about and he says: "I'm not thinking, Emmie, I'm just thinking."'

'Delayed shock, Em. The papers print every day of how many thousands are suffering from post-war shock. It'll pass.'

'No,' said Emmie, 'it's worse than that. He's happy in 'is own world, though.' With that, she gave them a nod and left.

'You know what I think, Max?' said Jessie once she heard the street door close. 'I think she came in especially to talk to us about that, she knew we were by ourselves. Dolly and Stanley having a lie down and the kids next door. She's really worried.'

'And with good reason. Too many men have gone down the same road. He was in the First World War and no doubt he enjoyed a pint before that too. I've read the statistics, Jessie, at least fifty per cent of those who returned from that war are now alcoholics. That's what's affecting Charlie's memory, he's becoming what's commonly know as "punch drunk". He wants and needs a drink but his brain can't take it as it used to.' He smiled reassuringly. 'He's got a good few years left yet, so don't worry. He could live 'til he's eighty.'

'But his memory'll get worse?'

'Who knows, love?'

Chapter Eleven

While Dolly, Stanley and the children were excitedly collecting things they wanted to take on their weekend holiday in Suffolk, Tom was busy at High House, trying to get his workforce to speed things up. To his mind they went at a snail's pace and to them he was in far too much of a hurry. But Tom was paying their wages so they showed willing, but only when he was watching them.

In one corner of the grounds, next to the lovely natural pond, the new play-park area was almost finished; but almost wasn't good enough for Tom. The hardstanding had been laid and the slide, swings, see-saw and merry-go-round were in place. However, the sand for the custom-made pit, next to the specially designed paddling pool had not arrived.

With just a week to go before the big day, Tom was getting agitated and even the assurances of the foreman couldn't ease his mind.

'It'll he here, Mr Thomas, you can take my word for it,' said Jim, confidently. 'The lorry's being repaired by a good mechanic from Ipswich, and by all accounts, it'll take no more than a few days, if that, to put it right. You'll hev your sandpit come rain or shine.'

'Just as well, Jim, because if it doesn't arrive you take up the pit, brick by brick, tile by tile; and don't expect payment. You made a promise and we shook hands on it.'

'Well, you say that; but really and truly, we ent had *that* long. My men have worked hard and they've done a pretty good job of it... all things considered. You got a park there. A private playground park, that's better'n any kiddies' park behind any village hall. All they get is a blooming swing or two. I shouldn't think your niece and nephew'll complain even if the sand don't arrive, which it will!'

'Good. I'll take your word for it *and* you to the cleaners if it don't come in time.'

'Well, you can't say fairer than that, can you?' said Jim, thinking he'd like to punch Tom in the face. 'You can't say fairer than that.' He smiled at him and doffed his cap.

'Yeah, go on then. Get on with what you 'ave to do.' Dealing with Suffolk men was entirely different from East Enders. They were even more cunning and Tom was only just beginning to discover it. But he respected them for it. He respected anyone who wasn't as thick as two planks.

'So you'll be having some company,' said Jim, 'that'll be nice for you. Your sister, wasn't it?'

'Family is what I said,' said Tom, turning away.

'So you did,' murmured the foreman, a curious smile on his face. 'So you did.'

If Tom was as sharp as he thought he was, he would have realised that Jim was gently probing and not just being friendly. He wanted to know more about this stranger, who, by all accounts and some local gossip, used to never allow anyone into his grounds – but that was before the war. The story which Jim had heard was that the man from High House was a bit on the eccentric side. Some even said he was a recluse – a Londoner who lived alone and chose to see no one. This man did not fit the bill, neither did he answer too readily when addressed as

Mr Thomas. Jim thought that as rather odd, but who was he to judge? Still, he felt a mystery here...

'Pr'aps the war had something to do with it,' Jim murmured to himself, as he leaned on his fork and rolled a cigarette. 'Maybe he's had some real bad experiences.'

Once inside the house, Tom clenched his fists and punched the air, beside himself with joy. He had created his private play-park for his children, as good as the one in Victoria Park and Bethnal Green Gardens. If the sand arrived in time it would be great, but if not, it would hardly matter. Jim's squad had done an excellent job and had worked really hard, which, to Tom's mind, was how it should be. He was giving them work when there wasn't much about and he was paying them in pound notes. What more could they ask for?

'Got to keep the lazy bastards on their toes,' he said to himself as he picked up the receiver of his telephone. His next port of call was Harrods in London. They had served him well with the delivery of two sets of bedroom furniture and bedding, one for a girl and one for a boy. But he had forgotten to order toys for their rooms. He pulled the list from his pocket, it read: rocking-horse for Emma; train set for Billy; soldiers for Billy – and a fort. Teddy bears and dolls for Emma. If they couldn't deliver within a couple of days, he wouldn't place the order, Tom was fast learning how to get things done; money was the entrance ticket that opened *every* door. The order was taken – delivery promised. Tom loved his new lifestyle!

Back in his favourite room, in his favourite brown leather armchair, Tom was satisfied that he had done as much as he could for the time being. Warming his brandy with his hands, he stretched his legs in front of the crackling log fire and watched as the flames reflected in the large

Georgian copper jug in the hearth. He thought about Jessie being there with him, in the other armchair, the rich red and gold tapestry one, with its worn edges. He imagined her, legs curled underneath, a cushion tucked under one arm and in the other, a book. Jessie liked to read but only when she was relaxed. Here she wouldn't have to dip her slender fingers into soapy water, here she would have a live-in maid. He imagined Billy in his own bedroom and Emma-Rose in hers. He pictured the nursemaid going from one to the other, making sure that their every need was being taken care of.

Deep in his fantasies, he stretched a leg towards the tapestry chair and pushed off his shoe. He then moved his foot towards where Jessie's lovely firm buttocks would be and ran his toe down her imaginary leg. Smiling to himself, he remembered how she hated to be touched in that way, especially when she was deep into a book. He wondered if she did still like to read or if perhaps that dozy lapdog, Max, read to her. It wouldn't have surprised him. 'What a dozy bastard you are,' murmured Tom, slowly shaking his head. 'Soft as putty and brainless.' He tried to fathom what Jessie could see in the feeble-minded drip that he assumed him to be.

'Money, I s'pose,' he said, lighting a cigarette. 'You always did like a bit of money, Jess, didn't you? Not your fault, you was used to it.' He drew on his cigarette and blew a smoke ring.

'You weren't exactly brought up with a silver spoon in your mouth, but you never sucked on a cheap old metal one either. No, not you, Jess, your snooty mother saw to that.' He kicked off his other shoe.

'Well, if money's what it takes to win you over then Max is losing the race.' He laughed out loud, imagining

Jessie's face when he showed her the thick wad of notes he kept tucked away for emergencies. He visualised her face when he would bring her to High House and enjoyed every second of his fantasy.

'Silks, satins and gold, Jess, that's what you'll 'ave and why not? You were born to it and I found it – on a bloody train of all things.' He raised his glass, 'Good on you, Archibald John Thomas, and here's to your mother as well!'

Content that things couldn't be going better for him, Tom switched on the wireless and listened to some nice relaxing music and drank himself into oblivion, which was fast becoming his regular practice. Here, in his state of intoxication, nothing could touch him. All the cares of the world and even his own family, could not come uninvited. To Tom's way of thinking, God had created alcohol to help man get through the burdensome world He had lumbered them with. Most women were high on that list of burdens.

'But,' said Tom, addressing the flames of the fire, 'do women realise why they've bin put here? This is the question. I don't think they do, but if they was to think about it... it stands to reason. Why else are women *so* good between the sheets *and* very good at ironing shirts and cooking dinners as well? Hah! Answer me that one!'

Enjoying his one way argument with the fire, he slumped further down in the armchair and laughed to himself before he broke into the little ditty he had made up. Working the words to fit in with most music was something he rather enjoyed and believed he was rather good at. This evening he tried to sing it to the time of 'White Cliffs of Dover' fitting the words in as best he could:

'I've just returned to England,
From somewhere overseas,
Instead of love and kisses, my wife gives me the breeze.
Seemed to prefer another to try and get some fun,
A little car... a lovely country run.
My faithless, English Rose, who couldn't care less.
My teenage sweetheart, my lovely, lovely, lovely, Jess.'

'Well, Max...' drawled Tom, 'now we'll see who she fancies more. It's a level playing field now, old son, seeing as money is no object to the pair of us.' Tom raised his glass to the air and made the toast: 'To our Jessie...' he said, '...who won't believe what she sees!'

Later that night, much later, before dark turned into dawn, Tom woke up to the dying embers in the fireplace. Half asleep, he swallowed the last of the brandy from the bottle and staggered up the dark oak staircase in dire need of his big comfortable double bed, which had more to offer right then than any mistress. 'Sometimes,' slurred Tom, 'a man needs a soft mattress to sink into instead of a sexy woman.' Ten minutes later, Tom, fully clothed, was fast asleep on top of his bed, snoring like a foghorn. There he stayed until almost eleven o'clock the next morning, when he heard the tipper lorry arrive with the sand.

Swallowing his remedy for a hangover, he grimaced. He still hated the sensation of beaten raw eggs slithering down his throat. 'Bloody booze,' he murmured, 'gonna 'ave to cut down, Tom boy.' He drank a glass of water to wash away the sickly taste before settling at the kitchen table to drink his cup of tea.

'You've got a lot to answer for, Jess. Causing a man to turn to drink.' In reality, Tom had no one to blame but himself for letting alcohol become a bad master instead of a good servant. With Jessie still on his mind, he thought about ways of snatching the children when they were in Bury St Edmunds. Rachel, his current girlfriend, had gone along with the idea of sending the letter for him and had said that if he wanted her to, then she would talk to Jessie; try to get her to understand that a father needed to be with his children sometimes. That had made Tom smile, although he never let on. Jessie would go for both of them with claws sharpened, if he suddenly showed up out of the blue with a girlfriend on his arm.

What a joke! He was going to have to come up with a better plan than that. Perhaps he could entice the kids away without her knowledge. But try as he might he could think of no easy way round it. To charm his children away would be easy sailing, but what of the consequences? Jessie would raise the alarm and the Suffolk police would be out in force. Attracting *their* attention was not something he relished.

A few hours later, the foreman knocked on the kitchen door to say that the sand was in place and the workforce would be leaving soon.

'See, just shows what you *can* do when you're pushed, eh?'

'Mmm… now we did say cash, didn't we?' Jim was not amused.

'Dunno, did we?' said Tom, knowing full well that that was the deal. A good price for the job if it was pound notes and not a cheque. The taxman was everyone's enemy after all.

'We did. Of course we hadn't calculated as we should hev done, as to how many man hours all of this would take.'

'Well, if you 'ad of done,' said Tom, enjoying a bit of East End banter, 'I might 'ave given the job to someone else.' He hunched his shoulders and splayed his hands, 'We've all gotta get the best for ourselves, money don't grow on trees.'

'But we'll say no more about the extra hours,' said the foreman, quick off the mark. All he wanted was to be paid, and then get away.

Tom paid up, and once he'd seen the men off his land, he went to admire the brightly coloured park equipment and the sandpit. It was a dream come true for any child. How could Jessie possibly refuse to let their children play here? As he sat on the new ornate iron bench, close to the red and green see-saw, he came up with another idea. He could be honest about the whole thing. Write a note to be handed to Jessie on arrival at the hotel, saying that he had seen the group on their last visit and would like to join them for a cup of coffee in the lounge. He could sound humble and he could credit Max for looking after his family for him. He knew how to win Jessie round, but would it work?

He could say that soon after he left Grant Street, feeling depressed, he had managed to get kitchen work, and had continued, working his way up to assistant chef in hotels round the country. He could write that he had slaved away with every hour God sent and tell her that he'd built up his savings in the hope that he might be able to open his own little restaurant, one day, so that he could return to start afresh and make a good future for his family.

He could go on to say that good fortune had followed his hard working reputation in the business and that he was offered a partnership in a new small chain of milk and coffee bars, which he had taken up and had gone onward and upwards from there.

To score a few points, he could add that he'd kept out of the way so as not to upset and confuse the children. Once he had delivered the note and given Jessie enough time to take it all in, he could make an appearance and drive them all to High House.

Tom looked out through the old diamond-leaded window on to the grass tennis court and imagined himself and Jessie playing a game and having a really great time. He visualised Billy and Emma-Rose in the background in their own private play-park with their nanny watching over them.

'Ponies,' murmured Tom. 'I should 'ave got a couple of ponies in. Ne'mind, all in good time.' Smiling, he pictured his children in riding gear, jumping at shows to the cheers of onlookers as they cleared every fence. Why his luck had changed like this he had no idea nor did he care. As far as he was concerned, the rich were up there because they got more than their fair share of luck – born to it or come by it. He was no different from the upper classes except for one thing – *he* knew what it was like to be broke and now *he* knew what it was like to be rich.

'Good will out. I'll do you proud, Archibald John Thomas, I'll do you proud!'

Going into his study, he picked up the photograph of Billy and Emma-Rose. Soon he would have them out of the slums and the two-up, two-down, which probably now had Max's fingerprints all over it. Anger surged through his veins again, he wondered what his children were making of it. In his mind's eye he could see them in that tiny backyard, having been sent out there to play and bored to death with nothing to do. 'No one should 'ave to live like that, especially not my kids,' he said aloud.

This way of thinking was very different from not so long ago, when his and Jessie's terraced house was, to him, a little bit of heaven. *Their* little bit of heaven. Clearly, Tom was falling into a trap and couldn't see it. Sipping champagne was becoming a regular occurrence – drinking ale from a bottle a thing of the past.

Was he beginning to lose his grip on reality?

–

Meanwhile, back at Jessie's house, things were going with a swing. Stanley, who had now signed the necessary contracts for the sale of his house and the purchase of the two cottages, was passing the drinks round. The celebration was taking place at Jessie's because Dolly had packed everything into tea chests and stored them and their furniture in old man Lipka's shed next to his stable where he kept his cart-horse and goat. Taking advice from her mother, Dolly hadn't left anything to the last minute. Rose had badgered her into thinking ahead and it had paid off. The buyer for their house had brought forward the date of completion and was to move in the very next day. The cottages, however, were uninhabitable at the moment and so Dolly and Stanley were sleeping in Emmie's spare room with plans of camping in one of the cottages until the other was fit to live in.

'Well,' said Stanley raising his drink and beaming, 'here's to me and Dolly turning into country bumpkins!'

'And here's to me,' said Emmie, 'who's got to put up with the pair of you till your dream home is shining like a pin!'

There were cheers and good wishes all round, even Billy and Emma-Rose had joined in.

'And here's to all of us,' said Jessie, 'who'll have relatives living in the country whom we can visit whenever we fancy!'

'No you bleeding won't,' said Dolly. 'You'll wait for a proper invite. Ain't 'aving you lot trundling down whenever you fancy.'

'Try and stop us, Doll,' said Charlie, enjoying himself, 'try and stop us.'

'I will stop you, right at the front gate and send you packing. You can stop with the gypsies.'

'I never knew there was gypsies there,' said Emmie.

'Course there are, proper old Romanies.'

'And,' said Stanley, filled with pride, 'they live in proper wagons, the old painted ones. Beautiful they are, ain't they, Doll?'

'Yep. Got inside fires as well. Last week when we took one of Stan's mates to see the cottages, we went for a walk and there was smoke coming out of a chimney.'

'I never saw any Romany wagons when I was there,' said Jessie, 'but then I never went much further than Alice and Jack's cottage really only as far as the pub.'

'Well then, you wouldn't 'ave done. This one was at the further end of Fen Lane and set right back next to the river, near the rabbit field. I'm surprised you didn't take Billy down there, Jess, it's where all the little kiddies go. Sit quiet for ages they do, waiting for the rabbits to pop out of their holes and skip about.'

'Well,' said Jessie, regretting having ever left the village, 'I might have seen 'em, sooner or later, if Tom hadn't come along and dragged me and little Billy away from

Alice's house. We were really happy and settled there. It were downright selfish of him.'

The room went quiet at the mention of his name. Emmie and Charlie didn't want to be reminded of the way Tom had treated Jessie throughout the war. They didn't want to think about the way he had treated her and the children after his discharge from the army; and especially, they didn't want to think about his present whereabouts. But Jessie was stirred by all the talk of Elmshill. She was jealous.

'I take it you've not 'eard from Tom *either*, Emmie?'

'Course I haven't. I would 'ave said.' Emmie knew that Jessie was just letting them all know that she hadn't forgiven Tom for taking off *again*. 'But don't you fret, Dolly and Stan won't 'ave need for two cottages, you'll see. Max can buy one off 'im later on and you'll 'ave a little place of your own in the country. Not to live in mind, just to visit at weekends and that.'

Smiling back discreetly at Emmie, Jessie was warmed by the closeness of her mother-in-law who knew her as if she was her own daughter. 'Max ain't that well off, Em,' she said, 'Not now perhaps, but you wait. It's written all over 'im.' She looked at the clock on the mantel shelf. 'Shouldn't you be getting his tea ready? He'll be in from work soon.'

'We're 'aving fish and chips. Max'll go out and get 'em later on.'

'You've got a good one there, Jess,' said Emmie, though deep down she was sorry that it wasn't Tom they were talking about.

'Anyway,' said Dolly, changing the subject. 'We won't be making do and camping out in the cottage this weekend. Oh no. *We* shall be staying at the Cherub Hotel.' Her mock posh voice wasn't far off from the real thing.

'But, but, but will there be rabbits?' said Emma.

'Not in the hotel, silly. But there will be once we go to the cottage.'

'I thought we wasn't gonna sleep there?' said Billy.

'Course we ain't gonna sleep there,' said Stanley, pushing his face close up to his nephew's. 'We're only going to 'ave a look, see what's what that's all. To show you the village where we'll be living an' that.'

'I've bin there anyway,' said Billy, his bored tone back.

'Oh and you remember it *all*, do yer?'

'Yes!'

'Jessie…' said Charlie, interrupting the flow. 'I've been wonderin' where your mother is, I thought she'd 'ave bin here today.'

Jessie looked to Emmie for an answer. She wasn't yet properly versed in how to treat Charlie's short-term memory loss. He had already asked about Rose three times and had been given the same answer: Ted had taken her to see a decent size workshop – once a doll factory – in an alley just off Cambridge Heath Road and was hoping to persuade Rose to buy it. But to go ahead she would have to sell the cobbler shop, and she just couldn't make her mind up. Jessie and Emmie had advised her against it, but they knew that at the end of the day, Rose would do what she thought best. They believed that instead of thinking in a businesslike manner, which Rose was more than capable of, she might, on this occasion, let her heart rule over her head.

'She's gone with Ted to look at a workshop,' said Emmie, as if for the first time. She had given up trying to jog his memory and it seemed kinder to let things ride. Jessie was the only one she had confided in.

'Workshop?' said Charlie, surprised. 'Whatever for?'

'So that he can get back to what he's good at – restoring furniture.'

'Oh… so he used to do that did he…?' Jerking his head as if he'd suddenly seen the light, he slapped his knee and laughed quietly. 'Course he did!' He then proceeded to tell Emmie all that Ted had told him as if she'd never heard it before.

Emmie's patience was no longer stretched by this familiar scenario because she had got used to it. Early on, though, she wondered if it was herself going mad. But now she knew that Charlie was sick. And whether it was brought on by too much drink or any other cause, didn't really matter. Now she simply went along with anything he said.

The only real problem she had to deal with was when Charlie wanted to help in the kitchen – with the cooking. This was so out of character that she had to use all of her self-control not to yell at him to get out of her way, but she managed to cope with it. But the worry of him placing a pan on a gas flame and then going out into the garden and forgetting he'd done it, was something she couldn't brush off. Four times she had smelt burning fat and rescued a smoking pan from the heat – just in time.

'You all right, Em?' said Jessie, taking her mother-in-law aside.

'Course I am, why shouldn't I be?'

'You know what I mean?'

'Not now, Jessie love, not now,' Emmie swallowed against a lump in her throat. 'He'll be all right, back to his old self in no time and don't you worry about me. I'm as strong as a wild horse pulling against the reins.'

There really wasn't much Jessie or Emmie could say or do about Charlie. Obstinate as ever, he refused flatly to believe there was anything wrong with him and he became angry with Emmie when she had suggested he see a doctor. It seemed an insoluble problem since poor Charlie could have no idea that he'd forgotten something he had no memory of in the first place.

A knock on the street door was a timely intrusion.

'Get that for me, would you, Em?' said Jessie. 'I'm gonna make a pot of tea to go with the bread pudding you made.'

'It's all right, Dolly's gone to answer it.' Emmie squeezed Jessie's arm. 'We'll have to 'ave a little chat soon.'

'He's not getting any better, is he?'

Emmie pursed her lips and shook her head. 'No, not really. He's as fit as a fiddle but his mind's so confused.'

'I *know* what you mean, Em. You don't 'ave to try and explain to me.'

'Thank God for that,' said Emmie. 'I honestly thought at times that it was me going round the twist. But you've seen for yourself… that *is* a relief. I can't tell you…'

'Where's the tea then? I'm gasping!' Alfie had arrived. 'All right, Jess?' he said giving her a hug. 'And how's my favourite mother-in-law?' he said, winking at Emmie.

'How d'yer make that out?' said Emmie, amused as ever by Alfie.

'Well, you're Jessie's ma-in-law *and* Dolly's, and they're my sisters so… fair's fair – can't 'ave you all to 'emselves, can they?'

'Well, I don't want you, saucy bugger.'

'What?' he feigned disappointment. 'How am I gonna manage without a mother-in-law?'

'Get married,' said Emmie.

'Ah! Now there's an idea; I might just do that. But if it went wrong, though, you'd 'ave a guilty conscience for pushing me into it and you wouldn't want that would you?'

'It's no good, Em, you can't win with him,' said Jessie. 'Trouble is, he 'as you believing everything he says with that charming smile of his.'

'What smile?' said Alfie, presenting his deadly serious face.

'Where's Hannah and David? I thought you were coming with them,' she said, trying to get some sense out of him. 'I 'ope you're not gonna say they've got a previous engagement.'

'As it happens, yeah, they've bin at the court all day, so 'ave I. Looks like Dave might be sent down, Jess.'

Shocked by the news and his offhand sentiment about something that serious, she waited, quietly, for him to explain but Alfie wasn't going to explain. He looked round the room for Max and then drifted off towards the kitchen, leaving Jessie and Emmie to themselves.

'I take it he *was* joking?' said Emmie.

'He was being serious.' Jessie was furious with the way he behaved at times. 'You know, sometimes, I really don't like Alfie. He's getting too cocky.'

'I can't find your boyfriend, Sis,' said Alfie, coming back from the kitchen and biting into a piece of bread pudding he'd helped himself to. 'Not 'ome from work yet? Must be coining it in!'

'That's right, Alfie, coining it. If he keeps this up he'll be a millionaire in a couple of years,' retorted Jessie.

'Good timing that for when David gets out then, eh?' he chuckled. 'You can all go on a world cruise together, can't you?' He took another huge bite of the bread pudding and spoke with his mouth full. 'Mind you, knowing Hannah, she'll 'ave spent most of Dave's savings by the time he does get out.' Again he laughed, almost choking on the food.

'Yeah, well enough of this. I'd best get back into the kitchen, that pot of tea won't make itself. You coming, Emmie?' It wasn't help that Jessie wanted. She needed to let off as much steam as the kettle and knew that Emmie was a bit confused by Alfie joking at Dave's misfortune. Of course, Jessie herself was used to his ways and although sometimes aggravated by him, she had always gone along with his laid-back outlook on life.

'Don't you wanna know what David's going down for then, Jess?'

'Not really, Alfie, no. With the kind of life he leads you learn to expect anything. So long as Hannah's all right about it…' she shrugged. 'And by the sounds of what you've told us, she seems to be fine. Let's hope she enjoys her spending spree, eh?'

Leaving him to stare after her, she went into the kitchen, followed by Emmie who immediately sat down on a kitchen chair. 'What's going on, Jess?'

Pleased with her performance which had left Alfie speechless, she started to laugh. 'Emmie, I don't think I care any more. Live and let live.' She kissed her on the forehead and told her not to worry. 'Hannah's going through a phase that's all. She'll be back with us once the life she's bin leading loses its sparkle.'

'Puts my worry over Charlie in the shade, don't it?' said Emmie, bemused by it all.

'It certainly does, so long as he's happy in that funny old world of 'is – so what? We love 'im to death and he knows it and that's all that counts.'

'Well,' said Emmie, 'I might 'ave lost a son but I've got myself a daughter in Tom's place, haven't I?'

'You certainly 'ave. By the way where's Dolly? She should be out 'ere in the kitchen. It's her celebration after all, she's the lucky cow who's gonna be living in seventh heaven.'

'In the garden with the kids. Practising for motherhood,' said Emmie. 'You're not jealous of her are you, Jess?'

'No, not now. I was at first but…. well, I'm a Londoner, ain't I? I love the markets, pubs, shops and the hustle and bustle of everyday life. You don't get that in a country village.'

'Well, let's hope they settle down to it.' Emmie found herself smiling. 'She's in for a bit of a shock. Taking the kids to that posh hotel. She'll be on edge all right.'

'I know. Still, it'll do 'er good and give me a nice peaceful weekend. Me and Max'll go out for a meal, I reckon, up Danny's Steak House in Aldgate.'

'Now then, what about that mother of yours? Selling the shoe-menders and buying a workshop for Ted, don't like the sound of that.'

'Well, she 'as been going on about it for a while.'

'I know that, but I never really took it seriously, did you?'

'I didn't know what to think to tell the truth,' said Jessie, cutting Emmie's bread pudding straight again after Alfie had hacked his piece off. 'Now I s'pose I am a bit worried. But should I be? After all, it's Mum's business and Ted's her husband now and she does look happy.'

'Yeah, I've told myself all that as well. Personally, I think he's a confidence trickster.'

Laughing, Jessie saw the funny side of Emmie's statement, never mind the expression on her face. 'Course he's not. He might be trying to rearrange things a little too soon for our liking but I don't think he's—' She stopped dead when Max came into the kitchen. 'I don't think he's that bad, Em.'

'Who're you talking about?' said Max, breaking off a tiny corner of the bread pudding and popping it into his mouth.

'Ted. They're looking at a workshop for 'im,'

'And you're not happy about that?' he asked Emmie.

'Well, it's none of my business really.'

Max leaned on the sink, ready for one of his debates. 'Of course it is. You're a very special and close friend to Rose, it's good that you're thinking for her. You think she's making a big mistake then?'

'Well, no, but...'

'But what? Come on you can tell us.'

'Max please...' protested Jessie.

'No, let Emmie get if off her chest.'

'There's nothing for her to get off her chest. We were just chatting that's all.'

'You sure nothing's upset either of you?'

'Max...' said Jessie, a warning tone in her voice.

'Rose is a wise woman,' said Emmie, hoping to end it. 'She won't be badgered into anything nor will she let any man hoodwink her.'

'So you think Ted's hoodwinking her then?'

'*Max!* Take your coat off, hang it up, and pour yourself a drink, then go and talk to Alfie. *He's* in a chatty mood as well, and he's got something to tell you about David. See if you can worm some more out of him.'

Taking another piece of the bread pudding, Max said: 'Talking of Alfie, he's asked me if I could lend him five pounds. What do you think, should I give it to him?'

'What's he want it for?' Jessie hoped it wasn't to pay off a gambling debt. She knew that Alfie spent more time at the dog track than was good for him.

'Someone he knows has got a motorbike with sidecar they want to get rid of. He thinks it's a snitch at that price.'

'Wake up, Max. He's had a hot tip more like, *another* hot tip. He still owes *me* ten shillings.'

'You think he's gambling heavy then, do you?'

'I don't know *what* he's doing and I don't care. If you're going to lend him any money then ask if you can have a look at the motorbike first, so you can advise him whether it's a bargain or not,' said Jessie, hoping that would be the end of it.

'What you're really saying is that you don't think there's a bike for sale at all?'

'I don't know, Max! All I *am* saying is don't let my sod of a brother pull the wool over your eyes, that's all.'

'And you think he would – if he could get away with it?'

'Max, please...' said Jessie, her patience gone. 'Sit down and shut up or get out of the kitchen.'

'Right then I'll ask him if he really does need the loan *and* what for,' said Max, 'I'm sorry, Em, but once he starts with the questions he never stops. And half the time I don't think he really takes in the answers you give 'im.'

'Don't apologise to me, Jessie, it's Max I feel for. I can't believe the way you spoke to 'im,' said Emmie. 'Don't you think you were a bit hard on 'im? Tom would never 'ave put up with that, and you know it.'

'No, I don't suppose he would. But Charlie would though, wouldn't he?' she said, smiling knowingly. 'I suppose me and Max are as close as you two. We've known each other a long time, remember. I met 'im when I was fourteen you know. Courted for three years, and then I met Tom and… well, the rest you know.'

'That's what it must be, then. That's why you can talk to 'im the way I talk to Charlie.'

'Probably, Em. I think I love him the way that you love Charlie. With Tom it was quite different. More passionate in a way, but—'

'Shh, all right, Jess I know what you mean. Never mind, love, never mind. It'll all turn out right in the end. No doubt Tom'll turn up one day with a woman on 'is arm. Let's just 'ope you don't go and change your mind when he does – we can all do without any more upsets.'

Chapter Twelve

The train journey from St Pancras to Bury St Edmunds went more smoothly than Dolly had hoped for. Both the children slept for half the journey and when he was awake, Billy was too excited to grumble about anything. Jessie had made packed lunches for all four of them and as a treat, she had put in a bottle of cream soda for the kids and two bottles of Guinness for Dolly and Stanley. When the children weren't watching cows out of the train window or sleeping, they would absorb themselves in the comics which Emmie had bought for them before they left. Billy tried very hard to read the short words in the Dandy, while Emma was quite content to just look at the cartoon characters in the Beano, So, by the time they walked away from Bury St Edmund's lovely old railway station, towards the centre of town and the Cherub Hotel, all four were in a very good mood. A happy holiday-time mood.

'What, what, what if I wet the bed, Auntie Dolly?'

'I've brought a rubber sheet to put under the hotel sheet.'

'But, but, but the *hotel* sheet will be wetted!' she said, stopping in her tracks and splaying her hands. 'What will they do?'

'Maybe put you up a bleedin' chimney wiv all the other bed-wetters.'

Standing dead still, Emma looked to Stanley for the truth. 'Will they, Uncle Stanley?'

'Course they won't. Auntie Dolly's teasing you again, I keep telling you not to take any notice of 'er. Come on, were on 'oliday now. Pecker up!' He took her small chubby hand and squeezed it. 'We're gonna 'ave the best time of our lives,' he said, winking at his niece.

'Granddad said they'll give us oysters. Will they? I ain't eating 'em if they do.' Billy was beginning to get excited. 'Nan said I'm to ask for jelly and custard big enough for Desperate Dan.'

Unable to resist, Dolly chuckled quietly. 'Nah, I phoned and asked about that. They don't 'ave jelly and custard in posh hotels but they are gonna give us cow pie, just like the ones that Desperate Dan eats.'

'What...! With horns sticking out?' said Billy, eyes wide.

'Yep. Bloody great horns that will probably poke you in those big eyes of yours.'

'Great! I love cow pie.'

'Not, not, not me; me won't 'ave it, eh?' said Emma.

'No, sweetheart,' said Stanley, shooting Dolly a look to kill. 'Take no notice of them two,'

Arriving at the reception desk of the Cherub, Stanley began to explain about the letter they'd received but Claud simply raised a hand and smiled. 'Welcome, sir, we've been expecting you and many congratulations on your prize.' He handed over the key to a family suite. 'Enjoy your stay and please don't hesitate to ask if there's anything we can do for you.'

'Oh,' said Stanley, impressed. 'So we don't 'ave to—'

'You don't have to do anything, sir, except enjoy your short break. Dinner will be served in the dining room from seven until nine. If you'd prefer to have yours brought to your room on account of the children being tired, just let me know and I'll arrange it for you.'

'Yeah we would, actually…' said Dolly, '…like our meal in our room. Breakfast as well, if that's all right with you?'

'Breakfast in your room it is.'

'What's wrong with us eating in the dining room, Doll?'

'Billy,' she said, 'that's what.' She looked at her nephew. 'Do you wanna sit in there?' She nodded towards the palatial dining room.

'Nah, not really. Too many grown ups.'

'See. I can read 'im like a book,' she said, walking towards the lift, swaying her hips for the fun of it – much to Claud's amusement.

To his mind, Dolly was the target; she was the reason why Mr Thomas had arranged this little drama. He started humming the 'White Cliffs of Dover' and then, as if inspired, he changed the words of the wartime favourite, singing quietly: 'There'll be fireworks a merry, in the quiet town of Bury… sparks will be flying… just you wait and see…'

Everyone, these days, seemed to have their own version of Vera Lynn's popular song!

—

As Dolly eased open the door into their suite she gasped, wide-eyed. 'Blimey, Stan, this can't be right!'

'Course it is. Come on, get inside.' He didn't have to tell the children, Billy and Emma were in like a shot. They had been given the best suite of rooms in the hotel with thick red carpets and pale gold and cream

226

soft furnishings. In the main room was a carved light oak four-poster bed with silk drapes tied at each corner post. There was a leather-topped writing desk, two luxurious cream armchairs and an occasional table on which lay that day's newspapers and a lady's magazine. In the huge bay window which looked out on to the square the dining table had been laid ready for breakfast the next day.

'We gonna sleep with you and Uncle Stanley?' said Billy, his nose screwed up at the thought of it.

'Course not, silly.' Stanley looked across the room to the adjoining doors. 'Now, I reckon one of them doors is gonna be the bathroom, and the other one... another bedroom – for you two.'

The children lost little time in trying them both. Of course, Stanley was right and within seconds both the children were bouncing on the twin beds, leaping from one to the other. Neither Stanley nor Dolly was going to stop them. The kids were having a wonderful time, shrieking with laughter and bouncing as high as they could. The walls seemed to go up for ever until they reached the ceiling and the ornate cornice.

'Well,' said Stanley, chuffed with the whole thing. 'Better unpack 'adn't we? Then go for a nice walk round the town, check out the buses and that.'

'They'll probably be able to tell us the bus timetable at reception,' said Dolly, sliding on to their four-poster bed. 'I ain't goin' nowhere, I'm not leaving this room. It's a bleeding palace. You can take the kids for a walk if you like.'

'Oh come on, Doll, there's loads of places to visit, this is an historic town ain't it? We'll start with the museum...'

'You will,' she said, yawning and spreading herself on die silky eiderdown. 'Take the kids to the Abbey Gardens as well. They'll love that.' Turning on to her side, she curled her legs and closed her eyes. 'But, don't spoil 'em,' she said, drifting off into luxurious sleep.

'Can we, Uncle Stanley?' said Billy, out of breath from all the jumping. 'Can we go to the gardens and the park?'

'Not, not, not a museum?' said Emma.

'It's all right, Emma,' said Billy, 'Auntie Dolly's snoring. We won't 'ave to go to a museum now.' He looked up pleadingly at Stanley.

'Nah, all right then. Come on, we'll leave 'er to unpack for us. Who fancies a glass of lemonade and a bag of crisps?'

Their shouts of joy were the answer. 'Shh...' said Stanley, 'don't wanna wake 'er up now do we? Come on, let's see what that posh room, where they serve the drinks, is like.'

'What, we gonna 'ave our lemonade in the hotel?' said Billy, not fancying the idea of that. 'I don't fink they'll allow us to go in the pub bit.'

'It's not a pub, it's a family bar. Come on. Emma, what you doing in that bathroom?'

'Looking in the mirror at my, my, face.'

'Still there, is it?' said Stanley, ever amused at his funny little niece.

'Nanny said I 'ad to look at it every time be-be-before we went out in case it was grubby. But, it's not; it's not grubby,' she said, admiring her reflection. 'Good, come on.'

'I need a wee-wee first.'

'Oh Gawd...'

The sound of the bathroom door closing was a relief, at least Emma could manage to see to herself. 'You'd better go as well once she comes out, Billy boy.'

'I'm all right,' he said, using his grown-up voice. 'I'll go to the lavatory in the bar if I 'ave to.'

Dolly was sound asleep when they left the room. Stanley locked the door and directed the children towards the lift which they would take down to the ground floor.

There was only one other passenger in the lift with them: an elderly lady wearing a fox fur round her neck. Stanley just prayed that neither of the children would make any comment about the dead animal. Billy had already sniffed slyly at the fur, said nothing, but exchanged a knowing look with Stanley. He knew when to keep his mouth shut.

'Why was the lady's dog asleep round, round, round her neck?' said Emma as the old lady walked out of the lift.

'No more questions,' said Stanley, leading them into the family bar. 'Now go and sit down over there, at that table, by the window, so you can look out. I'll fetch the drinks and that.'

'Don't 'ave to,' said worldly wise Billy, dropping in a chair. 'That man gets 'em for yer. He's a servant.'

'Oh right, yeah, course,' he said, sitting down with the children, uncomfortable in the plush surroundings without Dolly by his side. Dolly never gave a toss where she was or whom she sat next to, she changed for no one. 'This is all right, innit?' said Stanley, trying to relax.

'It's lovely,' said Emma.

'Elbows off the table, Emma,' said Billy, parroting his grandmother Rose.

'Ah, leave 'er be. Just keep your voices down and we'll be all right. So it's two lemonades and two bags of crisps, yeah?'

Emma nodded and laid her hands in her lap. She then leaned forward and whispered to Stanley: 'That lady keeps smiling at us.'

Stanley glanced sideways at the beautiful young woman, who *was* smiling at Emma. She looked gorgeous in a simple red dress. Her dark auburn hair was thick and straight and cut in a forties version of the twenties cropped bob. Her skin was tanned and she wore no make-up except for a deep red lipstick to match her frock. Her big brown eyes didn't need to be underlined or colour shadowed. Embarrassed that she'd caught his eye, Stanley nodded and felt himself going pink. 'All right?' he said, scratching his chin, a nervous habit from childhood.

'You must be very proud of them,' said the woman. 'They're so well behaved.'

'Yeah? Oh right, s'pose they are really. Not always though, but they're on their best behaviour today. It's that or a clip round the ear.'

The woman chuckled quietly, 'I don't believe that for one minute. They're devoted to you, anyone can see that.'

'He's not our dad, you know,' said Billy, putting her straight. 'He's our uncle.'

'*Proper* uncle that is,' said Stanley, 'if you know what I mean.' Since the war had ended many *new* uncles had appeared in the life of the women who had become war widows.

'And you've brought them away for a break. Aren't you lucky children? Not many uncles do that sort of thing.'

'It was Aunt Dolly who wanted to come,' said Billy, 'but, she's gone to bed though, *and* she snores.'

'It's the ba-ba-baby snoring,' said Emma, her face earnest. Billy burst out laughing. 'It *is* the baby doing it! Auntie Dolly said it, didn't she Uncle Stanley?' Emma insisted, shaking her head, the bottom lip curled yet again. '*I* never said it.'

'She's four months gone,' said Stanley. 'Some baby it's gonna be if it's snoring already.'

'I know this is going to sound a bit strange… I mean you don't even know me…' said the woman, '…I'm a local school teacher, with time on my hands today, and at a bit of a loose end. I was thinking of taking a walk along to the fairground… perhaps the children would like to come with me…'

'Oh… er, I'm not sure 'bout that. Um… and you're a teacher, you say? So why aren't you at school today?'

'I used to teach in school, but now I'm a private tutor, and as it happens, I don't have any students today.' She smiled, warmly, at Stanley.

'Can we, then?' said Billy. 'Can we go with the lady to the funfair?'

Stanley looked at their pleading faces. 'I'm not sure if—'

'Oh, pleeeaase, Uncle Stanley!' chorused the children.

'It's not far. Only ten minutes by car if that,' said the teacher.

'A car ride as well…' said Stanley, finding this very difficult. 'Yeah… well, it is a little holiday this, innit? Might as well make the most of it.'

'Yippee!' The children leapt to their feet.

Stanley pushed his hand deep into his trouser pocket and pulled out a handful of change. 'Here,' he said, 'that's for rides and that.'

'Oh, fanks, Uncle Stanley,' said Billy, grinning from ear to ear.

'Don't be too long, will you?' said Stanley, still not quite certain if he was doing the right thing. What will

Dolly say? Come to think of it – what would Jessie say, if she ever found out? She'd have his guts for garters, he was sure of that. Still, if the kids can't be safe with a teacher…

She looked into Stanley's face and smiled. 'Will a couple of hours be all right… something like that?'

'Yeah. Sounds fine.' He still didn't seem too sure.

'Don't worry, they'll be fine, I promise you. Why don't you join your wife for a rest?'

'You're joking, ain't yer? Nah. I'll be all right down 'ere.' He looked across the room to where some men were playing cards. 'Might join that lot.'

'Right then, children, shall we get off?' She smiled at Billy and Emma.

'Go on, you two, see you later. Have a good time.' Stanley's mind was now on a game of cards. 'Room for another one?' he said, approaching the card players.

They looked from one to another before a silverhaired gentleman spoke. 'We're playing poker… you might find—'

'That's my *game*,' he said smiling. 'And don't worry about this,' he nodded to his empty jacket sleeve. He slipped his hand into his inside jacket pocket and pulled out a beautifully polished maple, playing-cards holder, specially made for him when he was a POW.

'A chap from up this way made this for me. We were in a Japanese prisoner-of-war camp together.'

The silver-haired gentleman stood up, pulled a chair from another small round table, and motioned for the card players to inch round to make room for one more. 'Honoured to have you join us, sir,' he said, smiling.

'Thanks. The name's Stanley. Pleased to meet you all.'

Once the obligatory introductions were made, one of them suggested they played for matchsticks, thinking that

Stanley would prefer that. He soon made it clear that he was happy to play for money and hinted that he had won a hand or two, in his time. In fact, Stanley was a brilliant card player and next to pontoon, poker was his game.

Having slipped out of the hotel with Emma and Billy, before Stanley had fully realised the implications of what he'd done and perhaps changed his mind, the woman walked quickly away from the hotel and through the town with her charges.

'So what's your name then?' said Billy, looking up at the beautiful woman who was holding his hand. 'I'm Billy and this is Emma.'

'My name's Rachel.'

'What kind of teacher are you?' asked Billy.

'I'm a private teacher.'

'What's that mean?'

'It means I teach children in their own houses. I could be *your* private teacher.'

'What… and we wouldn't 'ave to go to a school?'

'That's right. You have your lessons at home. Reading, writing, arithmetic… and you don't have to go out on freezing cold mornings and sit in a boring old classroom.'

Billy was beginning to like the sound of it. 'I might ask Mum to get *us* one of you.'

'Well, if you lived up here you could have the real thing – me… instead of *one* of me.'

'Why, why, why we walking quick?' asked Emma, her little legs struggling to keep up.

'Are we? Oh dear… I am sorry.' Rachel slowed her pace but there was nothing she could do about her heart which was pounding. She could see nothing wrong with taking two children to see their daddy but an inner voice

233

was screaming at her to turn back. 'Is that better, Emma?' she said, having slowed down.

'Yes.'

'Is it far to the fairground,' asked Billy, already thirsty.

'Not really. It's at a park in a nearby village.'

'Where's your car then?'

'You'll see. I think you'll be surprised but no more questions now or you'll spoil things.' Smiling at one and then the other, she led them across the road, down Angel Hill towards Eastgate Street alongside the Abbey ruins and gardens.

'Could we buy some lemonade first?' He had seen a small sweet shop. 'I'm really thirsty.'

Stopping suddenly, she smiled broadly. She could now see the parked car with Tom drumming his fingers on the steering wheel. 'Do you see that cream-coloured car, just along the road there?' she asked the children.

'Course I can see it,' said Billy, 'it's blooming well brand new – it's a beauty!'

'Well how would you like to go for a ride in a car like that?'

'It's only got two seats,' he said, pointing out the obvious. Of course he would like to go for a ride in it. Anyone would. 'Where's *your* car then?' he said.

She walked slowly towards the gleaming, cream Triumph Roadster, with its bright chrome headlamps and cream leather seats. 'As a matter of fact, there are two little dickey seats for children tucked away in the boot of the car.'

'How do *you* know?' said Billy.

'I just do. Well, here we are, you can have a closer look now. I told you that you were in for a surprise – guess who this is?'

'Hello, kids,' said Tom, taking off his dark glasses. 'What d'yer think of Daddy's new car then?'

–

Waking up after two hours of delicious sleep, Dolly took her time in the stylish bathroom: bathing, brushing out her hair and putting on fresh make-up. To her, this was a once in a lifetime experience and she was more than happy to make the most of it. She considered ordering afternoon tea to be sent to her room but thought better of it. Stanley was easygoing but she didn't want to push her luck. Slipping into a clean pair of slacks, blouse and cardigan, she checked herself in the ornate full-length mirror. Pleased with the way she looked she gave herself a wink. 'This is the life for you, Dolly girl,' she said, 'you was born to it.'

A quiet tapping on the door brought her back to reality. She expected it to be Billy, having found his way up to the room by himself. But when she opened the door, a stranger stood in front of her. The man was dressed in tweeds and his hair was unkempt. She looked at him and waited, puzzled.

'Is my brother in there?' he said.

'No... I think you must 'ave the wrong room.' She waited for him to go but he just stood there, looking at her. 'What room number is your brother in?'

'Oh, he's not supposed to be stopping here, I am. I'm trying to get away from him you see, he follows me everywhere. Wherever I go on holiday he turns up; is he in there?'

'No. There's only me here.'

'I think he *must* be in there. I can't find him anywhere else; he might be hiding.'

'He's not in 'ere, honest. I would say if he was.'

'But you wouldn't *know*. He's devious. Might be hiding in the bathroom.'

'No. I've just come out of there and he definitely wasn't in the bathroom. Why don't you go downstairs to the reception desk, eh? They might know where he is?'

'I've asked. They haven't seen him, he's very cunning you see, he won't let me go anywhere without him. Can I just look in your bathroom just in case he's there, he always goes for bathrooms – I don't know why.'

Feeling sorry for the poor devil when perhaps she should have been on her guard, Dolly opened the door wide. As far as she could see, this man, in his thirties, was obviously simple-minded and hopefully harmless! 'I suppose you can 'ave a look.'

He walked past her and towards the bathroom. 'You go in first and see if he's there,' he said.

She opened the bathroom door. 'See, no one.' She went inside and went through the motion of looking for him. 'Nope. He's definitely not here.'

'Can I come in and see for myself?'

'If you like.'

Cautiously, the man stepped in and faced the mirror. '*There!* I knew it! Why are you following me everywhere – why can't you leave me alone?' he said to his reflection.

Bemused to say the least, Dolly was at a loss as to what she should say or do. She didn't want to laugh at the poor devil but it wasn't easy not to. 'That's not your brother,' she said, standing next to him. 'This is only a mirror.'

'What is it you want?' he said, peering at himself. 'I don't owe you anything. Why don't you go away?' He turned to Dolly. 'Why is he tormenting me like this? If I leave the bathroom, he leaves it, if I come in, he comes in. I can't shake him off.'

'Look,' said Dolly, 'this is you. And that,' she tapped the mirror, 'is your reflection.'

'If I go out, he will too. It's always the same.'

'Well, he would do, wouldn't he?' she said, stifling her laughter.

'Look, you and your sister go out and see if he follows you.'

'Sister?'

'She's standing there right next to my brother.'

'Oh right… I wonder what she's doing here?'

'He's put her up to it.' He pushed his face closer to the mirror. 'Stop behaving like a child, you should be ashamed of yourself.'

Turning away, Dolly left him to it and waited for him to leave.

'He's still here, your sister's gone but *he's* still here!' he called.

'Well bloody well leave 'im there, then!' she called back. 'Come on, let me buy you a cup of tea downstairs. We'll lock him in!'

He came out of the bathroom. 'Quick,' he said. 'If we're quick enough he might not see us go. Come on!' He grabbed Dolly by the arm and pulled her out of the room.

'Why did you come on holiday by yourself? Haven't you got any relatives or friends?' Dolly asked as they descended in the lift.

'They wouldn't come with me, they know what *he* gets up to. They'd be taking two of us and they won't have that. Do you always go away with your sister?'

'Oh yeah. We go everywhere together!'

237

Once downstairs at reception the man walked away towards the main door. 'Excuse me,' she called after him, 'I thought we were going to have a cup of tea?'

He looked genuinely taken back. Shaking his head at her, he tut-tutted at the loose women of the day and strolled out of the hotel, leaving Dolly to gaze after him, wondering if she'd dreamt the whole crazy scene.

Going into the family bar, she looked round for Stanley and the children, not really expecting them to be in there. So she was rather surprised when Stanley called out to her.

'Over 'ere, Doll!'

Turning round she saw Stanley at the table with the card players. She couldn't see Emma or Billy anywhere in the spacious room. There were other families, other children, but no sign of her niece or nephew.

'Where are they then?' she said, smiling at the other gentlemen round the table.

'Gone to a fairground wiv one of the hotel guests. I gave them some money for rides, and that.' He leaned back in his chair and grinned, 'Look at my winnings. Twenty-two bob in a couple of hours, not bad eh?'

'*What* guest, Stanley?'

'A woman – a teacher. We got talking and she offered to take them off our 'ands for a little while. I said you was 'aving a rest and—'

'For Gawd's sake, Stan! Where is this fairground?' She was not amused.

'Dunno. But they'll be back very soon, d'yer fancy a drink?'

One of the men coughed quietly, an indication that they should be getting on with their game. Stanley picked up on it and winked. 'Deal me out the next round,' he said leaning forward and almost whispering. 'I'll leave me winnings on the table so you know I'll be back. Best not upset the missus, she's in the family way.' He tapped his nose.

There were knowing smiles and sighs all round. 'I should settle her down then,' said the silver-haired gentleman. 'You know what women are like if they get upset.'

'Not half,' said Stanley, rising. 'Won't be long.'

Joining Dolly, who had gone to the reception desk to ask where the fairground was located, Stanley took her arm. 'The woman was in the family room, Doll, she's a regular. A schoolteacher in fact, so there's no need to worry. Teaches little kids like our Billy; I think she might 'ave bin a bit, you know... lonely.'

'Was she old and ugly, Stan?'

'Nah, course not. Gorgeous as it 'appens. Why?'

'If she was gorgeous, she wouldn't be lonely for long, now, would she? Not in a place like this... I mean, I've just 'ad a man in our bathroom.'

'You what?'

'Later. I wanna find out where this fairground is. Silly sod. Letting 'em go off with a stranger, nutcases are roaming round this place, I'm telling yer, Stan. I just met one and I'd not even bin out of the room!'

'Honest?'

'Yeah, he had bats in the belfry all right. Perhaps that's why they let sane people come 'ere *free*. You sure it's a hotel and not a mental institution? The blokes you was playing cards with looked like they could do with a bit of sunshine as well.'

'Can I help you, madam?' said the somewhat patronising receptionist.

'Probably. The fairground… could you give us directions?'

'Fairground? I didn't realise it was in town. It'll be in the grounds of the Abbey ruins I expect, or failing that, the park green.'

'Oh, right.'

'Is anything wrong, madam? You look pale.'

'One of your guests took it into her head to child-mind for me. Not that my husband couldn't 'ave managed them but then there *was* a bit of gambling going on in the family room and Stan's always been a bit partial to…'

'Oh, we don't call that gambling, madam, they play for matchsticks.' The fixed smile was still there. 'One of our guests, you say, mmm, I'm just wondering who that might have been. Was it a man or woman?' she asked, a concerned expression on her face.

'A gorgeous woman, apparently. Stanley?'

'Well, you know, nice looking and nice manners. Dark 'air, red dress, big brown eyes.'

'Doesn't ring any bells with me, I always familiarise myself with our visitors. I can't say…'

'She's a teacher, by all accounts.'

'Perhaps she booked in when I was off-duty. I'll look out for her when she comes down for dinner this evening.' She scribbled a few words on her notepad. 'We'll leave a little something on her table. A little thank you for the hospitality she's shown to a fellow guest.'

'So the fairground's not far then?' said Dolly, peppery in this woman's company.

'A twenty-minute walk I should think, maybe a little more.' She handed Dolly a street map of the town, compliments of the hotel.

'We might as well wait 'ere for 'em, Doll. We might miss each other and they'll end up going out looking for us.'

'Well, I can't just sit 'ere and wait, we don't even know who she is. What if she's a kidnapper?'

'Oh, I hardly think so,' said the receptionist.

'I don't give a toss what you think, Miss. We're talking about my niece and nephew going off with a complete stranger.'

'If she's a guest of the hotel then—'

'What d'yer mean, *if* ? Are you saying that any Tom, Dick or Harry can walk in 'ere and sit in the family room, or the lounge, whatever you wanna' call it?'

Sighing heavily, the receptionist asked Stanley the name of the lady in question. Her expression changed when she registered from his guilty face that he didn't actually know. 'You mean *today* was the *first* time you'd met her?'

'We only booked in round two o'clock, of course he'd never seen 'er before.' Dolly, now panicking, turned on Stanley. 'Did she say what 'er name was?' Shamefaced, Stanley hung his head. 'No.'

'Oh Gawd,' said Dolly, 'Jessie'll kill us.'

'Oh, come off it, Dolly, they'll be all right. Just calm down.'

Taking a deep breath, Dolly tried to relax. 'You're right. I'm just a little bit shocked that you could let the kids go with a stranger.' She turned away from him, more upset than she was letting on. 'I just hope that game of cards wasn't why you let 'em go.'

'Course it wasn't! The woman 'ad already won the kids and me over on the idea before I even saw the game was on!'

'I think,' said the receptionist, 'that we should give it another hour or so, and if they're not back by then we should consider phoning the police to be on the safe side.'

'You won't do nothing of the sort, we'll wait in the family room and *we'll* decide what the next move'll be.'

'As you wish, but if you could give a description of the woman, I might check with the staff and see if anyone can identify her. At least that way we'll know if she *is* a guest staying in the hotel or just a passer-by in for afternoon tea.' The woman's voice had softened and Dolly felt a tremor of guilt.

'Well, yeah, that sounds helpful. Look, I'm sorry if I was rude but it's just one thing after another today. I hadn't been 'ere long when I had this weird bloke knocking on my door asking if his brother was in my bathroom.'

'Oh that'll be our resident guest, Mr Thomas, he's harmless enough. Been with us for months; shell-shocked you know. They sent him home before the war ended. He doesn't seem to have *any* family from what we can make out, so, he prefers to live here. After all we do boast a family atmosphere,' she said, proudly.

'Poor sod,' said Stanley, remembering others who'd gone through the same thing. 'Still he must 'ave a few bob if he can afford to live 'ere.'

'I'll tell the waitress to make your afternoon tea a special one, to make up for all the upset.' The receptionist was doing her best to make them feel at home.

'You was a bit hard on 'er, Doll,' said Stanley, taking her arm, as they walked away.

'Shouldn't 'ave acted above 'er station then, should she – stuck up cow. Still, at least she came round in the end, and I'm not finished wiv *you* either. If they're not back in an hour I'm gonna scream blue murder.'

'That's all right,' he said, 'I'm used to it.' Stanley's light-hearted tone was a cover for the concern growing inside him. Things had been going through his mind: the teacher was a bit on the pushy side and she didn't waste much time in making her offer, and... she had made a pretty quick departure.

Chapter Thirteen

After just a few hours at High House, Billy and Emma, in their new world of make-believe come true, were happier than they had ever been. They loved their bedrooms, their toys, and, especially, their play-park. The fact that there was no funfair didn't seem to bother them, there was so much on offer. They loved the house, they loved the grounds, they loved… everything. The long pine table in the breakfast room which had been spread with any child's favourite foods and treats had hardly been touched – there were too many distractions.

Once Billy had tried out every piece of equipment in the play-park, he explored the outbuildings: an old barn with a hayloft and ladder, a bike shed, the gatehouse with its own sitting room, kitchen and bedrooms.

Emma's major discovery was an old railway carriage which had once been pulled by one of the first steam trains in Britain. It had been brought to High House and set down in a corner of the orchard long before Tom's time in residence.

While pushing Emma on a swing, Rachel wondered about the children's mother. Tom had told her that he'd left his family because he had found out that his wife had been seeing another man while Tom was away fighting for his country. He could never forgive her. Other than that he hadn't mentioned his family again. But she couldn't help wondering why, with Tom's obvious wealth, *they* lived in the East End of London. This information she had elicited from Billy with only a little prodding. By the sound of things, the house was very small with only two bedrooms and a box room where Emma slept; the garden sounded more like a backyard than anything else.

'You can stop pushing now,' said Emma, 'I can manage.' Her little legs were working like mad.

'What's your bedroom at home like, Emma? Is it nice and big like the one here?'

'No,' said Emma, pushing herself forward on the swing. 'And we 'aven't got a play-park, neither.'

Rachel could see she was struggling to keep the swing going so gave her a helpful push. 'Here comes Daddy and Billy, I think it might be time to go. Your brother looks in a bit of a mood. I expect he wants to stay.'

'We can't stop 'ere, Billy!' yelled Emma. 'Auntie Dolly'll be woke up now!'

'So?' said Billy, sulking.

Arriving at Rachel's side, Tom winked at her and then whispered in her ear, 'Seems like I've made an impression, he wants to stop overnight.'

'Come on, Emma, we've gotta go,' said Billy, none too pleased.

'Can we come back again though?'

'Course you can, darling,' said Tom, lifting her off the swing and hugging her. 'Daddy'll come and fetch you in his motor car, yeah?'

'I don't really like that hotel,' said Billy, dropping on to the grass. 'And they don't 'ave any toys or anything there. It's too quiet!'

'Ne'mind,' said Tom, chuffed. 'You'll be going 'ome tomorrow.'

'Yeah, after we've bin to look at the old dirty cottages.'

'Cottages?' said Tom, wary.

'Yeah. Auntie Dolly and Uncle Stanley are going to live in them, but they're gonna live in a gypsy caravan first.'

'Auntie Dolly? So she's come with your mum, 'as she?' Tom was confused.

'No. Mum's stopped at 'ome. Uncle Stanley brought us all on the train.'

'Right,' said Tom. What was going on here? 'So Dolly and Stanley are gonna get married are they?'

'They already did.'

It was one surprise after another. He had intended to drop the children off outside the hotel but now he was thinking that perhaps he would go in and have a pint with Stanley. Find out what was really going on and how much Max Cohen featured in all of this.

'You can 'ave another ten minutes while I go and see to things inside, then you can come in and choose which toy you wanna take back home with you. You'll 'ave to carry it so pick something small.' Leaving Rachel to sort them out, he went into the house.

'I might run away from 'ome,' said Billy. 'I know 'ow to get on the train and that. I might come up 'ere to live.'

Emma looked up at Rachel, 'He wouldn't do that, would he?'

'Not if he's as smart as I thought. He'll wait until your Daddy comes to collect you both, which might be next weekend for all you know.'

'I'm going with Granddad down Petticoat Lane next Sunday, to pick out what I might want for Christmas. I'll be able to come the next week though.'

'Christmas? That's a couple of months away.' Rachel tried not to laugh at him.

'You 'ave to look ahead you know. Fings sell out quick – decent fings anyway, Granddad said.'

'You see a lot of your grandparents then?'

'Yeah, they live next door. Nan might come up as well, not Granny Rose though. I'm glad 'cause she's too strict. Every time I—'

Tom's urgent call to Rachel stopped Billy in his tracks. 'Come in a minute, would yer – just you, leave the kids out there.'

'Oh dear, not another unwelcome surprise, I hope,' she murmured.

Going back into the house, Rachel wondered what it would be like living with Tom but she didn't relish the thought of mothering his two children. 'What's the matter, Archie?' she said, on seeing Tom's pinched expression.

'I don't wanna take 'em back, Rachel.' He slumped down onto a chair. 'They're my kids as much as hers; they'd be much happier with me. I can offer them more than she can.'

'You want to keep them, permanently, Archie – are you sure? I would have thought a weekend every now and then would be plenty for you and at Christmas and holidays, of course.'

'We'll see,' he said, not really caring what she thought. 'Get 'em ready to go, I'll drop you off at the bus stop.'

'Oh, I'm to get a bus home, am I?'

'Nothing wrong with that is there? You usually go everywhere by bus.'

'Well, yes, I suppose I do. I just thought that I should go back to the hotel and return the children to their uncle.'

'No. I'll drop you off.'

'But we'll have to pass the hotel to get to the bus stop.'

'So? Bloody hell, it's nearly seven o'clock, no wonder it's getting dark. Go and get the kids.'

'Pardon?'

'It's late, Rachel. Fetch the kids – it's time to go.'

'So I'm a servant now, am I, Archie?' she half-joked.

He eyed her cautiously, sensing she was a bit on the tetchy side. He would have to keep her happy as she still figured in his plans, especially since she'd won Billy over. 'Gimme a smile, sweetheart, and I'll give you a present.'

A devilish smile spread across her face. 'You can't buy *me*.'

'Don't 'ave it then.' He pulled a very small, black leather box from his pocket. 'I'll give it to my sister-in-law, Dolly. She loves rings.'

'Please yourself.'

'Here… you know you want it—' he pushed it into the palm of her hand and gave her a kiss on the cheek '—and it's for the right hand not the left.'

'I wouldn't accept it if it were.'

'Is that right? Good – well, open it then.'

With the tip of her thumbnail she flicked open the lid to find a stunning three-stoned sapphire ring. 'Archie, it's beautiful!'

'There's more where that came from. Now will you go and get the kids?' He winked and nodded towards the door, a clear indication for her to do as she was told.

With mixed emotions, she placed the ring on her finger and decided there and then that it would come off for no one. He could love her and leave her the next day if he wanted for this was a good enough pay off. 'Thank you for the present, Archie, I love it,' she said, bowing as she retreated just like a geisha girl.

Employing an impish sense of humour, she never failed to arouse him with her play-acting. 'I'll tell you what, Rachel, you stop 'ere while I take the kids back, you can be warming the brandy by the fire. You'll find a pair of my red silk pyjamas in the oak cupboard on the landing, so you can be warming them for me as well... and make sure you keep yourself warm.'

'Anything you say, Master...' she said, seductively.

In the car, on the way back to the hotel, both Billy and Emma were quiet and Tom was beginning to feel edgy. He hadn't seen his brother Stanley for months and the last time had hardly been convivial. Stanley *had* been loyal in telling him about Max and Jessie, but then, as far as Tom was concerned, his brother had changed tack, praising Max and defending Jessie, saying that they were probably just good friends. Now he had married Jessie's sister and it all sounded a bit too chummy for Tom's liking. He thought about Jessie's twin sister, Hannah. She had been his childhood friend, his *best* friend, if he was honest about it. He wondered where her loyalties lay now: with him or with Jessie?

'You all right in the back there?' He glanced over his shoulder to check the kids.

'I need the lavatory,' said Emma, quietly.

'Can you wait?' said Tom. 'We're nearly there.'

'I can... just.'

'Good girl, you all right, Billy?' There was no answer. 'Billy!'

'I'm all right, keep going, Dad.'

'Course I'll keep going. What's up?'

'Nothing!' Billy was enjoying the speed and thrill of the ride.

'Sorry I spoke,' said Tom, going quiet. Then his thoughts began to turn to home again, but this time thinking of his mum and dad. 'How's Nanny?' he said.

'All right,' said Billy, preoccupied.

'Granny Rose got married,' said Emma, surprising him yet again. 'And Auntie Han.'

'Don't tell fibs, Emma,' said Tom, adoring the way his little girl spoke, 'your tongue'll drop off.'

'No it won't,' said Billy, ''cos she's not fibbing. Seems that everyone's getting married. That's what Granddad said anyway.' And Charlie hadn't been far off the mark, the number of romances after the war were still keeping churches and register offices busy.

'Granny Rose said that Mummy should marry Uncle Max,' said Emma, innocently.

This struck Tom like a bolt of lightning, but he kept silent and waited for the children to open up a little more. They did.

'*Only* if she gets a divorce, Emma,' said Billy, knowingly. 'Mummy don't know where you buy them from anyway. I asked Granddad for 'er and he said in Woolworth's and she said that was silly.'

So, there had been talk of Jessie marrying Max. It shouldn't have hit him like a thunderbolt and he shouldn't have felt shocked but it *had* shaken him and caught him off-guard. Divorce proceedings looked inevitable.

'Uncle Max 'as bin round a lot then, has he?'

'He lives wiv us,' said Billy, matter-of-factly.

'Oh right,' said Tom, as casual as he could be under the circumstances. He was beginning to feel uneasy and, unless he misread the signs, just a little guilty. So wrapped up in his new life, he hadn't given much thought to things back home, believing that nothing much would change over the year he expected to be away. But things *had* changed and he didn't like it one bit! Putting his foot down on the accelerator his transient remorse was easily replaced with bitterness.

Cursing Max for sneaking in and pulling the rug from beneath his feet, Tom screeched to a halt in front of the hotel. He needed Stanley to tell him exactly what had been going on: everything that Jessie and Max had been up to. Filled with aggression he got out of the car but didn't notice the police car parked outside the hotel under the streetlight. As he was about to let the children out of the car, he caught sight of Dolly across the square, talking to a policeman. She was obviously distressed.

'All right, kids, stay where you are,' he said, 'I forgot to stop off and get some crisps and lemonade for you, we'll just nip back to the shop for them.'

Within seconds he was back in the driving seat and away. Not quite knowing what to do next he drove out of the town and stopped outside a small pub, his mind working fast. Suddenly he came up with an idea. 'Oh dear,' he said, 'Daddy's left his wallet back at the house. We're gonna 'ave to go back—'

'Good,' said Billy. 'We can sleep there.'

'You'd like that would you?' he said, pulling away again. 'Yes.'

'What about you, Emma?'

'She is asleep! Nuffink'll wake 'er up now and she's wet 'erself.'

'Ne'mind, Rachel can wipe the seats over. Best get 'er to bed straight away, I reckon, don't you, son?'

'Yep, I reckon that's for the best.' Billy was more than pleased with the way things were turning out. 'We won't 'ave to get up early and go to that old cottage now, will we?'

'No. I'll phone the hotel and explain what 'appened. They'll tell Uncle Stanley and that'll be that. You can stop over till Monday, if you like, and I'll run you 'ome to London in the car.'

Billy could hardly believe it. His eyes lit up. 'What about school?'

'You can 'ave the day off, a couple of days if you like. Say you've got a cold; I'll write a note for you.'

'Mum ain't gonna like that,' he said, shaking his head.

'Well, I'm your Dad and I haven't seen you in a long time.'

'I know,' he said, a touch of worry in his voice. 'But what about school? We might get into trouble.'

'Well, you won't be playing truant, will yer? If you stop up 'ere for the week, that'll be called an holiday and they can't say nothing about that.'

'Could we stop for a *whole* week?'

'Don't see why not. Have to buy you some clothes though but I don't s'pose you'd mind that.'

'No.'

'Good. That's what we'll do then. I'll send a telegram to your mother.'

Having no intention of phoning the hotel or sending a telegram, Tom commended himself on his quick thinking. Happy to be on top of things, he hummed a tune as he drove, until the reality sunk in – the *police* were at the hotel! Taking a bend too fast he swerved and momentarily lost control of the wheel much to Billy's delight. Pulling to a halt, Tom lit a cigarette and wondered what his next step should be. Obviously they believed that the woman who had taken the children to the make believe funfair and not returned with them, was suspect to say the least. At least he never left his address when using the hotel for his overnight stays and Rachel had never slept there with him. As far as he knew, she had never before been inside the Cherub.

The more he thought about it, the more he realised that he had actually effected a watertight abduction. No one knew that Billy and Emma were with him at High House, he could keep them there for as long as he wanted. When they were ready to go back home, or if the police did trace them, he would lie. Say that Jessie knew he had arranged to have them collected from the hotel, for a holiday with their dad. Getting Rachel to go along with the lie was his only problem. Smiling to himself, he decided on a bracelet to match the ring, he couldn't imagine any woman turning that down.

'Nanny and granddad could live in the gate'ouse,' said Billy, miles away, in a promised world. 'And Rachel could come in and be our teacher so we wouldn't 'ave to go to school.'

'Anything's possible, son,' said Tom, 'anything's possible.'

Pulling into the grounds he saw smoke coming out of the huge chimneys and guessed that Rachel had lit a fire in the drawing room as well as the master bedroom. 'You'll 'ave something to eat, Billy, then a nice warm bath and straight to bed. All right?'

'Yep.'

'I might go out later, once you're asleep,' he lied, 'back to the hotel and let Uncle Stanley know what's 'appening. You'll be all right with Rachel, I'll get 'er to stop overnight so she can see to you in the morning as well. Get breakfast and that, then we'll go shopping.'

'All right.'

'So you're happy with that, are you?'

'Yep. You'll 'ave to carry Emma in and put 'er to bed, she never wakes up once she falls asleep.'

'Fair enough. Rachel can see to 'er.'

'Yep.'

Hugging his little girl close to him as he strode along the tree-lined avenue towards the entrance to the house, Tom wondered how he could work it so that he would see more of his children. He imagined them living in comfort and style at High House, Jessie could make up her own mind. If she chose to carry on committing adultery with Cohen, then so be it. If she was sorry for all she'd done he *might* forgive her. After all, he had had quite a few women, so to his mind, he had got his own back. He felt sure there would be a hundred Jessies out there who would do anything to be his wife. Not Rachel though. She was all right as tarts went but, after all was said and done, that's all she was – a paid tart.

–

By ten thirty that night, Jessie was tucked up in bed reading a paperback while Max, lying beside her, was drifting off into a comfortable sleep. The sound of a car pulling up outside the house went unnoticed, she was too involved in the story she was reading. The three sharp knocks on the street door however struck her cold. Tom came to mind immediately. The one thing she had always dreaded was that he just might turn up out of the blue.

Turning to Max, she shook him. 'Get up, Max!'

'What?' he turned and peered at her. 'What's up?'

'Someone's at the door. Quick, go to your own room, it might be Tom.'

'Tom?'

She was out of bed in a flash and pulling on her house-coat. 'Yes, Tom. If he catches you in here, he'll kill you. *Move* yourself!'

'This is ridiculous,' he grumbled, getting out of bed. 'The sooner you get your divorce the better, we shouldn't have to—'

'Not now, Max, save it for the morning.' She left and went downstairs, praying he would remember to take every bit of the clothing he'd stripped off.

The police standing on her doorstep made her blood run cold. Her first thoughts were that Tom had been killed in an accident and that they were here to break the news. She looked from one police officer to the other and their grave expressions made her fear the worst. She didn't know what to say to them – her mind had gone blank. She simply gazed at them, waiting.

'Mrs Smith?'

'Yes,' said Jessie, her voice no more than a whisper.

'May we come in?'

Standing aside, she nodded towards the door of the front room. She just knew that something awful had happened. Once in her sitting room, with the dying embers of the fire still glowing, she waited for them to break the news.

'Has something happened to my husband?' she said, finding her voice.

'No. Not as far as we're aware.'

She heaved a sigh of relief. 'If Tom's in trouble with your lot, I can't help you,' she said. 'I haven't even got a clue where he is. He walked out months ago and I've not heard from 'im since.'

'Do you think he might be living in Suffolk by any chance?' said one of the officers.

'Suffolk? I've no idea. *Has* he done something criminal?'

'We understand that your children went to Bury St Edmunds with your husband's brother and your sister – Stanley and Dolly Smith?'

Confused, Jessie couldn't imagine what this was about. 'Well, they did, yeah, but I don't understand. How do you know that and what's it got to do with Tom?'

'Would you say that your husband and his brother are close?'

'Of course they are, they're brothers.'

'Why did Stanley and your sister take the children to Bury St Edmunds instead of you? Would you say that your brother-in-law, Stanley, *persuaded* you to do that?'

'No.' What was going on? Why were they here? If Tom was in trouble, she wouldn't want to say anything to make things worse for him.

'Look, if you're about to tell me that Tom's lying low somewhere and his brother and my sister have gone for a nice family visit…?'

'Stanley blames himself for your husband walking out in a jealous temper. We wondered if somehow he might want to make up for it, you know… do the decent thing…?'

'Like what?'

'Maybe go along with some half-baked plan to take the children to meet their dad… spoil them for the day, that kind of thing.'

'There would be no *need* to,' said Jessie, irritated. 'I'd be happy if my husband took the trouble to spend some time with the kids. He's not bothered *so* far!'

'Mrs Smith. Earlier on today your brother-in-law handed over the children to a complete stranger. A woman.' He paused, watching her reaction. 'She'd offered to take them to a funfair in her car. Now we don't want to have the entire Suffolk and Norfolk police forces out looking for your children if they're with your husband. We wondered if he could have put this woman up to it and—'

'You're telling me that my children are *missing*!' Jessie paled.

'*Is* your husband living in Suffolk?'

'I don't know!' Intuition warned her that Tom must have been involved with this prize that they had won. But how? Why?

'Did he ever mention going to live in Suffolk?'

'No.' She didn't want to get Tom into any more trouble with the police – no matter how irresponsible he'd been towards his family. What was *really* going on? She had to know more.

Max came into the room, having heard most of what had been said from the other side of the door.

'Jessie, what's going on?' said Max. One of the policemen turned to Max and his expression spoke for itself; *Who are you?*

'I'm not sure what's happened, Max.' She turned to the officer who had given Max a dark look. 'This is Max Cohen. He's a family friend who's renting a room,' she said, embarrassed to have her lover in the room. 'Since my husband walked out it's not been easy to make ends meet.'

'I see…' The officer shook Max's hand. 'It's not unusual for a father to want to spend some time with his children; it's only natural. We *hope* that that's what we're dealing with here. Either that or the woman has had trouble with her car and if that's the case the Suffolk police will have picked up on it by now.'

'What makes you think he's in Bury St Edmunds?'

'We don't know where he is exactly, Mrs Smith. But the Suffolk police have brought this to our attention. Remember, you were the one who came in originally and reported your husband missing. Perhaps it's just coincidence, but we have to check it out.' Trying to reassure her he added, 'This "unknown" woman may be perfectly innocent and it's possible that her car broke down and that your children may well be back in the hotel by now.'

'The sooner I get there, the better,' said Jessie, trusting her intuition.

'So you think your husband might be involved then?'

'I don't know, anything's possible where Tom's concerned.'

Smiling; the officer stood up. 'Don't worry, he won't get into trouble if he's not involved, but wasting police time and funds is a serious matter – especially with someone who *has* a record for wasting our time. It was very annoying having to chase after army deserters.'

'He didn't desert,' said Jessie, 'he just took a bit of time off now and then.'

'We'll be off then, Mrs Smith. I'm sure you'll find your children unharmed.'

Once outside, the officer chuckled quietly at his younger colleague. 'Tom Smith's behind this all right; I knew he would be. He was a fly-by-night before the war *and* during it.'

'But what makes you so *sure*?'

'Lover boy in there. It's obvious that he's got his feet under Smith's table. He had a choice: knock his wife's lover black and blue or get back at the wife by worrying her sick. She's not really worried though… she knows as well as I do what's happened.'

Inside the house, Jessie was pacing the floor. 'Max, will you come with me to Suffolk? I won't *ever* forgive 'im for this. This time he's gone too far, I'll kill 'im.'

'So you don't think it could be a kidnap—'

'Oh, Max, please! The children of wealthy parents get stolen for ransom money not the likes of us. The woman's probably his girlfriend and they probably 'ad fun setting this up. She must 'ave a bit of money, though if she's got a car and could pay for the hotel.'

'You think they set up this prize weekend then, is that what you're saying?'

'Yes, Max. I should 'ave smelt a rat first off. It wasn't on hotel letter heading. Actually, it crossed my mind, but then I brushed it off, never in a million years had I put Tom behind it then. I thought the hotel might do this kind of thing for publicity you know a reporter there with a camera to get a shot of the lucky family, that kind of thing.'

'But, Jess, if he went that far just to see his children and to get you up there—'

'No, Max, don't. If Tom loves me and the kids that much why didn't he simply come down 'ere and knock on the door? No… he's shacked up somewhere round Bury St Edmunds with some rich woman. It's so bloody obvious I don't know how I kept my tongue still when the police were here. See, I still protect 'im even after the way he's treated us. You must think I'm really thick.'

'Of course I don't. As a matter of fact, just before we went into that hotel in Bury, I was almost certain that I saw someone who reminded me of Tom. Didn't look like an exact double but something struck me at the time...'

'Max... I'm now certain it was him. He saw us as a cosy foursome and took the bit between his teeth. He's looking for some kind of revenge.' She shook her head slowly. 'Once I've got my kids back home, I'm putting an order on 'em, he'll never get near 'em again unless I'm there.' She looked into Max's worried face. 'What is he doing in Bury St Edmunds of all places? It's spooky, Max. I've gone cold, I don't like it.'

Chapter Fourteen

'There's nothing to beat this, is there?' said Tom as he sat on his big, soft comfortable armchair by the roaring log fire.

'No,' said Rachel, sipping her glass of champagne, 'there's nothing quite like it.' Her red silk dressing gown was carefully arranged to reveal the sexy red silk pyjamas. She stretched her legs and curled them across his knees. 'You know… I could get used to this kind of life,' she said.

'Yeah,' smiled Tom, 'it's fine while the kids are sleeping like angels. What about when they demand attention? Would you 'ave the patience for that?'

'I'm a teacher, don't forget, and infants were always my favourite. Virgin minds are like blotting paper: soaking everything in… and you can choose what to give them to soak up.'

'Is that right?' said Tom, stroking her ankles.

'Tell me more about your wife,' said Rachel, the drink giving her courage to mention something which he never wanted to talk about.

'Tell you *what* about her?'

'Anything you like; her shortcomings, her good points, whatever you want. Tomorrow I will have forgotten it so…'

'It won't be mentioned again?'

'That's right, and if you like, I'll tell you about the man I very nearly married. My tall, dark, handsome Norfolk poet who preferred to live in a shed rather than a house.'

'Preferred or had no choice?'

'Preferred. His parents are very rich. That's what happens you know – with the children of the wealthy – they rebel against all things that only money can buy.'

'Yeah, until they're broke, then it's a different story. Silly bastards. Not me,' said Tom, running a hand up her leg. 'I've worn rags as a kid and now I wear silk. I don't wanna wear rags again.'

'Michael would never *have* to wear rags, he inherits a million pounds when his mother dies never mind what he comes into when his father kicks the bucket.'

'Should 'ave married 'im then, shouldn't you?'

'I would have if he wasn't so boring. His favourite occupation was to read his poetry *aloud*. I didn't always manage to fall asleep.'

'So, it's not just my money you're after,' said Tom, slowly unfastening her dressing gown.

'Oh, no… it's your body *and* your money,' she said, smiling.

'Good. That's what I like to hear. It's *your* body I want now.' Taking the glass of champagne from her hand, he removed her pyjamas then laid her back on the velvet settee. He kissed her frill, soft lips; her firm breasts and every inch of her until he found that spot which had her writhing and moaning.

'The children might hear,' she said, almost too breathless to speak.

'Forget them, they're out to the world,' he murmured, as he gently caressed that fleshy, familiar warm place between her legs.

'You're a sexy vixen,' said Tom, moving his body on top of hers. 'A red-hot devil.'

'And all yours,' she said, panting. 'So take me, you *bastard*,' she said, wrapping her legs round his back.

'You *bitch*,' he said, 'you've really asked for it this time!'

Their lovemaking was violent and intense and Tom was more than satisfied with his prowess as a lover. When he had had his fill, he sent her off to bed and poured himself another large brandy.

Leaning back on the settee, he closed his eyes. He was left alone with his thoughts and foremost among them was how and when he might return the kids to the hotel. Much as he wanted to keep them, the situation was too risky and he had too much to lose. He *had* to avoid the police at all costs.

–

Lying next to Max in the hotel room, Jessie was too tired to sleep. Tired and wide awake. When they had arrived in the wee hours there was only a night porter to greet them and he had been asleep at the desk. Most of the hotel was in darkness and there was no sign of activity whatsoever. Jessie had imagined she would find the police there, but she had been wrong. The night porter hadn't even heard of the so-called kidnapping.

'If this was London the place would be crawling with the law. For all they know some bloody lunatic's got my kids.'

'Jessie, try to relax, you'll be dog tired tomorrow and—'

'Relax! How can I? I don't know where he's shacked up or what my kids are feeling like; they might be crying for me…'

'No they won't. He's their father, don't forget, he'll have lavished presents and sweets on them and done everything he can to win them over. They'll be all right.'

She went quiet. 'Max, am I right – it must be Tom behind this? It can't be a deranged woman, surely? They must be with Tom, mustn't they? You don't think I've been too—'

'Jessie, please, I told you. Tom saw us when we were here with Dolly and Stanley, of course it's him up to his tricks. Stop going over and over it.'

'We don't know for sure it was him you saw.'

'I do now, I might not have then but I do now. I *know* it was Tom.'

'I wish I could believe it one hundred per cent. I just can't understand what was going through his mind. He must have known the police would be called in; Tom's not a complete idiot.'

'Maybe he phoned the hotel very late and explained.'

'Explained what? That he'd stolen my children?'

'No. That her car broke down, or something, it's only over one night don't forget. Try and get some sleep and tomorrow we'll find out more.'

'I can't, I want my babies back…' her voice trailed off as she began sobbing. 'I'm scared, Max, I'm really really scared. I don't know where they are or what they might be going through.'

'I know,' he said, stroking her hair. 'But there's nothing we can do until it's light. We'll trace him in no time; the hotel will have a record of his name and address, if not the police will soon find him. Tom Smith's a common enough name but a cockney having moved up here will be like a sore thumb sticking out. And remember, his girlfriend is obviously known at the hotel if not in the town.'

'You think I'm worrying for nothing, then?' said Jessie, wiping her eyes.

'No, you're bound to be worried. I don't want you to break down on me over it, that's all. I don't want you to get ill. You're all I've got and everything I want, Jess.' He kissed her lightly on the cheek. 'I love you and I hate to see you like this.'

'I know, Max.' She snuggled down and turned on her side holding him close. 'I'll be all right now, I'll doze off soon.' Ten minutes later Max was asleep, but Jessie lay there with her children on her mind.

–

At the same time, in High House, her son was lying awake in his bed. He was confused over the woman who was living here with his father; Billy felt sad and mixed-up. So when Emma crept into his room and asked if she could get into the bed with him, he was glad of it.

'Don't take up too much room, though,' he grumbled, making space for her.

'I didn't like it by myself,' she whispered.

'That's because you're only four.'

'The house is *very* big.' Emma lay on her back and stared up at the ceiling. 'Will the wood bits up there fall down?'

'No. Dad said they're called beams and they hold the house up.'

'But, but, but he's not really our dad, is he? Not *really*.'

'Mum said he is and so did Granddad.'

'But Nanny never said it, did she?'

'Yes, she did. I don't think he is though, I think Uncle Max is, but they don't want us to know. I think the one downstairs is a war spy.'

'But, but, but not the Bloody German, eh?'

'Course not. Don't swear, Emma.'

'I never swore, Billy.' Her lip began to tremble. 'I *didn't*.'

'Bloody *is* swearing.'

'No it's not…it's a German. Granddad knows, he says "Bloody Germans". 'Cos of all the blood from the bombs.'

Billy wasn't listening. 'I never knew that he was rich, Granddad never said he was rich.'

'The Bloody German?'

'No, Daddy. If he is our dad. Nanny and Granddad ain't got no money, why didn't he never give them some of 'is if he's not a spy?'

'Granddad 'as got money. I've seen it – in a toffee tin, in the little cupboard next to 'is chair.'

'That's beer money that Nanny don't know about. It's a secret, so don't tell.'

'Will he let us keep our toys?'

'I'm taking mine 'ome with me. That's why they're in that comer over there. We'll take yours an' all.'

'He didn't say we could.'

'I don't care, I'm taking 'em anyway. I might not come back again.'

'What about the play-park? It's ours but we can't take that, can we?'

'We can go to Victoria Park with Granddad.' Emmie went quiet and then spoke in a whisper. 'Don't you like 'im?'

'He's all right, but I like Max better.'

'I love Uncle Max,' said Emma. 'He reads us stories.'

'Yeah.'

'Shall we go to sleep now?'

'You can, I'm not tired.'

'But, but, but you won't run away, will you?'

'I might do in the morning, if he don't take us back.'

'Wouldn't he?'

'Not if he's a spy. Granddad said you 'ave to watch out for spies.'

'But you won't run away without *me*, please say you won't, Billy?'

'I'll ask Rachel in the morning about 'im being a spy.' Billy lay very still, thinking things through. Rachel was, after all, a schoolteacher so they were safe while she was there. If the man really was his dad and a *good*, rich man, *she* would know. 'Don't wet the bed, Emma,' he murmured. But Emma was dead to the world; sound asleep and looking like an angel. Sliding down under the bedclothes, Billy sank his head into the feather pillow and closed his own tired eyes, wishing he was back home, with his mum.

–

While Stanley was pacing the floor of the hotel room in Bury St Edmunds, Dolly lay on the bed, sobbing. They had no idea that Jessie and Max had arrived at the hotel and were in one of the nearby guest rooms. Neither of them could sleep. Stanley was extremely agitated and angry, furious in fact that the police had questioned him for over an hour. Made him feel like a *right* criminal.

'How could they think I'd do a thing like that? What sort of people are they up 'ere?'

'Horrible,' sobbed Dolly. 'I hate all of 'em, I wish we'd never come. I don't wanna live in that cottage any more, I don't want us to buy it. I just wanna go home...'

'I'm talking about the law – what do they *think*? That me and Tom are *dumb*, just 'cos we was brought up in the

East End. As if we'd even fink of doing something like that. Plotting a weekend just so Tom could see the kids? Silly bastards.'

'Don't swear, Stanley.'

'They make you wanna swear, there's no word that's not swearing that covers this farce.' He shook his head, livid. 'That's what it is. A bloody farce! They should be searching for that bitch, she's obviously not right in the 'ead. Can't they see that!'

'Stanley, stop it!'

'I'm sorry, Doll,' he said, dropping down on to the bed. 'I can't 'elp it.' He leaned forward and covered his face and started to cry. 'Where are they? Where's little Emma and Billy boy?' he sobbed.

Dolly wiped her eyes and blew her nose. 'I dunno. I don't understand the way the police go about things either. The kids 'ave bin stolen and everyone's gone to bed, how can that be right?'

'It's not right. They shouldn't be leaving it till the morning, and what about Jessie? She don't even know. If it's in the papers in the morning and she reads it... I'll swing for someone, Doll, honest I will.'

'There wasn't a reporter down at the station was there?' This new thought made Dolly go cold.

'No. I just 'ope there wasn't one snooping round this place, it's a small town. The fact that the police were 'ere and took me away should 'ave bin enough to have 'em all pouring in for the gossip.'

'I would 'ave known if they were here. I was hounded by 'em when Dad 'ad the accident in the docks. Not that they cared about *us*, they was only interested in the story: "Docker ordered to drive overloaded crane!" "Docker sent to his death!" "Docker burned alive in flaming crane!" "Docker plunges into the Thames, burning alive!" I'll never forget those headlines for as long as I live.'

'No, I don't s'pose you will love.' He shook his head, despairingly, 'I don't know about you Doll, but I can't sleep. There's no point in getting undressed.'

'Come on then, we'll go down and get the porter to open up the bar.'

'If *he* won't, *I* will. The kitchen an' all. I'm starving.'

'We might 'ave to slip 'im a ten bob note,' said Dolly, checking herself in the mirror. 'Be worth it though. I can't sit up 'ere all night worried sick. Be worth it for two reasons.'

'What's that?' said Stanley, pulling on his shoes.

'Once you've got 'im chatting, I'm gonna have a little search round that reception desk, see what I can find. I can't believe that woman walked into this place on her own, just on a whim, and then walked out again with two kids.'

Stanley eyed her cautiously, worried that she was getting too uptight. 'How do you mean?'

'I dunno, but there's something fishy about the whole thing. I did doze off earlier for ten minutes and when I woke up I had this feeling that there was more to this than meets the eye. That's 'ow I feel, Stanley. As if someone's up to something and it's staring us in the face, but we just can't see it – yet.'

'I know what you mean, it don't add up. Unless the wicked cow goes round hotels hoping to find kids to nick, and if that's the case she must 'ave done it before so she'd 'ave a record. I gave a good description of 'er, right down to the nail polish.'

'Oh, you noticed that then?'

269

'Yeah,' he said, trying to make her smile. 'So long as I don't touch, can't stop the mind from thinking what it wants, Doll. She wasn't my type but...'

'Yeah, yeah all right. Let's get down there and see what we can find out, we've wasted enough bloody time. I'm not gonna—' A soft tapping on the door stopped Dolly mid-sentence.

Stanley was there in a flash, yanking the door open.

'Excuse me, I saw the light under your door, is my brother in there?'

Peering at the stranger, Stanley said, 'What d'yer want, mate?'

'I can't find my room. He was in there again so I came out but now I can't find it.'

Stanley looked over his shoulder at Dolly who was half smiling. 'He's the one I told you about earlier on,' she whispered.

'Who was in where?' Stanley asked their visitor.

'My brother, I think he might be in your bathroom.'

'Yeah? Well, let's leave 'im there, shall we? Look, mate, were just going downstairs for a drink – we couldn't sleep either – you can join us if you like.'

'I only drink champagne, won't touch any other stuff.'

'Fair enough, we'll 'elp you get through a bottle. Come on, Dolly, move yourself.' Glad of the diversion, they made their way downstairs.

'Bin 'ere long 'ave yer,' asked Stanley, 'nice long 'oliday is it?'

'There used to be a mirror in this lift,' he said, vaguely.

Dolly pinched Stanley, daring him not to laugh. 'What 'appened to it then?' she said, keeping a straight face.

'I unscrewed it, took it down. But they put it back up again. They weren't as quick as me though.'

'You took it down again,' said Stanley. 'And why not, eh?'

'*Eleven* times in all, they soon gave up. I've never forgotten the spider in the cave with that Scottish King Robert Bruce: You must never give up. I'm working my way round the house, removing all the mirrors.'

Looking into the man's face, Stanley reckoned him to be in his early thirties. 'House?'

'They say it's not mine, but it is you know.'

'What… this hotel?'

'It's not an hotel, they call it that to dupe people. They collect all the moneys. But I'm on to it.'

'What's your name then?' said Dolly, warming to him.

'They all seem to think it's Henry but I think *he* switched it years ago. I have a feeling that my brother is Henry – Henry Thomas. If I'm right then I must be Archibald, but I don't let on. Best they don't know everything. I'm not that bothered really.'

'Archibald, eh? Archie for short, I s'pose,' said Stanley, stepping out of the lift. 'We'll call you Archie, all right?'

'Why would you do that? My name's Henry – Henry John Thomas.'

'Fair enough, mate, fair enough.'

Finding no one at the reception desk they went in search of the night porter, who was, as Stanley guessed, in the lounge, reading a paperback and enjoying the freedom of the bar.

'Well, if it isn't you, Henry, and what might you have been up to now?'

'Is my brother in here?'

'I haven't seen him, to be sure. I'm thinking he might be in your bathroom. Sleeping it off.'

'Well, if he is he can bloody well stay there.' He motioned with a wave of a hand that the porter was to stand to attention. 'One of my bottles of special,' he said. 'I'm entertaining this evening.' He turned to Dolly and Stanley, 'Please do make yourselves at home. You'll find the sofa by the window to be more than comfortable.'

'No, I'll tell you what, Henry. You escort my wife over while I just go and 'ave a Jimmy Riddle.'

'Yes of course. But I think you'll find that Richard, here, isn't up to cocktails. Nice chap though he is but not worldly.' He took Dolly's arm and like a practised gentleman at court, led her to the cosy snug in the comer.

Stanley caught the porter's eye and grinned. 'Got a right one there, ain't yer?'

'Oh he's not so bad, harmless enough.'

'Really thinks he owns the place?'

'Yes indeed. But then you know, none of us can be sure. He's been a resident for years so they tell me.' He leaned forward and looked Stanley in the eye, 'Look, I *know* you're worried about the children and I'm sorry I can't help you. We've not heard anything new from the police and your wife looks so tired. Wouldn't it be best for her to try and get some sleep?'

'Nah, we can't sleep. We'll just wait for news. Fancy a game of cards to pass the time?'

'Well, I just *might*,' he said, smiling. 'Take our minds off this sad business. Best get his champagne over to 'im first, mind, we'll be needing *two* bottles for the four of us. He'll insist you have a drink with him, we get through a bottle between the two of us. He loves his bubbly, does Henry.'

'Look, I know you said that you'd never seen this woman before. The one who took the kids but—'

'*No one* had seen her before.' He looked pitifully at Stanley. 'Management called a meeting. We have a full description from the police. I know what you must be going through, but I can't help you. There's nothing more I can tell you. I wish I could, I *can* understand how you feel. And their poor mother upstairs – what *must* she be going through?'

'Mother? You mean Jessie's *here*?'

'Oh of course you won't know, they didn't arrive till late, must have been gone one o'clock this morning.'

'Oh right...' said Stanley, pushing his hand through his hair, all at sixes and sevens. 'Blimey... don't know what to think, should I go up or what? I can't think they'd be asleep. Bloody hell, you've taken the wind out my sails.'

'I can see that. But at least it's put a smile on your face.'

'What is the time anyway?'

The porter checked his watch. 'Almost three thirty.'

'Gimme their room number, I'll go and see if a light's coming out from under their door. If they're—'

'There's no need,' chuckled the porter, 'look who's come in.'

Spinning round, Stanley was very happy and relieved to see the familiar faces of Jessie and Max. Dolly, of course, burst into tears as soon as she saw her sister. Within seconds, they were embracing, clinging on and crying. 'I'm sorry, Jess,' said Dolly, 'I'm really so sorry.'

'It's all right, Dolly, it's all right. I know who we have to blame for all of this and it's not you.'

'I don't blame you for being angry with 'im, Jess, but don't be too hard, eh? He's gutted over it – really gutted.'

Jessie pulled back and looked into Dolly's face. She could see that she'd had no sleep and her eyes Were puffy and red from all the weeping. 'Not Stanley. *Tom!*'

273

'Tom?'

'Yeah. I'll explain once I've had a drink. I've tried to get some sleep but it was impossible; poor Max, he must be dog tired.'

Once the group of night owls were settled down in a corner of the bar, they relaxed and swapped ideas as to what might or might not have gone on during that day. Henry Thomas was pleased enough to be in their company, nice people who weren't trying to get rid of him but carrying on as if he wasn't there. He was a good listener *and* he had his champagne.

Stanley went over his story again trying to put Jessie in the picture as to how innocent the whole thing seemed at the time.

The story of the woman who had taken the children told, there wasn't much else to say. Jessie felt sure that Tom was behind it and Dolly couldn't see how that could be.

'But what made *you* think it was Tom you saw last time we was 'ere?' said Stanley, peering at Max through tired eyes.

'You know what it's like sometimes… you see a face… you think it's someone you know but it isn't. It really wasn't much more than that. And of course once he got into the car, well, that was it. I knew, or at least I thought I knew, it couldn't have been him.'

'Why not? What was wrong with the car?'

'*Wrong* with it? What could be wrong with a brand, spanking new convertible Triumph Roadster? Long cream bonnet with two large chrome headlamps.' He shrugged. 'Once I had seen that I thought no more of it.'

'It is *not* brand new, my friend,' said Henry, the resident guest.

They all turned to him slowly. What did he know that they didn't?

'It's not brand new. I should know.'

'It looked it.'

'Hardly ever used, that's *why*!'

Dolly was ready to signal to them that he wasn't all the ticket, when he said, 'It was Mother's car – *one* of them. *I* didn't want it. Why drive when you can get someone else to do it for you and why live in a house when you can live in a hotel?'

'She sold it then, did she?' asked Max.

'Mother didn't sell things. She *bought* things. It was the chrome headlamps. My brother first started to follow me when I took over the car, so I parked it at one of the houses and left it there.'

'What house was that?' asked Max, feeling as if they were on to something.

'One of mother's. Too big,' he said, floating a hand through the air. 'This needed doing, that needed doing. Why live in a bloody great house when you can live in a place like this and have someone do everything for you?' He looked round him, 'I hope to God I don't own *this* place.' He leaned closer to Max. 'If you see my brother, will you tell him to go away, to leave me alone for good. He can have it all – Mother's fortune – I don't want it. A millionaire fell madly in love with her once, you know. She was a beautiful woman and very rich – *before* he came along. So you can imagine…'

Henry had, by now, drunk almost a bottle of champagne and the only effect it had on him was to turn his cheeks rosy and put a sparkle in his dull eyes. His speech wasn't in the least bit slurred.

'So the car,' said Max, 'is it possible that someone might have stolen it? The man who was driving it the other day?'

'Who knows? I don't care, it's only a motor car, after all.'

'It's such an interesting story,' said Max, eliciting more information.

'What is?'

'Your mother marrying a millionaire and you leaving your car at a house that you'd forgotten about.'

'I did *not* say that my good man. Mother married no one! I did *not* say I had forgotten anything. I have an excellent memory.'

'What about your beautiful mother – is she still alive?'

'Good gracious, no. He took her from us somewhere between the wars, can't quite remember the exact day. We adored her you know, my brother and I, she loved us to death. A wonderful woman and a wonderful mother; she was very, very beautiful. The men kept on coming: men from all walks of life, well-bred; oh yes. She once entertained a prince you know. I've got a photograph of her in my room but I won't take you up there. What's the point, he'll be in the bathroom and you might want to use it, and that would never do.'

'So you're from a very wealthy family,' said Jessie. 'I've always wanted to meet a rich man and you're not in the least bit a snob either.'

'Snob? I should say not. If you knew how my mother made her fortune you might snub me,' he said, averting his eyes.

'Don't you believe it. Dig around any family history and you won't find one that's snow white,' said Jessie. 'Far from it, especially among the rich. In the north of England they've got a saying: "Where there's muck there's money".

In the East End we've got one: "Where there's money there's muck".'

Max opened his mouth about to ask the man if he enjoyed living in the hotel, but Dolly kicked his shin and nodded at Jessie. She was giving him a message to keep quiet and let her sister carry on. Dolly knew what Jessie was doing, she knew *exactly* what she was doing.

'Do you know what would be really lovely, Henry?'

'Oh lots of things I should think. Not that I can think of any in particular.'

Jessie feigned deep concentration. 'You know what my wish would be if I was granted just one? I would love to look round one of them country houses which we passed on the way here. Just to 'ave a look you know, and admire—'

'Well, you could have the key to one of ours if I could only remember where they were—' he looked upwards and thought about it – 'there's one in London but that won't do; then there's one in Ipswich somewhere but I think that's falling to bits – Mother let it go once it started to need repair. We had some lovely times there as children, my brother hated it, he would've been better off living in the London squalor. Bit of an oddball.'

'What about the car? The lovely cream Triumph Roadster, is that kept in the garage at the house in Ipswich?'

'Not if you've seen it on the road it isn't. I should think someone must have stolen it from High House. Don't care really, it was never my—'

'High House...' said Jessie, '...that's the one in Ipswich?'

'Is it?' Henry looked puzzled as he tried to remember. 'No, no, High House was in good order. I never liked that place, too morbid with all those black oak beams everywhere: on the ceilings, on the walls, up the bloody staircase; too dark for me.'

'Sounds horrible,' said Jessie. 'I s'pose that one's up north, is it?'

'No,' he said, shaking his head. 'Mother *never* bought in the north. Suffolk – that's where it is – in Suffolk.'

'Which is where we are now,' said Jessie brightly, keeping it going.

'Are we? I thought we were in Bury St Edmunds, but then it doesn't matter where we are so long as we are happy.' He leaned back in his chair and looked up at the ceiling. 'I remember the railway station. Now that I *did* like.'

'Have some more champagne, Henry,' said Stanley, filling his glass. 'All this talk about High House and the railway station. You'll be coming up wiv the name of the village next. Bloody good memory, I'll say that for you.'

'The village? Oh that's easy – Stowmarket. There.'

'Stowmarket, eh? Go on, I thought that was a small country town.'

'It is my good man, well done.'

'Oh, so High House ain't in a village then, it's in a town?'

'Never. It was never in a town, no, it was in the village of Elmswell. I should know.'

Stanley raised his eyes to meet Jessie's, she was thinking the same thing. Had he got it slightly wrong? Did he mean Elmshill? Elmshill where the cottages were, where he and Dolly were going to live? 'Oh right, I've seen signs to *Elmshill.*'

'Different place entirely, *that* village is on the Suffolk Norfolk border. Elmswell is in the heart of Suffolk, I should know. Is anyone hungry?'

'Starving,' said Stanley.

'Really? Well, we can't have that,' Henry waved the porter over.

'I don't think he's gonna be very happy about this,' said Jessie.

'He will be if we get into the kitchen and get on with it, I bet,' said Dolly.

She was right. The porter was more than pleased to have another supper himself. He showed them downstairs to the kitchen and the huge refrigerator where there were plenty of eggs and some bacon. 'Shall we?' said Dolly.

'Why not?' said Jessie.

'Then it's off to Elmswell by the sound of it.'

'Soon as dawn breaks.'

'You think Tom's hiding there don't you?'

'Don't you?'

'I don't know, Jess, but that horrible dread in my stomach's gone. I think the kids are with 'im.'

'You can bet on it. I've worked it out, Dolly. Now I know for sure that I'm married to a *real* con man. I reckons that Henry's brother was the bloke who chucked himself under a train, leaving Tom with 'is kitbag. He told me all about it not long after his demob. I bet you there were papers in that kitbag and I bet that Tom's done the same as some of the men he told me about: taken on another bloke's identity – a rich bloke's identity.'

'Sounds the kind of thing he'd do. The leopard never changes his spots. Does what's best for 'im and sod what worry he puts others through. I can see now what you were trying to tell me during the war. He's a cunning, selfish sod. Lovable… once, not any more though, what he did was wicked, taking the kids like that. What worries me is, did he intend to bring 'em back?'

'Course he did, can you imagine 'im looking after Billy and Emma-Rose? And he's not daft, he'd 'ave known the entire blooming police force'd be out looking for 'em. If it wasn't for that poor sod up there – Henry the mad – looking for 'is brother, we'd still be in the dark.'

'It all sounds a bit incredible, Jess.'

'No, not really, and to tell you the truth, Doll, when we came last time, I had a strong feeling that Tom had been in the hotel. When I came out of the dining room and went through to the cloakroom, I swear… it was as if I could smell him.'

'Brylcreem, Jess, most men smell of it.'

'No, it wasn't just that, it's hard to describe. I never mentioned it 'cos it might have sounded as if Tom was always on my mind.' She thought back to the day. 'It was as if he'd walked out a minute or so before I passed through. I wonder… I wonder if he *had* come in to arrange things at the reception desk that day, you know, once he'd spotted us?'

'Might 'ave done. Knowing Tom, he would 'ave wanted to act straight away. He's got a nerve, I'll say that for 'im.'

'I suppose…' Jessie sighed and leaned against the refrigerator… 'it must 'ave looked bad, booking into a hotel with Max as my partner.'

'We *never* booked in for the night, remember, we came for a midday meal.'

'But Tom wasn't to know that was he?'

'True, which is probably why you could sense him in the reception area. He was probably checking up, and no doubt that's when his bright idea came to 'im.'

'All the same, it could've upset 'im.'

'Oh for Gawd's sake, Jessie. D'yer think Tom's bin living like a monk… with all that money and crying into 'is champagne all lonely and sad? Is that what you think? *You* could 'ave done with some of that money. Scrubbing floors in the morning at the library while he's lordin' it up 'ere – bastard.'

'You think he's shacked up with someone then?'

Dolly rolled her eyes and sighed. 'And you don't…?'

Chapter Fifteen

It was the sound of a peacock's cry that woke Tom from his sleep. Feeling cold, now that the fire had gone out, he reached across the settee and pulled the rug, which had earlier been wrapped round Rachel, over himself, hoping to get warm. Five minutes later he was up and pulling on his Aran jumper. Longing for a cup of tea he went into the kitchen and lit the gas under the kettle. Dawn was breaking and the sun was coming up but still it felt cold – October cold.

Thinking of his mother, Tom felt a wave of guilt creep over him. For all he knew, she or his dad could be ill or just worried sick and no one would know where to find him, but he hadn't wanted to be found. However, his plan for staying away as long as possible was now under review since the day he'd seen his wife go into that hotel with Max. To Tom, it seemed that Jessie was *always* responsible each time he fell flat on his face.

Yeah, he thought, Jessie and Max – one way or another they always managed to pull the rug from under his feet. When he was taking leave from the army, it was Max who knew where he was staying so only he could have informed the military police. He had had to go to the Kent hopfields to bring Jessie back home where she belonged and on the train home, once again, the military police were after him. Had he not been sharper than they were, he would have been arrested on the train instead of escaping just as it was pulling out of the station.

'And then, when I was doing all right by myself, you 'ad to turn up with your bit on the side and crush me. Well sod you, Jess, you can worry yourself silly over the kids 'cos they're stopping right 'ere with me. I'll make *all* the decisions now.'

Smiling, he lifted the steaming kettle off the Calor stove and poured boiling water into the teapot. This small ritual of tea making always helped when he was mad at Jessie. And he *was* mad: she could still sneak her way into his dreams and taunt him with her naked body. He couldn't escape from the cow, not even when he was asleep!

Warmer now and more relaxed, he sipped his hot tea and planned his next move. He would send the most expensive bouquet of flowers to Emmie and a gift pack-aged bottle of malt whisky to Charlie, via Harrods of course. He would tell them that he had the children and was giving them the best holiday of their lives and loving every minute. He would also send them a registered envelope containing more money than they had ever seen. Stanley and Dolly too; they would get a handsome wedding present by post. But the best bit for Tom was thinking what to send to Jessie's mother, Rose; this had to be something special. It had to be the best... something that she couldn't resist keeping. Yes, he would rub it in, rub salt into the wound. Rose never considered him good enough for Jessie and now *she* wasn't good enough for him.

With a feeling of well-being, he unbolted the kitchen door and went outside to greet the morning – the garden was at its best at this time of day: full of colour and with the scent from the roses and the last of the honeysuckle

Wafting in the air. Strolling through the grounds, he made his way to the play-park. His chest swelled. 'What more can a man do for 'is kids than this?' he said, proudly.

Going back inside he went upstairs to take a peep at Rachel, still sleeping soundly. This was the best time to see a woman and it was the best time to smell her, to taste her, to make love to her. Taking off his jumper, he was about to climb in beside her when he heard a sound from downstairs and realised that he hadn't closed the kitchen door behind him. Damn!

Cursing, he went down to bolt the door, already aroused by the mere sight of Rachel curled up under the silk eiderdown. He couldn't wait to join her in bed, but he had time for a quick drink. Stopping at the well-stocked drinks cabinet in the smoking room, he poured himself a dram of his best malt whisky. Sipping it slowly, he closed his eyes, enjoying the sensation as it warmed his throat. He loved his new life, and nothing or no one was going to take it away from him...

'Hello, Tom.' The soft, familiar voice drifted across the room.

'Wha—' He didn't move. Was his imagination playing tricks? It couldn't be her... she was in London, he was in Suffolk. 'Too much drink last night, Tom,' he mumbled to himself.

'Where are my children?'

Spinning round, he came face to face with Jessie. 'What are *you* doing 'ere?' The blood drained from his face.

'My question exactly! Where are my children...? I want to take them home.'

Shaken, he cleared his throat and then peered at her. She was definitely for real and not a figment of his imagination. 'They're in bed – nice and comfy and fast asleep. *Not* to be disturbed.'

'I suppose you think you're clever?'

'I do, Jessie. I do. In fact, I think I'm Ace. Ace of spades.' Now he was feeling smug. 'I'll show you round, if you like. Show you the play-park I 'ad specially built for 'em.'

'I'm not really interested, Tom. All I want are my kids.'

'*Your* kids…? Sorry, Jessie, but you're gonna 'ave to get used to the idea that they're *my* kids now. I'm taking over from now on in. I don't think it's healthy for 'em to be in the same house where their mother's playing a whore.'

'You bastard! You know I'm not playing a whore. I'm gonna divorce you, Tom, and marry Max. I should've done it ages ago. He'll be here shortly so you can tell him what you've just told me. You know… the bit about me being his whore.'

'Stop it, Jess, you're scaring me,' he said, grinning at her. 'What d'yer think of my little place then? Came up on the pools, didn't I? Sorry now, are you? You could 'ave 'ad a life of luxury, still, there you go. A flat above a shop is all he's got to offer, ain't it? S'pose you'll have to settle for that.'

She really wanted to tell him all she had found out from Henry at the Cherub but her instincts told her to keep quiet. 'Stanley and Dolly'll be here soon as well, I asked them to wait down the lane. I thought it might be too much for you if we *all* walked in.'

'It would, Jess, you're right. But they're not gonna walk in and you… you are gonna walk out – right now. This is my home and you're not welcome.' He sipped a little more of his whisky and winked at her. 'You're trespassing.'

'And you're *not*?' she said, unable to lose an opportunity to have him wondering just how much she knew.

'Course I'm not trespassing. I know it's hard to believe, but I'm a landowner now. Rich as you like. The world is my oyster, Jess, and there ain't no room in it for you.'

Hearing slippered footsteps, Jessie hoped that this was going to be the woman who had dared to lure her children away. When she appeared, her description fitted the one Stanley had given. Jessie wanted to smack her round the face.

'What's going on?' said Rachel. 'I heard voices... who's this?'

'The mother of the children that you kidnapped,' said Jessie.

'Ah, so we meet at last...' she said with a condescending smile. 'But I would hardly describe it as kidnapping. Stanley was quite happy for me to take them to the funfair, but I brought them here instead... to their own *private* play-park.'

'Tell that to the police. They should be here soon.' Jessie was lying and enjoying it.

'Take no notice, sweetheart,' he said, throwing Jessie a filthy look. 'The only one in the family that the law are interested in is her brother, Alfie. Or is he already inside, Jess?'

'Alfie's gone straight, if you must know, it must 'ave bin your influence, Tom. Soon as you were out of the picture, he got himself a proper job. Know what? He thinks you're waste of time.'

'So you went to the police,' said Rachel.

'Actually, *they* came to me. And it won't be long before they come for you.' She turned to her husband. 'You've not been as clever as you think, Tom. You didn't know that Archibald John Thomas had a brother, did you? A brother who lives in a hotel. A hotel which you know very well – the Cherub. Now isn't that amazing… what a stroke of luck for me, don't you think?'

A cold bolt of terror shot through him. But Tom being Tom, he covered it well. 'Look, just do me a favour, Jess. Go away. I'll fetch the kids back to the hotel once they've 'ad breakfast.' But his face had paled and there were beads of sweat appearing on his forehead. 'I really don't know what you're on about, so just go will you. You're upsetting Rachel.'

'You mean she doesn't know about it?' She turned to Rachel and shrugged. 'The real Archie is dead. Killed 'imself, and poor Tom was left holding a dead man's kitbag with all his papers inside. I'm sure you can work the rest out for yourself.'

Rachel looked to Tom for an explanation. He simply waved a hand in the air. 'She's always been a jealous cow. You're better looking than 'er, Rachel, that's what she can't stand. She's lying through 'er back teeth. Always did when things didn't go her way.'

'Tom, it didn't take much for us to wheedle the story out of Henry Thomas. And, when we had all the facts,' she lied, 'we took them to the police. They'll come here. So if you're smart you'll get out while you can.'

'You've bin reading too many paperbacks, Jessie.'

'Oh, by the way, your mum and dad are well. A bit shocked when the police car turned up, and even more shocked when they said the children had been kidnapped. But there we are, Tom, what do you care – you never did think about consequences or other people's feelings, did you?'

The gravity of the situation was sinking in rapidly and Tom could not disguise his anguish. He was worried – very worried. 'Oh I'm not listening to this. Go and pack

your things, Rachel. We're leaving.' Stunned by this revelation, Rachel was rooted to the spot.

'I said go and pack, Rachel.' Tom spoke between
clenched teeth.

'Of course I will darling, but you shouldn't let your
wife upset you like this.' She looked at Jessie and offered
a smile. 'He's a very sensitive man, you know.'

'Is that a fact... you dozy cow,' hissed Jessie.

'She wants a settlement, that's what she's come for.
Well you can 'ave it, Jess. Tell you what, you can have
this place, I've enjoyed it here, but I'm bored with it now.
The country life should suit you and your boyfriend.' He
unhooked a bunch of keys from the wall and tossed them
at Jessie. 'Here... keys to my kingdom. But a very *small*
part of my kingdom. See 'ow generous I can be.'

Rachel turned on Jessie. 'You only had to ask and Tom
would have given you whatever you wanted. He's the
most considerate man I've ever met.'

'With someone else's money, who wouldn't be? You
seem to have lived a very sheltered life, Rachel. But you'll
learn love. You're welcome to him.' She began to back out
of the house. 'I'll join the others in the car and once you've
gone, we'll all come in and have a look round. Unless you
want to see Stanley?'

'No, I don't want to see Stanley. As far as I'm
concerned he's welshed on me so I disown him. I only
had one brother in my books, Johnnie... and Johnnie's
dead. Come on, Rachel, get your handbag and coat. We'll
take the Bentley and leave 'er with the Roadster and her
boyfriend can 'ave my clothes – told you I was generous,
Jess. Tomorrow, we'll go shopping, Rachel. Never been
inside Harrods, 'ave you?'

Seeing Tom in this light, Jessie shuddered. He had always been the lovable rogue, but he had turned into something else, something more sinister. The war *had* changed him.

'No I can't say that I have.' Rachel was disturbed too. The smile had gone from her face and now she looked concerned.

'And they say that money's not everything. I think someone got it wrong somewhere, don't you, Jess?'

Jessie did not respond to his taunting. 'I'll find the children's room and get them dressed,' she said, her voice no more than a whisper.

'No you won't, not yet anyway. I need to talk to 'em first, explain that I'll be back one day. That's not too much to ask, is it?'

'If you must. I'll just go and tell Stanley and Dolly what's happening.'

'And Max... don't forget to tell Max,' said Tom, glaring into her face. 'I know he's out there, bound to be.'

When they saw Jessie approach, her arms folded and head down, both Stanley and Dolly were out of Max's car in a flash. 'Well?' said Dolly. 'Are the kids there?'

'Yeah. In bed. Tom's saying goodbye to them. He doesn't want you to go in. He's er... he's packing,' she said, trying not to hurt Stanley's feelings.

'Doesn't want us to? Leave off. Wait there for us.' Stanley swaggered off, calling back over his shoulder, 'Who does he think he is — Lord of the Manor?'

'Yes!' said Jessie. 'That's it exactly!'

'Come on, Max,' said Dolly, 'let's go and see 'ow the other 'alf live.'

'No,' said Jessie, 'Wait till they've gone. His girlfriend's in there too.' She sighed heavily. 'He's changed so much,

Dolly. Gone a bit strange in the head, I think. I just hope he don't throw Stanley out.'

Going inside the house, Stanley gave the downstairs a quick once over and then went in search of Tom. He could hear whispering and followed the sound. 'Well, you fell on your feet, mate, didn't you?' he said, walking into the master bedroom, happy to see his brother again.

Seeing Stanley proved too much for Tom and he couldn't ignore his feeling of emotion for his brother. 'Go and make a cup of tea, Rachel,' he said, waving her out of the bedroom. She left the room but had no intention of brewing tea. She listened from the staircase, wanting to find out more about the man that she had known as Archie but whose real name was Tom.

'What's going on, brother?' said Stanley. 'I can't make head nor tail of any of this.'

'It's a long story but to cut it short, I've landed on me feet, Stan. I've lost Jessie for the moment but it won't be for long. She'll come running back once she's fed up with Max. I'm a bit disappointed in you, you know. How come you or Dad didn't kick 'im out?'

'He's all right, Tom, and he looks after the kids. At least Jessie don't 'ave to scrub floors any more.'

'No, I bet she don't. Don't mean she's not a scrubber though, does it? What's this I've heard about you getting married?'

'Yep, me and Dolly.' He leaned his head forward and spoke out of the side of his mouth, 'She's pregnant, you know. I'm gonna be a dad.'

'Oh right, case of having to, was it?'

'Nah, I was gonna marry 'er anyway. I've always liked 'er, you know that. She's all right, is my Doll.'

'Look, Stan, I would offer you a cup of tea, but now that Jessie's been in and upset my girlfriend, all I want to do is get out of here. She always messes things up.'

'Oh, I dunno, Tom,' said Stanley, still slightly miffed by his brother's attitude.

'Well, you wouldn't. She's always kept one face for me and one for everyone else. "Good girl Jessie", that's how she likes to come across. Still, think what you like, I know 'er better than anyone.'

'Stands to reason you must do,' Stan said, sadly. This hadn't been what he'd expected from his brother. Determined to lift things, he nudged Tom and grinned. 'Clever sod. How'd you manage all this? Taking a bloke's identity ain't that uncommon, lots of them went out married with five kids and came back single men to start all over. But this—'

'Stan... I'm in a bit of an 'urry. Why don't we get together for a beer in a couple of weeks? I'll write to Mum now that Jessie's blown it. I was biding my time so I could surprise the lot of you and move you all in with me. That's 'istory now though, thanks to Jessie.'

'Yeah all right then, Tom, don't let me 'old you up.' Stanley looked and felt awkward. 'So how you gettin' away with it all? Forging 'is signature and that? 'Cos if you are and the law catches up with you' – he sucked air through his teeth – 'you'll be in for a long stretch.'

'Like taking ice cream from a baby,' said Tom, glancing at his gold wristwatch. 'Must rush, I'll catch up with you though. Help yerself to whatever you fancy. Don't 'ave to worry about ration books and coupons while you're at High House – the cupboards are well stocked.'

Making it clear that there was nothing else to talk about, Tom gave him a nod. A nod that said, *Time to go Stan, move yourself.*

'Right. I'll leave you to get on then.' Stanley gave him a friendly punch to the arm and left. With mixed emotions he went back to the car and the others. He sat quietly on the grass verge pondering over what his brother had told him. Suddenly he stood up. 'Come on. I'm not putting up with this, we'll all go in. And when we do, Doll, you put the kettle on and behave as if you've got every right to be there. We'll sort out the pair of 'em.'

Dolly knew her Stanley well enough to see that he was seething. 'Whatever you say, lover. Come on, Jess, and you, Max,' she said, giving them an encouraging look.

Tom didn't look at all surprised when they bowled into the house. In fact, he knew it would happen. Billy had woken up but had been ordered to stay in bed; Emma was still asleep. Tom had thrown a few things into a small suitcase, including all of his files. He was leaving nothing incriminating behind. Rachel, having had second thoughts on whether to get out or not, had decided to stay with Tom. She had experienced enough to know that life with him would be more exciting than teaching in a country town. Besides which, they were from the same mould – two of a kind.

Coming into the kitchen where they were gathered, Tom nodded at Dolly and ignored Max. 'Make yourself at home. This is Jessie's place now, or hasn't she told you? I'll 'ave it signed over once I get to London, my lawyer's there so it shouldn't take long.'

'So 'ow you bin keeping, Tom?' said Dolly, as chirpy as you like. 'You certainly look different with your coloured hair and that, but I can still see *you* in there, behind that disguise.'

'It's not a disguise, Dolly, just a change of looks that's all.' He looked at Max and grinned, 'You look a bit nervous, mate. Don't worry, you can relax, I ain't gonna lay a finger on yer.' He chuckled with a look of restrained menace on his face and left them to it. 'Come on, Rachel, we're going to London!' And just like that, Tom walked out, his kingdom in his suitcase, and wads of notes in every pocket with Rachel at his heel, knowing she could run off whenever she wanted.

'Blimey,' said Dolly, sinking down on to a chair. 'What *'as* bin goin' on, Jess? Look at this place, it must belong to a millionaire.'

'It does,' she said, 'it belongs to that lovely man who would rather live in a hotel where there's company, and I for one don't blame 'im. Let's hope one day he can find 'imself someone to love and be loved by.'

'Well, I fink we should leave 'im be. He's as happy as Larry where he is,' said Dolly. 'Meanwhile, we could come up here and enjoy this place whenever we feel like it. You're not to know that Tom was lying, Jess, if he told us he came up on the pools, who are we to argue? He said it was yours and he was gonna sign it over.'

'We couldn't,' said Jessie. 'Don't be daft.' But she was hoping they would overrule her. It was a once in a lifetime opportunity to throw caution to the wind and Jessie was ready to do that — more than ready. She had never been as free spirited as her sister, Dolly, but equally she had never been as earnest as she had been of late, staid was the word that came to mind. Yes, thought Jessie, it was time she lived a little dangerously, Tom had dropped a unique and glorious gift into their lap. His parting present, even though it wasn't rightly his to give, made up for all the grief he had caused her. 'I don't think we should but if I'm outnumbered…'

'You are, Jess, so shut up. Tom's used his brain and come up trumps. This is 'is legacy to us and I, for one, ain't gonna chuck it away, And by the sounds of it, he's got somewhere else to go and plenty of dosh to go with it. *I'm* for coming up 'ere for 'olidays, what d'yer reckon, Stan?'

'Wants freshening up a bit… white-wash'll do the trick. Yeah, not a bad little place in the country is it? Put the kettle on, Doll.'

'And what if Henry Thomas turns up with the police in tow to get back his property?'

'We say we're sorry and leave. We can face that, Jess, when we come to it.'

'There's a bit of live woodworm,' said Stanley, checking a beam, 'but I can sort that out.'

'We wouldn't 'ave broken the law, Jess. How were we to know it wasn't Tom's place? Ignorant, ain't we? Just a bunch of ignorant East Enders.'

'I agree… it's tempting,' smiled Max, bemused by the whole thing. 'But first things first, I'll drive into Bury and let the police know that it was Tom's girlfriend who took the children.'

'Yeah, and you make sure you tell 'em that he meant to fetch 'em back after a couple of hours but 'is car broke down. Say it's all bin a mistake and now it's hunky-dory.'

'I suppose we could do it,' said Jessie, placing best bone china cups on to saucers. 'We could visit you at your cottage and you could visit us when we're up'ere.'

'Yeah, once the cottages are done up. Till then, *this* is where we'll be lodging, thank you very much.'

'You can't do this,' said Max, laughing. He was about to tell them all the reasons why not when Emma-Rose appeared in her lovely Harrods nightie and rubbing her eyes. 'Mummy!' she cried, throwing herself at Jessie. 'What you, you, here for?'

'I fancied a day out, love. Soon we'll all go home. Uncle Max'll take us back in his car.' She watched her daughter's reaction.

'No, not yet, please!' She screwed her nose up and shook her head. 'We've gotta play-park. Don't go 'ome yet, eh?'

'That's all right sweet'eart, don't you worry; You go back upstairs and tell Billy that from now on we'll be spending 'olidays here, and some weekends. Uncle Max will bring us.' She glanced sideways at Max, a certain smile on her face. 'You'll fetch us up, won't you… Uncle Max?'

'Doesn't look as if I've got much of a choice.' He spoke in his usual deadpan voice, hiding his joy. He loved the place. 'Just as well my claim came through, we'll need some spending money.'

'What claim?' said Jessie just as Stanley came back into the room.

'Never you mind.' Max eyed Stanley and gave him a warning look.

'Burgled, wasn't he? Lost everything, all them family heirlooms.' Stanley shook his head, regretfully. 'I'll tell you what, Doll, them curtain's want 'anging out in the fresh air. Cigar smoke and Gawd only knows what living behind 'em.' He peered at Jessie. 'What you smiling about?'

'Oh, nothing.'

'Yeah,' he said, glancing round the room. 'Bit of distemper to freshen it up, that's all it wants. Me and

Max'll do that in no time, and Dad. We'll fetch 'im up as well and Mum's gonna love this place. Imagine 'er face, she's gonna be as proud as punch. Her Tom came up trumps in the end, eh? Giving us a place like this.' He looked from one to the other, 'Well, we've *gotta* do it – for Mum and Dad. They've had so much bad luck it's time it changed for them.' He turned to Max. 'Fancy a drink?'

'It's a bit early in the day, Stan.'

'Yeah, but is it morning or still last night?' He reached out and pulled a bottle of champagne from behind the door where he'd hidden it. 'You're not gonna believe this, but I found a cellar. And it's full of every drink you can fink of. Bit grubby down there but a bit of whitewash…'

Ten minutes later they were toasting their good luck with Archibald John Thomas's best champagne. 'Who we gonna drink to?' said Stanley, thinking it just had to be Tom.

'To family and friends,' said Jessie. ''Cos without them, I for one wouldn't have got through that ruddy war.'

Glasses raised, grins on their faces, a chorus rang out and filled the room. 'To family and friends!'

'Especially Tom!' blurted Jessie, surprising herself as well as the others. She had seen Billy and Emma arriving. 'This was the best present he could 'ave given to us and that play-park is the best he could 'ave given to his children!'

'To Tom!' Stanley raised his glass 'And especially to Archibald John Thomas, may you rest in peace you lovely man!'